"While you a
to conduct yo
in a ladylike fashion," Eddie said.

Linette's nostrils flared. "You mean play the lady of the manor."

He had his doubts as to whether she even knew how a lady conducted herself. Like his father said, the Edwards family didn't fit in. Softly he asked, "How do you see your role here?"

She ducked her head so he was unable to see her expression. "I suppose I thought you meant to marry me." She lifted her head and faced him with her eyes flashing courage and challenge. "I will make a good pioneer wife."

"I never got your letter, or I could have warned you I'm not desperate for a wife. Besides, you can't simply substitute one woman for another as if they are nothing more than horses."

"Why not? Are you madly in love with Margaret?"

Love? There was no such thing as love in an arrangement like theirs. "We suited each other."

"She doesn't seem to share your view of suitability."

Books by Linda Ford

Love Inspired Historical

LINDA FORD

lives on a ranch in Alberta, Canada. Growing up on the prairie and learning to notice the small details it hides gave her an appreciation for watching God at work in His creation. Her upbringing also included being taught to trust God in everything and through everything—a theme that resonates in her stories. Threads of another part of her life are found in her stories—her concern for children and their future. She and her husband raised fourteen children—four homemade, ten adopted. She currently shares her home and life with her husband, a grown son, a live-in paraplegic client and a continual (and welcome) stream of kids, kids-in-law, grandkids and assorted friends and relatives.

The Cowboy's Surprise Bride

LINDA FORD

Love Inspired

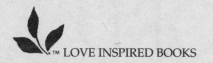 ™ LOVE INSPIRED BOOKS

ISBN-13: 978-0-373-82947-7

THE COWBOY'S SURPRISE BRIDE

Copyright © 2013 by Linda Ford

www.LoveInspiredBooks.com

Printed in U.S.A.

I have set before thee an open door,
and no man can shut it.
—*Revelation* 3:8

Without cowboys our part of the world would be a much different place. This story is dedicated to the cowboys of the West and those who love them. To both past and present cowboys and to those who entertain at the greatest outdoor show in the world: the Calgary Stampede, which celebrated its 100th anniversary in 2012. Thank you.

Chapter One

North-west Territories, Canada
October 1881

For the first time she was about to meet Eddie Gardiner. The man she intended to marry. The answer to her prayers.

Linette Edwards parted the curtains on the stagecoach—meant to keep out the dust and cold. The first few days of their trip, dust had filtered through them, and now cold with the bite of a wild beast filled every inch of the tiny coach. Four adults and a child huddled against the elements.

"You're letting in the cold," her traveling companion complained.

"I fear we are in for an early snowstorm," one of the male passengers said.

Linette murmured an apology but she managed to see the rolling hills and the majestic mountains before she dropped the curtain back in place. Since they'd left Fort Benton, headed for the ranch lands of the Northwest Territories of Canada, she'd peered out as much as she could. The mountains, jagged and bold, grew larger and larger. A song filled her heart and soul each time she saw them. This was a new country. She could start over. Be a different person than she'd been forced to be in England. Here she would be allowed to prove she had value as a person. She ignored the ache at how her parents viewed her—as a commodity to be traded for business favors.

She shifted her thoughts to the letter of invitation hidden safely in the cavernous pocket of the coat she'd acquired in Fort Benton. She longed to pull it out and read it again though she had memorized every word. *Come before winter.*

"I expect more than a shack," her friend Margaret had fumed when she'd read an earlier letter from the same writer. "After all, he comes from a very respectable family." With bitterness edging each word, Margaret read the letters describing the cabin Eddie assured her was only temporary quarters. "Temporary? I'm sure he doesn't know the meaning of the word. A year and a half he's been there and he still lives in this hovel."

"It sounds like an adventure." Linette could imagine a woman working side by side with her man, being a necessary asset to establishing a home in the new world. It sounded a lot more appealing to her than sitting and smiling vacantly as a female spectator. She'd been raised to be the lady of the manor but she wanted more. So much more.

Margaret had sniffed with such disdain that Linette giggled.

"I have made up my mind," Margaret said. "I cannot marry him and join him in the wilds of the Canadian West. I expected far more when he asked for my hand before he left to start a Gardiner ranch out in that—"

she fluttered her hand weakly "—in that savage land."
Her shudder was delicate and likely deliberate.

"Oh, Margaret, surely you don't mean it."

"Indeed I do. I've written this letter."

Seated in the overstuffed parlor of Margaret's family
home in London, Linette had read each word kindly but
firmly informing Eddie that Margaret had changed her
mind and would not be joining him now or anytime in
the future. *I expect it makes me sound small and selfish, but I can't imagine living in a tiny house, nor being
a woman of the West.*

"But what about your feelings for him? His for you?"

Margaret had given her a smile smacking of pity. "I
enjoyed his company. He was a suitable candidate for
marriage. There are plenty other suitable men."

How often she'd envied Margaret the opportunity to
head to a new world with so much possibility simply
for the eager taking of it. "But he's counting on you.
Why would you want to stay here when the whole world
beckons?" Wouldn't he be dreadfully hurt by Margaret's rejection?

"You should marry him. You're the one who thinks
it would be a lark." Margaret was clearly annoyed with
Linette's enthusiasm. "In fact, write him and I'll enclose
your letter with mine."

"Write him? And say what?"

"That you're willing to be his wife."

"I don't know him." A trickle of something that felt
suspiciously like excitement hurried up her limbs to her
heart. But it couldn't be. It wasn't possible. "My father
would never allow it."

Margaret laughed. "I think the Gardiner name would
make even your father consider it a good idea. And

would it not provide an escape from the marriage your father has planned?"

Linette shuddered. "I will not marry that old—" Her father had chosen a man in his fifties with a jangling purse of money and a drooling leer. His look made Linette feel soiled. She would do anything to avoid such a fate. She'd been praying for a reprieve. Perhaps this was an answer to her heartfelt petition.

Yes, the Gardiners were an old family, well respected, with a great estate and vaults of money, as her father so often said with utmost reverence in his voice.

"Of course," Margaret started, considering her with a mocking smile, "if you're dreaming of love and romance—"

Linette jerked back. "All I'm thinking of is escape." Love did not enter into a suitable marriage, which was fine with her. She fully intended to keep her feelings out of the picture. A trembling in the depths of her heart warned her that love would make her weak, vulnerable, ready to give up her personal goals. Not something she intended to let happen. She grabbed a piece of paper. "I'm going to do it. Anything is better than what my parents have in mind." Being a rancher's wife in the new world suited her fine. She was weary of the social restrictions her parents insisted on and not at all loath to living the kind of life she'd heard existed in the new world. There, women marched side by side with their men. They were even allowed to own land! Doubtlessly they'd be allowed to get their hands dirty and be involved.

Before she could change her mind, she'd penned a short letter. *A marriage of convenience if it suits you. Please reply to Margaret's address.* She knew her father would read any letter that came to the house. Much better to know she had a positive answer from Mr. Gardiner before confronting her father. If she had to be part of a business deal, it would be on her terms. She'd say who and where.

She clasped her fingers on the answering letter that had carried two tickets—one for herself and one for a traveling companion. The missive was brief. Not much more than an invitation to come. Her heart had danced for joy. Margaret was right; her father had glowed at an invitation from a Gardiner.

The stagecoach swayed to a stop. "Hello, the house." The driver's call shivered up and down Linette's spine. They'd arrived at Eden Valley Ranch.

It wasn't as if Eddie were a *total* stranger. She'd read his letters to Margaret. He sounded like a strong man, an independent thinker. She had no trouble imagining herself sharing his life. Yet her insides clenched in trepidation.

She squeezed right back in protest. She would not let nerves weaken her resolve. She'd prayed for such an escape and God had generously provided. *Hitherto hath the Lord helped me.* Renewed faith filled her, driving away any doubts and fears.

One of the two men who also rode in the coach flicked aside a curtain. "Looks like a fine establishment."

Linette parted the curtains again and peeked outside. The coach had drawn up before a log cabin with only a narrow door and small window in the wall facing them. This must be where the man lived. She pressed her tongue to the roof of her mouth and refused to think how small it looked. Hardly big enough for all of them. Never mind. Nothing could deter her now. She'd prayed her way from London, over the Atlantic Ocean, and across most of the North American continent. The rooms she'd had on the trip had left barely enough space for stretching. Although vastly different from the spacious home she'd grown up in, she'd gotten used to it readily enough. This cabin would be no different.

The door of the cabin opened and Linette took a deep breath. A man stepped forth, ducking as he crossed the threshold. This had to be Eddie Gardiner. She'd seen his likeness in pictures, but they failed to do the man justice. Despite the chill in the air, he hadn't bothered to grab a coat or hat and in the bright sunshine his brown hair shone. He dressed like a range hand—dark denim trousers, a blue shirt that had faded almost colorless on the sleeves with dark remnants of the color in the seams, and a leather vest that looked worn and friendly.

Her heart jumped to her throat. She hadn't expected to feel anything for him. Surely it was only excitement, combined with a touch of nerves. After all, despite the letters, he was a stranger. She wanted nothing more or less from him than a marriage of convenience.

His gaze sought the parted curtains and his dark eyes narrowed as he tried to make out the face in the dim interior.

She flicked the curtain closed and turned to her traveling companion. "You keep the child while I meet him." The boy would remain a secret for now. Seeing her intention, one of the gentlemen stepped down and held out a hand to assist her. She murmured her thanks as Eddie strode forward.

He slid his gaze over her as if she were invisible and looked toward the stagecoach. "Is Margaret inside?"

Linette shook her head trying to make sense of his question. Surely he'd mistakenly spoken her name out of habit.

"Is she at Fort Benton? If so I'll go for her immediately." He glanced at the sky as if already trying to outrace the weather.

Her mouth felt like yesterday's dust as she realized what he meant. "You're expecting Margaret?" It took every ounce of her stubborn nature not to stammer.

"Any day. I sent tickets for her and a chaperone to come before winter."

Come before winter. She remembered the words well. They'd bubbled through her heart. But she thought they were meant for her. "Did you not get the letter?"

At that the driver jumped down. "'Spect any letters you'd be wanting are in here." He waved a small bundle. "Seems you haven't picked up your mail for some time, so I brought it."

Cold trickled across Linette's neck, dug bony fingers into her spine and sent a faint sense of nausea up her throat. She swallowed it back with determination. If he hadn't received her letter, then the tickets he'd sent hadn't been meant for her. He didn't know she was coming. He wasn't prepared to welcome her and accept her as a suitable helpmate on the frontier. Now what?

She stiffened her shoulders. She had not crossed an ocean and a vast continent to be turned back now. Her prayers for escape had been fervent. God held her in the palm of His hand now as He had on the journey. This was her answer. She nailed her fears to the thought. Besides, nothing had changed. Not really. Margaret still wasn't coming and he still needed a wife. Didn't he? She sought her memories but could not remember that he'd ever said so in clear, unmistakable terms. Had she read more into his missives than was meant?

Eddie took the bundle of mail and untied the strings. He flicked through the correspondence.

Recognizing Margaret's handwriting, she touched the envelope. "That one." Her own message lay inside, unseen by the man she thought had invited her to join him. She sucked moisture from the corners of her mouth and swallowed hard.

He slit the envelope and pulled out the pages in which she'd offered to take Margaret Sear's place. *I look forward to being part of the new West.* He read her letter then Margaret's, his fingers tightening on the paper as he understood the message. A flash of pain crossed his face before he covered it with a harsh expression.

Her heart twisted. He expected Margaret and instead got his hopes and dreams shattered. If only she'd known. But what could she do about it now? Except prove she was better suited to be a woman of the West.

Thankfully he did not read the letter aloud, which would have added to her growing embarrassment as the three men listened intently—one peering from the inside of the coach, one standing at its side where he remained after helping her alight, the other pretending to check on the horses though he made certain he could hear what was said. Even so, her face burned at their curiosity about an obvious misunderstanding of mammoth proportions.

Eddie jammed the pages back in the envelope. "This is unacceptable."

Her muscles turned to warm butter. It took concentrated effort to hold herself upright, to keep her face rigid. She would not let him guess that the ground threatened to rise up and clout her in the face.

One hand clasping the mail bundle, he jammed his fists to his hips and turned to the driver. "You can return her to the fort."

The man tipped his hat back on his head and shook

his head. "Ain't goin' a mile more'n I have to. It's about to snow."

The wind bit at Linette's cheeks but the cold encasing her heart was not from the wintery weather. She could not, would not, go back to London and her father's plans.

The coach driver went on in his leisurely way of speaking. "I'm taking these two gentlemen to the OK Ranch then I'd hoped to make it back to Fort Benton where I intend to hole up for the winter. I don't fancy being stuck in Edendale." He made a rattling noise in the back of his throat. "But it looks like I'll be stuck at the OK for the time being."

Linette cared not whether the man was returning to the tiny cluster of huts bravely named Edendale or back to Fort Benton. She wasn't going anywhere.

The gentleman who'd helped her down still stood at the steps, waiting and watching. "The girl is strong. Tough. Takes a special kind of lady to take care of travel arrangements and her traveling companions. Not a lot of young women are prepared and able to do that. You could do worse than have her at your side in this brave new frontier."

Linette gave the man a fleeting smile of appreciation then turned back to Eddie.

Eddie met her gaze. He must have read her determination though she hoped he hadn't seen her desperation. "We need to talk." He grabbed her arm and marched her around the side of the house, out of sight and hopefully out of earshot of the others, where he released her to glare hotly at her.

She tipped her chin and met his gaze without flinching even though her insides had begun to tremble. Where would she go if he sent her away? Not back to the marriage her father had arranged. Perhaps money would convince him. "I have a dowry."

"Keep your money. I have no need of it."

"I came in good faith. I thought you'd received my letter." *Come before winter.* The words had seemed so welcoming. She'd made preparations as quickly as she could. How was she to know he didn't respond to her letter? Hadn't even received it. She stood motionless. She wouldn't let so much as one muscle quiver.

"Obviously I hadn't." He stared at the bundle in his hand, sounding every bit as confused as she felt. A contrast to the anger her parents had expressed when she'd informed them she would not marry the man of their choosing and meant to go West. Only after she showed her father the letter from Eddie and only because the Gardiners were a well-respected family had he agreed. With many constraints. Her father knew her too well. Knew she would avoid this marriage, too, if she had the means to strike out on her own. Knew she would not flinch before the dangers nor shirk from the challenges. That's why he'd allowed her barely enough money to keep from starving to death on the journey and made sure her dowry would be held until he had proof she was married. He'd made her understand he would allow her only enough time for the necessary documents to cross the ocean. Should they not arrive in a reasonable time he would send one of his henchmen to bring her back. She'd used the limited funds he'd provided caring for the sick and destitute she'd crossed paths with. She had not so much as a penny to her name.

She shuddered as she imagined one of her father's cruel servants poised and ready to pursue her.

There was no escape from her father's plans apart from this marriage.

She understood Eddie's shock. It couldn't feel good to realize Margaret had refused to come, refused his offer of marriage. She swallowed back a swell of sympathy, and resisted an urge to pat his arm. She brought her thoughts back to her own predicament. "I'm prepared to care for your home." As soon as she and Margaret agreed Linette should take her place, Margaret had reluctantly arranged for their cook to teach Linette to prepare food and run a house. She hadn't dared to ask for such instructions at home. Her father had often enough said they were rich and had servants to do menial work. Only the death of some distant relative of her mother's who'd made a fortune in India had changed the family circumstances from penniless to well off before Linette's birth. Father wanted everyone to believe they were landed gentry, but she often wondered how much of the inheritance still existed and suspected her father's plans for her were meant to add to the coffers. But how much was enough to satisfy her father? She wondered if enough existed.

"He should have servants to do those things," Margaret had fumed when Linette badgered her to arrange instruction.

"It will be an adventure to do something useful."

Unless Eddie changed his mind, her lessons seemed destined to be useless. She stiffened her spine. Failure was not an option.

Eddie turned his gaze back to her then with a great sigh eased toward the stagecoach.

She followed at his heels. "I'm a hard worker." She would press her point but she wouldn't beg.

The driver stood at his horses, staring at the horizon and shifting from one foot to the other. "Eddie boy, the wind has a bite to it. Winter is likely to clutch us by the throat any moment."

She'd wondered at the earliness of the snow, but the man in the coach had explained it was due to being in high country. "Snow can come early and stay or leave again. There's no predicting it."

Eddie turned to speak over his shoulder. "I'm to be stuck with you then. But only until the weather moderates then I'll send you back."

"Stuck? Seems you're getting the better part of this bargain." She had no intention of staying one day more than she must, but she silently prayed the winter would set in early and be long and cold, preventing travel. That would give her sufficient time to persuade Eddie to change his mind.

She would not—under any circumstances—return to her father and his despicable plan for her.

Despite her lack of funds, she considered setting off on her own but she must acknowledge the facts—her father would not let her escape his clutches. He had ways and means of tracking her wherever she went. And he wouldn't hesitate to use them. She knew she couldn't hide from him even if she found a means of surviving on her own.

Eddie still provided the only answer to avoiding her father's plans. Winter provided a reprieve. She would use the time to prove to him she was the ideal pioneer wife. She would make him want to keep her. He'd beg her to stay.

Eddie ground to a halt and turned to face her.

She blinked back her silent arguments lest he guess at her thoughts.

He edged forward, forcing her to retreat until they were again out of sight and hearing of the interested party waiting at the stagecoach. "You might want to re-consider this rash decision of yours. It's wild out here. There are no luxuries. No chaperones."

"I brought my own chaperone." If he found her arrival a burden, he was not going to like her next announce-ment. She tipped her chin and faced him squarely. Not for all the roses in her mother's garden would she reveal so much as a hint of trepidation. "And a child."

"A child?"

"Yes, I brought a child."

He swallowed hard enough to lose his Adam's apple. "You have a child?"

He thought the child was hers? Embarrassment, laced with a heavy dose of amusement, raced through her at the shock on his face. Her amusement could not be contained and she laughed delicately, feeling her eyes dance with merriment. "He's not mine."

"Then why do you have him?"

"I met his mother on the boat. She died in the cross-ing and asked me to take the child to his father."

"I'm not his father." The poor man almost choked at the thought.

She laughed again, thoroughly enjoying his discom-fort. "I didn't mean to imply you were. His father met us in Montreal and when he heard his wife had expired, refused to take his son." A dreadful scene had ensued as Linette tried to convince the man of his duty. "I had little choice but to bring him along."

Eddie choked again.

Maybe she would have to thump him between the shoulders, and found the idea rather satisfying. With every passing moment, he proved more and more an-noying. She'd expected a welcome of some sort, guarded perhaps, or even perfunctory. She assumed he would have made arrangements to have someone present to perform their emotionless union. But never in her many far-flung imaginings had she considered this possibility.

He cleared his throat. "I think a place the size of Montreal would have a foundling home. I think the nuns have—"

"Are you suggesting I should have abandoned him to strangers?"

"It's not called abandon—" He must have read the challenge in her eyes for he stopped short. "Seems to me that's what a sensible woman would have done. Besides, wouldn't he be better off there with schools and playmates?"

She pulled herself as tall as she could, annoyed she still had to tip her head to glare at him. "We better get something straight right here and now. I have no tolerance for the pharisaical affectations of our society. I refuse to stand by and not offer help to someone when it is within my power to give more than an empty blessing. I could not, nor would I, turn my back on a small child." Helping others was one of the many things she and her father had warred about. She expected things to be different in the British Territories of Canada.

She planned to make sure they were.

Eddie stared at her then scrubbed at the back of his neck. "All I have is a small cabin. Only one bed."

She had gained a small victory. No need to push for more at this point. "We'll take the bed."

"And I'm to what?"

"I understand from your letters to Margaret that there is a bunkhouse for men who work for you."

"I will not sleep with them."

His words had a familiar, unwelcome ring to them.

"Does it offend your sensibilities to share quarters with the men who work for you?"

"Not at all, but it would be awkward for them. I'm the boss. They deserve a chance to relax without thinking I'm watching them."

His reply both surprised and pleased her. She admired a man who thought of others. But her admiration did not solve what he perceived to be a quandary. She didn't see a problem. "I believe the cabin has two rooms. You can sleep on the floor in the other room."

"You are too generous." The look on his face made her want to laugh, but she sensed he did not share her amusement.

"Eddie boy," the driver called. "I'd like to get on my way before nightfall."

Eddie and Linette did silent duel with their eyes. Although their weapons were invisible she understood her life and her future hung on the outcome of this battle. Finally he sighed. "Come along. Let's get your things."

"There's something I better tell you first."

"You mean there are more surprises? Let me guess. Another child? A brother or sister? A—"

"My chaperone is a woman I met in Montreal. Her husband died and she has no family."

"You traveled from England without a chaperone?"

She flicked him an impatient glance. It was easy to see that rules meant a lot to him. She'd prayed he wasn't like her father. Now he seemed frighteningly so. "Of course not, but Miss Snodgrass was eager to return, and when she saw I intended for Cassie to accompany me, she got on the next boat home."

He waited, aware there was more.

"Cassie is a little…well, I suppose you could say she's having trouble dealing with her grief."

"Trouble? In what way?"

Words came quickly to her mind, but none of them seemed the sort to make him kindly disposed toward Cassie. Perhaps the less she said the better. "Let's just say she's a bit sharp." She hastened to add, "I'm sure she'll settle down once the edge of her grief has passed."

He scrubbed at his neck again. "Let's see what you have."

She hurried past him, fearing if he thrust his head in the door and ordered the pair out, the ensuing reaction would give them all cause for regret. The kind gentleman who had assisted her from the coach watched for her return, doubtless listening with ears cocked. She wondered how much he'd heard. Not that it mattered. He'd already managed to get most of the story from her as they bounced along for several days with nothing to do but stare at each other. He held the door for her and with a quirk of his eyebrows silently asked if things had gone well.

She gave a quick nod, grateful for his kindly interest, then turned to the other occupants. "Cassie, we're here. Come out. Grady, come here." She reached to take the four-year-old from Cassie's lap

Grady seemed to shrivel into himself. Only at Cassie's gentle insistence did he let Linette take his hand and lift him to the ground. He took one look at Eddie and buried his face in her skirts. She knew he would stay there until she pried him free.

Cassie grabbed her small travel valise and paused in the open doorway. The look she gave Eddie blazed with anger.

Please, God. Keep her from saying something that will give him a reason to put us on the stage again without any regard for where we'll end.

"He's passable, I suppose."

Linette's breath stuck halfway to her lungs. She stole a glance at Eddie. Surprise flashed in his eyes and then he grinned. He had a nice face when he smiled, but more than that, his smile made her feel he would be patient with Cassie, who often expressed her pain in meanness. Relief poured through Linette like a warming drink.

"Thanks," Eddie said.

"Wasn't meant as a compliment," Cassie murmured.

"I've been told worse." He held his hand out to assist Cassie, but she pointedly ignored him and accepted help from their traveling companion.

Linette's attention was diverted as the driver handed down the two trunks she'd brought. Grady had only a grip bag.

Eddie whistled sharply, causing Grady to sob. Two men stepped from the building across the way.

"Yeah, boss?" one called.

"Boys, take these trunks to my house."

Linette watched the two cross the roadway in long, rolling strides. Their gait reminded her of the sailors on the ship. They had on Stetson hats, worn and rolled, unlike the new, uniformly shaped ones she'd studied back at the trading post in Fort Benton where she'd exchanged her fine English silks and bustles for frocks she considered more appropriate for living in the wilds—simple-cut dresses of calico or wool. She'd procured a dress for Cassie too but the woman refused to wear it. "I am who I am and I'm not about to pretend otherwise," she'd said. Linette hadn't pressed the point. Sooner or later the old garment Cassie wore would fall apart and then she'd be glad for what Linette offered.

She glanced at her own dress. A little the worse for

wear after crossing the prairie. She'd clean up once they got settled in case Eddie took note of her rumpled state.

As they walked, the men jingled from the spurs on their boots. They yanked their hats off and squirmed inside their buffalo coats. "Ma'am." They nodded to Linette and Cassie.

"Miss Edwards, may I present two of my men, Slim—" he indicated the taller, thinner man. "And Roper." The other man was heavier built. Solid. Younger. And he watched Cassie with guarded interest.

Linette realized she hadn't introduced her companion and did so. "Cassie Godfrey." Then she indicated the boy half-buried in her skirts. "This is Grady Farris. He's four years old." He shivered enough to make her leg vibrate.

The men nodded then jammed their hats back on and took the trunks into the house.

Eddie spoke privately to the driver who then swung up to his seat and drove from the yard. Linette stared after the coach, knowing she now had no escape. She was at Eddie's mercy. Her resolve hardened. Only so far as she chose to be. She'd be no man's slave. Nor his chattel. Any arrangement between them would be based on mutual benefit. No emotions involved to turn her weak.

The stagecoach no longer blocked her view and she saw, on the hill overlooking the ranch, a big two-story house, gleaming in its newness. It had the unfinished look of raw lumber and naked windows. They must be expecting neighbors. People who put more value in their abode than Eddie. When would these people finish the house and move in?

"I suppose you would like to see your quarters." Eddie indicated they should step toward the low dwelling.

She turned from studying the house on the hill to

closer inspection of the cabin. It looked even smaller than she expected. But she didn't care. She'd escaped her father's plans and the future beckoned.

Eddie resisted the urge to squeeze his neck. It was tight enough to withstand a hanging. He'd expected the mail would contain a message to meet Margaret. He'd planned to marry her at the fort before bringing her to his home. He'd thought of her every day as he worked on the new house. He'd counted the days until she joined him.

Margaret was the ideal young lady for him. He remembered many a pleasant afternoon sharing her company in her family home in London before he'd left for the British Territories. He'd grown quite fond of her and she of him. Or so he thought. In time their affection would grow. He anticipated the day she would arrive and marry him. Margaret would grace the big house he would have completed by now except for the necessity of making sure the breeding stock he'd had shipped from Chicago was herded safely from Fort Benton to the nearby pens.

Instead, a ragamuffin of a woman stood before him in a black woolen coat that practically swallowed her. As it flapped open he saw a crude dress much like those he'd seen worn by wives on hopeful dirt farms and the half-breed women in the forts. She looked ready to live in a tepee or log hut, which was likely a good thing because the latter was all he had to offer her.

The cold wind reminded him he'd hurried outside without a coat. "We might as well go indoors."

How Linette managed to make her way to the house with the boy clinging to her side like a giant burr amazed him.

She was an Edwards daughter if he believed what she said. He wasn't prepared to believe anything about her at the moment. How had he ended up in such an awkward position? And with an Edwards woman! His father had had some business dealings with Mr. Edwards years ago and had expressed distaste for the other man. "A churlish man," he'd said. "Thinks because he inherited money through his wife it makes him an aristocrat, but he lacks any sense of decorum or decency. I vow I will never have business dealings with him again and I intend to avoid any social contact." Eddie couldn't think the Edwards daughter would warrant any better opinion from his father.

Slim and Roper hurried out and jogged back to work. Not, he noted, without a backward glance at the women. They'd be filled with curiosity for sure and spend the rest of the day speculating about this turn of events.

Eddie had always done his best to live up to his father's expectations. After all, he owed the man so much. Coming West and starting a ranch to add to the Gardiner holdings, establishing a home that would make his father proud provided him an opportunity to repay his father for giving him the Gardiner name. Randolph Gardiner had married Eddie's mother when Eddie was an infant. If not for that, Eddie would have been an outcast bastard child and his mother would have lived in shame and disgrace.

He held the door for the ladies and Linette stepped inside first. The sigh that whistled from her lips drove back the gall in his throat and made him grin. Had she been expecting something fancy? No doubt this crude cabin shocked her. It was only temporary and then would serve as quarters for a foreman. If the man was married and had a family, Eddie would add on to it but had not seen any need for that now. It had solid walls. It was warm and dry. It served as a place to put his feet up and have a cup of coffee and somewhere to catch a comfortable night's sleep. Not much else.

The letter clutched in his fist crackled. Margaret had changed her mind. As if he didn't measure up. His insides twisted in a familiar, unwelcome way.

He studied the woman he was stuck with. Linette was almost plain. Her eyes too direct. Her lips too narrow and stubborn, almost challenging. Her hair was light in color. Neither brown nor blond and coiled in a braid about her face. Her eyes were so pale they didn't deserve to be called brown. She was too small. Built like a struggling sapling out on the prairie. In fact, everything about her was wrong. Quite the opposite of Margaret. No way would she fit into his plans. His father's instructions were clear. "Find suitable land and build a house. A replica of our home and life back here in England." Eddie had been surprised his father had entrusted him with the task and vowed he would make his father proud.

Linette Edwards could not be allowed to ruin his plans.

But he couldn't send her away with the weather threatening to turn nasty. He'd shelter her until it moderated…which likely meant for the winter. Then, under armed escort if necessary, he would see her returned to England or wherever she might have a mind to go…just so long as it wasn't here.

Trouble was, she wasn't alone. Not that she should be. But the woman she'd brought along looked as if she'd been rescued from the gutter. Her clothes barely missed being called rags. Her untidy black hair and scowling face indicated she was not happy to be here. He snorted silently. At least they shared that. He wasn't happy to have any of them here.

Then there was the boy with a flash of blue eyes and a mat of blond hair sticking out from under his cap. He often thought of children to fill the rooms in the big house, but children bred with a woman like Margaret. Not waifs.

Cassie hesitated at the doorway. The noise that escaped her mouth was full of anger and discontent. "I had more room back in Montreal."

Linette laughed softly—a merry sound full of pleasure. She didn't seem the least bit distressed about the conditions.

"You slept in the train station after your husband died and left you stranded in a strange city," she said to Cassie. "Of course it was bigger. But it wasn't home. This will be home." The word was full of promise and warmth.

He figured he better make sure she remembered it was temporary. "Until better weather." Silently, he again acknowledged that might not be before spring and the thought made his neck muscles spasm. "Then you're headed back to your father."

"There's many a slip between the cup and the lip."

Her disregard of his warning made him chomp on his back teeth. It took an effort to release the tension so he could speak. "There'll be no slips here."

Cassie edged forward into the room and stood with her arms crossed. He figured her eyes would be crossed, too, and full of displeasure. Good. If both women found the situation intolerable… But it was a long time until spring. A crowded house with two women dripping discontent would be miserable for everyone.

What had he done to deserve this?

Margaret's letter said she didn't think she could face the challenges of frontier life nor live in small quarters. He'd meant the big house to be a surprise. Now he saw keeping it a secret had been cause for her to think she'd be confined to some sort of settler's shack. His mind kicked into salvage thoughts. Miss Edwards would see the house. She'd realize it was almost finished. She could report its fineness to Margaret. Margaret would change her mind. She'd be pleased to join him. Tension drained from him so quickly his limbs twitched.

He realized the interior of the little house lacked warmth and closed the door behind him. He'd been about to leave the cabin and had let the fire die to embers. "I'll get some heat in here." Deftly, he added wood, and in minutes welcoming flames sprang to life. Now he'd have to plan on heating the house all day. He'd have to get more firewood chopped. These women and the boy were going to be a nuisance as well as a threat.

"I didn't realize how cold I'd grown," Linette said, holding her hands toward the stove. "Is it usually this cold in October?"

"Snow comes early this close to the mountains, though I hope it holds off for a time yet. The cows are still up in the higher pastures."

"And you would prefer to have them where? Down here?"

"Yes. Down in the lower meadows where they'll be able to get to the grass."

"You don't feed them?"

She sure was full of questions. "Do you know anything about ranching?"

"A cousin raised cattle. He always kept them in barns and pens in the winter and fed them hay."

He chuckled. "Hard to build a barn big enough for

a thousand head or more." The way she widened her eyes in surprise gave him a moment's victory then he wished he'd kept the fact to himself. If she was a gold digger he'd provided her with more to dig for. "I have some hay. Most ranchers don't think it's necessary, but one of the first men I talked to when I came out here was Kootenai Brown. He's lived in the mountains for years and says only a buffalo can survive without hay. They dig through the grass like a horse. He told me if I want to succeed in this venture I should plan to have hay available." Why was he telling her all this? Surely she didn't care. But her pale brown eyes flashed with intelligent interest. Not the fake batting of eyelashes he'd seen from women who seemed to think any sign of intelligence would frighten off a man.

"Kootenai Brown? Isn't Kootenai the name of an Indian tribe?"

He couldn't hide his surprise. Didn't even try. "How do you know that?"

"I've read everything I could find about the Northwest."

He turned his attention to stoking the fire to conceal his reluctant admiration.

Cassie groaned. "And she likes to talk about it all day long." She moved marginally closer to the stove as if reluctant to allow herself any comfort her circumstances might provide.

Linette laughed softly. "I didn't realize I was boring you."

"You and that gentleman from the coach. Did he say he was going to another ranch?"

"Yes. I believe he said he was an investor with the OK Ranch and intended to check on its operation." She turned back to Eddie. "Would that be correct?"

"Could be. Good thing if it's true. The OK bunch has run into some trouble."

"What sort? Wild animals? Rustlers?" She practically quivered with excitement.

He studied her more closely. Was she the sort to be bounding into trouble just because it sounded adventuresome? He did not need that sort of aggravation. He answered her question first. "They lost cows by driving them north too hard. The rest of the herd is weakened. If they don't see them properly fed I fear they will lose the works." He intended to make sure she wasn't about to turn his life inside out and upside down and put his peace and security at risk—any more than she had already. "You don't find trouble to be exciting, do you?"

"If you think I'd be happy to hear of a herd of cows suffering—" Her eyes snapped with anger.

"I was thinking you seem overly anxious to think there might be wild animals or rustlers. I warn you I won't tolerate anyone deliberately putting themselves or others at risk simply for an exciting experience."

"What will you tolerate?" Linette demanded.

They studied each other with wariness. And a startling sense of shared determination that shifted his opinion of this woman. Of course, they shared that. Only in different directions. He was determined to carry out his original plan to marry Margaret and establish a home he could be proud of. She meant to upset his plans. "While you are here, I expect you to conduct yourself wisely and in a ladylike fashion."

Her nostrils flared. "You mean play the lady of the manor."

Behind her, Cassie snorted.

She'd no doubt been raised as such. Why didn't she offer to be so here? Not that it made any difference. He wasn't about to toss Margaret aside over a misunder-standing. Softly, he asked, "What do you see your role as here?"

She ducked her head so he was unable to see her expression. "I suppose I thought you meant to marry me." She lifted her head and faced him with her eyes flashing courage and challenge. "I will make a good pioneer wife."

"I never got your letter or I could have warned you I'm not desperate for a wife. Besides, you can't simply substitute one woman for another as if they are nothing more than horses."

"Why not? Are you madly in love with Margaret?"

Love? There was no such thing as love in an arrange-ment like theirs. "We suited each other."

"She doesn't seem to share your view of suitability."

He guessed she meant if she had, Margaret would be here instead of her. He pointed toward the window. "I mean to correct that. Did you see that house out there?"

She nodded.

"I built it for Margaret."

Linette's eyes widened. "But she said…" She looked about at the tiny quarters and shook her head. "I don't understand."

"I wanted it to be a surprise. I see now I should have informed her about the house. But you can write and tell her how special it is. Once she knows, she'll recon-sider and come."

She fixed him with a direct stare. "You really believe that's all there is to her refusal to come?" Her gaze de-manded honesty.

His neck knotted and he squeezed the back of it. He thought Margaret wanted to share his life. He still be-lieved it. Surely what he had to offer was acceptable to

Margaret. She only objected to meager quarters and that would soon be a thing of the past. He looked about the small room. "I obviously don't need help running this place. And I don't need or want a pioneer wife. My wife will have a cook and housekeeper to help her run the big house." He returned to confront her demanding look. "But with winter coming on—"

"You'll tolerate our presence until spring?" Her voice carried a low note of something he couldn't quite put his thumb on. Warning? Challenge?

He scrubbed the back of his neck again, wondering how much more tension it could take before something snapped. Most of his time was spent with animals who had little to say but *moo* and with cowboys known to be laconic. It didn't much prepare him to pick up on subtle nuances of social communication, but even a dolt would understand her question was more than mere conversation. "I expect we'll have to tolerate each other, crowded as we'll be in these quarters."

Cassie spun away to stare at the door. "I should have stayed in Montreal."

Linette gave her a tight smile. "You weren't exactly happy there, if I recall."

"Seems happiness is too much to hope for."

Linette hurried to her side and wrapped an arm around the woman's waist. "Of course it's not. We'll be happy here. About as happy as we make up our minds to be. All of us." The look she sent Eddie warned him to disagree or make it impossible. "Isn't that right, Mr. Gardiner?"

"I'm sure we can be civilized. After all, we're adults." Except for young Grady, and all eyes turned toward him. "I expect he's the only one we need to be concerned about." The child had been abandoned then put into the care of strangers. Which made Eddie that much more grateful to his father for the life he'd been given.

Seeing everyone watching him, Grady started to whimper. The boy's fears vibrated through the room.

Eddie thought of stroking the child's head to calm him but knew it would only upset him further. He was at a loss to know how to comfort the boy.

Linette knelt to face Grady squarely. "You're safe here. We'll take care of you."

"I want my mama," he wailed loudly.

Linette dropped to the floor, pulled the boy to her lap and crooned as she rocked him. "Mr. Gardiner, I believe Grady is hungry. Can you direct me to the food supplies and I'll gladly make us tea."

Food? He had no food to speak of in the cabin. "I've been taking my meals over at the cookhouse." Would they like to go to the cookhouse, too?

Grady wailed louder, as if Eddie had announced they were all about to starve. Seems Grady had answered the question. He would not be comfortable among so many strangers. Best to let them eat here. "I'll rustle up some supplies right away." Grateful for an excuse to escape the cabin, crowded as it was with bodies and feelings, he grabbed his coat and hat and headed across the yard.

Dare he hope the weather would moderate long enough for the stagecoach driver to decide to venture back to Edendale or Fort Benton? If so, he would have that trio on their way.

But he knew that scenario was about as likely as finding a satchel full of money on the ground before him.

Another thought sprang to life. After less than an hour his nerves were strung tight as a drum. How would he endure months of this?

Chapter Two

Eddie told Cookie the whole story as he waited for her to put together supplies for the unwelcome guests. "I intend to rectify the situation just as soon as the snow goes." With any favor from the Lord above, that would be sooner rather than later. Until then, he would simply make the best of it.

"She ugly?" Cookie demanded.

"She's passable."

"Cross-eyed?"

"No. Can you get things together a little faster?"

"I'm goin' as fast as these old legs will go."

Eddie let out a long, exasperated sigh. Cookie wasn't old except when it pleased her to be so. The rest of the time she kept up a pace that would wear out a horse.

"Then she's got those horrible teeth so many women have." Cookie did a marvelous imitation of a beaver with protruding upper front teeth.

"Didn't notice any such teeth when she smiled." Though he did note how she carried herself with such grace. She hadn't been raised to be a pioneer woman. Why would she choose it? "Now, how about some tea? You got lots or do I need to run to the supply shed?"

Provisions for the winter months were stored in a tight outbuilding lined with tin to keep rodents out.

"I got tea enough to spare. Smile, did you say? So she has a pleasant nature?"

"Look, Cookie. I've spent only a few minutes in her company. It's not enough time for me to form an evaluation of her personality." Except to note she had a cheerful laugh and—it seemed at first meeting—an equally cheerful nature. Matched by a dreadfully stubborn attitude.

Cookie laughed boisterously and clapped him on the shoulder hard enough to set him forward a step. "Guess you won't be able to say that after a winter together in that tiny shack."

Her husband, Bertie, came in with a load of wood for the big stove. "Bertie," Cookie roared. "There's two women and a little boy in Eddie's shack."

Eddie groaned at the blatant pleasure wreathing Bertie's face.

"Well, I'll be hornswoggled and hog-tied. This is turning into a real homey sit'ation. Eddie, lad, you've surprised us real good."

Cookie and Bertie grinned at each other like a pair of silly children.

"It's all a mistake, as I told Cookie. They'll go home come spring. I'd send them now only the stagecoach isn't running, and with winter—"

"Eddie, lad, I'm thinking this opportunity is a rare one. Don't be letting it slip through your fingers." Bertie nodded and grinned.

"I'm of like mind, my love. I'm of like mind." Cookie clapped her husband hard on the back.

Eddie wasn't a bit sorry for the other man when he shifted under his wife's hearty affections. "It's temporary. Why can't you accept that?" He grabbed the sack and stomped across the yard, their laughter echoing at his heels.

"He's not happy to have us here." Cassie's observation was almost laughable.

Linette simply smiled. "Then it's up to us to convince him otherwise." She had not come this far and prayed this hard to give up at the first sign of resistance. Though she hadn't expected to be resisted. No doubt his initial reaction was fueled by pain. It couldn't be pleasant to know he'd been rejected.

Cassie snorted. "Don't expect me to try to sweeten him up. If you ask me, I'd say the man is as stubborn as he is high."

Yes, he was a tall man. And well built. And he had a smile that drove the clouds from her mind. None of which mattered as much as a single gray hair. All that mattered was she had the winter—God willing and the cold weather continued—to convince him a marriage of convenience suited him. She saw no other way out of her predicament. "I'd say he has high ideals. That could serve us well."

Cassie stared as if Linette had suggested something underhand.

Linette sighed. Cassie seemed bent on seeing everything in some dreadful fashion. "I only mean that a man with honor can be trusted."

"No man is completely honest and honorable. Take it from me. They'll take your heart and treat it with total disregard."

Linette had no desire to know the details behind such a statement, so she ignored it. She had no intention of giving her heart to a man. Her only interest in a marriage to Eddie was escaping from her father's plans and gaining the right to act according to her conscience.

She turned her attention to the room. It was small. The stove was the tiniest she'd ever seen. It was nothing like the one Tilly, Margaret's cook, had taught her on. For a moment, she doubted her ability to prepare food despite all her reading. Everything was so different from what she'd practiced on or imagined. She stiffened her spine. She would do whatever needed doing, do it well and without complaint. A tiny table, one wooden chair and a small bookcase crowded with papers and books completed the furnishings. She longed to explore the book titles, but first things first.

"Help me get organized," she told Cassie. She hung her coat by the door and rubbed her hands together. "At least the table has wings." Flipped up, they would all be able to crowd around for their meals, assuming they had more chairs.

"We'll have to take turns lifting a fork to our mouths," Cassie predicted.

"It's perfectly adequate. Now let's organize the bedroom. I want to put Grady's things where I can get at them." She took the boy's hand and stepped into the tiny bedroom. With the two trunks beside the bed there was barely enough room to stand. The bed was narrow. Two would be cozy. Three crowded.

Cassie pointed out the fact. "We'll have to take turns sleeping."

Linette reached down and touched the fur covering. "It's as soft as down. We'll be just fine so long as we're prepared to manage." She faced Cassie squarely. "I seem to recall you complaining about not being able to sleep for fear someone would steal your bag. Or worse."

Cassie shuddered. "But at least it was warm and roomy."

"But here it's safe." She shoved the narrow dresser hard against the corner. There were nails driven into the logs across the end wall. She bundled Eddie's belongings onto one hook, freeing up the others. The scent of leather, horseflesh and something subtle, bringing to mind grassy slopes and warm sunshine, assailed her senses. A tremor of anticipation scooted up her throat. She dismissed the sensation and hung some of Grady's things. She placed her smaller items on top of her trunk.

Cassie stood in the doorway. "I don't see how we're all going to fit in here. A person will have to step outside just to change their mind."

Linette chuckled. "We'll simply have to make sure we don't all try to change our minds at the same time." She'd hoped for a small smile from Cassie but got nothing but a sigh of displeasure. "Come on, Cassie. Look on the bright side."

"I don't see that there is one. I'm a widow in a big country. A man's country, I might add. Need I point out that we are at the mercy of Mr. Gardiner? And if it wasn't him, it would be another man."

Linette hated the thought of being at his mercy, but it was true. But only to the degree she allowed it to be. "Then let's be grateful he appears to be honorable." At least he hadn't left them out in the cold.

They stepped back into the other room. It took only two dozen steps to circle the whole house, but as Linette pointed out, it was safe and Eddie was an honorable man so far as she knew. *Lord, keep us secure and help Cassie find peace. And help Eddie to change his mind before spring.* She had no doubt it could happen. Didn't the Word say "with God all things are possible"?

Grady shuffled toward the stove and stared at the black surface.

Cassie studied Linette with narrowed eyes. "Were you really prepared to marry Mr. Gardiner, a complete stranger?"

"Yes."

"Why?"

Before she could reply, a cold draft shivered across the floor and up Linette's shins. She turned to see Eddie standing in the doorway, three chairs dangling from one arm and a bulging gunnysack from the other. He kicked the door closed with his foot and stared at Linette.

"I'd like to hear the answer to that." His gaze burned a trail across her skin, making her cheeks burn.

She ignored the question and her reaction to his look, grabbed a chair and planted it beside the stove for Grady. Simply by turning it about, she could pull him up to the table.

Eddie dropped the other chairs and indicated the women should sit then turned the last chair to the heat.

At his approach, Grady pressed to Linette's side and whimpered. She wrapped her arm around his tiny shoulders. "Hush, child. You're safe here. Nice and warm."

Eddie dug in his pocket and withdrew six perfectly round stones and an assortment of interestingly shaped pieces of wood. Two were round knots. Four resembled crude animals and the other two were smooth lengths. "Grady, here's some things you can play with."

Grady buried his face against Linette's shoulder and wailed.

"It's not personal. He's feeling lost. He'll soon enough realize he's safe." It was her daily prayer. The boy had been inconsolable since his mother's death. She reached for the objects. Eddie dumped them into her palms. They were warm from his touch and her throat pinched tight. She told herself it meant nothing and she dropped them to her lap. "Look, Grady. This one looks like a cow."

The boy wasn't interested.

"Perhaps later." She turned away knowing natural curiosity and abject boredom would overcome fear in short order. "Thanks for bringing the chairs."

"There's food and other things I figured you might need in order to survive." He indicated the sack he'd dropped on the floor.

"Thank you." She started to edge away from Grady's grip. "I'll see to tea." *Please let there be something in that sack I can prepare.*

Eddie signaled her to remain seated. "First, I'd like to hear the answer to Mrs. Godfrey's question."

Linette shook her head and did her best to look confused, as if she didn't recall.

The way Eddie quirked one eyebrow she knew she hadn't fooled him. Nevertheless, he repeated Cassie's question. "Why would you cross the ocean and most of North America to marry a stranger? Surely there are interested men in England."

Linette's shudder was sincere. "Of course, and my father made sure all the men I met were suitable in his estimation." She tried to keep her voice strong but suspected everyone heard the tremor that came from the pit of her stomach. She swallowed hard and forced back her revulsion. "He agreed to a marriage between myself and a distant relative who to all accounts is rich in land and money." She clamped her teeth together to keep from revealing how disgusting she found the idea then released them to speak again. "He is a fat old man."

"How old?" Eddie's voice rang with doubt.

"He's fifty-one." Did he think she'd made up the age difference? Even that wouldn't have been so bad. It was the way the man looked at her, his eyes undressing her as he licked his lips like a hungry dog. Realizing she clutched at her upper arms as if to protect herself, she lowered her hands to her lap.

"How old are you?" He still sounded unconvinced.

"I'm twenty." She tipped her chin proudly. "Some might think I'm old enough to welcome any sort of a marriage, but I'll never be that old."

Eddie chuckled.

"You wouldn't find it amusing if you were in my position."

Cassie sniffed. "Men are never in that position."

Eddie sobered though his eyes continued to spark amusement. "I'm trying to guess what you said or did to convince your father to let you travel West."

"Your good name and your letter were enough." She ducked her head. "I also pointed out the nearness of a convent where I knew I could find shelter and protection." Her father had vowed all kinds of damage to the convent if she had actually gone there, so it wasn't really an option.

Grady edged a hand to Linette's lap and gingerly explored the largest rock.

"Do you know my age?"

She returned her gaze to Eddie. "Margaret said you're twenty-five." How must Eddie feel to be turned down by the woman he expected to become his wife? It hurt to think about it. "I'm sorry for your disappointment."

He held her gaze for a heartbeat. She read a distant hurt, then he blinked and let only his disapproval reveal itself. She would assuredly make a far better rancher's wife than Margaret ever would. But of course, the heart did not always see what the head knew was best.

"I was married at sixteen," Cassie said, rocking slowly, pulling Linette's attention to her. She wished she could erase the pain from the woman's expression. "We worked hard to save enough money for our passage. Then we worked in Ontario. I wanted to stay there. We had a nice house, but George heard there was good land along the North Saskatchewan River. He saved enough to buy an outfit and settle in the Northwest. We sold everything. But George got sick in Montreal." Her voice fell to a whisper. "I thought I'd die when he died. I used the last of our savings to have him buried," she moaned. "He deserved far better."

So did Cassie, but Linette didn't say so, knowing far too well the woman was given to bouts of discouragement and defeat.

Cassie gave the stove a bleak look. "Here I am not yet twenty-five, a widow. I'll be alone the rest of my life."

"God has a plan for your life. He says His thoughts toward us are of peace, and not of evil." She spoke of a verse she thought to be in Jeremiah.

"I've seen little reason to believe God wants to do me good." Cassie's voice shook. "Until I see otherwise, I think I'll trust my own resources."

"What is your opinion?" Linette asked Eddie. Even if he'd received her letter and agreed to a marriage of convenience, she'd made up her mind not to marry until she was certain of his convictions. He'd expressed his faith in his letters, but she wanted to hear it firsthand. She still wanted to hear it, though marriage now seemed but a distant possibility. But no, she would not abandon hope that God could work a miracle over the winter.

He gave his answer some consideration. "I believe God honors those who honor Him."

"Yes. I agree."

"And how do you suggest we do that?" Cassie demanded.

"I can't answer for everyone," Eddie said. "For me, it means doing my duty. Honoring my father and mother. Being charitable."

A man of honor, just as she'd guessed from the first. Surely she stood a chance of finding favor in his eyes. She tried to signal her relief to Cassie. But the other woman only stared at Eddie.

"So you think if we do what is right, God will treat us fairly?"

"That's my belief."

"So what did I do wrong to lose a husband and two babies? They were born beautiful and whole but never drew breath."

"I can't say. That's between you and God."

"Oh, no," Linette protested. His words sounded condemning, as if Cassie harbored secret sins. Linette found such reasoning to be flawed. "You can't reduce God to human intelligence and emotions. There are circumstances we aren't aware of. We don't see the big picture, but God does. That's where trust comes in."

Cassie made a sound of raw disbelief. "When you've lost everything, then you can talk to me about trust. Until then, it's only childish wishing."

Linette ached for Cassie's pain, but the woman was stronger than she realized to have survived such hardship. However, Linette couldn't imagine enduring such tragedies without God's help. "Whatever happens I will trust God." She wondered what Eddie thought and met his gaze, felt a jolt in her lungs at the way he studied her.

"I hope you never have occasion to believe in anything but the goodness of God." Did he sound just a little doubtful? As if he considered it possible? This situation was about as bad as things could get. And her faith had not faltered.

"'He will never leave me nor forsake me.' Now I'm going to make tea." She clapped her hands to her knees, startling Grady, who whimpered and buried his face against her shoulder. She put the toys on the floor, took his hand and drew him after her toward the sack.

Eddie jumped to his feet and accompanied her. "Cookie wasn't sure what you would want. She says if you need anything, just trot on over to the cookhouse."

"There's another woman on the place?"

Eddie chuckled at her delighted surprise. "Yup. Cookie."

Linette stepped past the sack to peer out the window. "Which is the cookhouse?"

Eddie stood close to her, bending a little so he could see out the window. "Can't miss it. It's the two-story building right across the road. Cookie—Miz Liza McCormick—and her husband, Bertie, live on the upper floor, but mostly you'll find both of them cooking and feeding the crew."

"Liza? Pretty name. How many are in your crew?"

"During the summer, there's twelve men, give or take, plus me and the McCormicks. Less once winter sets in. Six or eight men. Right now most of them are up in the hills, edging the cattle down. And best call her Cookie."

"Another woman. Isn't that nice, Cassie?"

Cassie showed marginal interest. But it didn't dampen Linette's relief. The place suddenly seemed a lot more civilized and friendly. She studied the building across the wide expanse Eddie had called a road. As soon as possible, she'd pay Liza—or Cookie, if she preferred—a visit. Eager to get on with this new life, Linette spun away from the window and almost pressed her cheek to his chest.

His eyes widened.

Something quivered in the pit of her stomach.

Their gazes held for a moment of nervous awareness at the realization they were going to be sharing these tight quarters for several months.

She ducked her head, lest he guess at the way her heart had come unsettled. She could expect such encounters throughout the winter. She must prepare herself. Learn how to keep her emotions under lock and key. She would not be controlled by feelings.

The winter…only a few months…but more than long enough for God to work a change in Eddie's heart. In the meantime, she had to prove to him how nice it was to have her around.

"Let's see what Cookie sent over." He hadn't meant to be drawn into questions about Linette's personal life. What did it matter to him if her father had chosen a marriage partner she didn't welcome? Yet the idea made his muscles tighten. He'd seen the way she held herself and knew she didn't make up her fears. It couldn't be pleasant to be controlled by a father who didn't take her feelings into consideration.

He could only hope something would change on her behalf before spring when he'd send her back to her father.

Linette tried to extract herself from Grady's clutches. "Look, Grady. Play with these things and I'll make you something to eat, but I can't work with you hanging from my arm."

Grady poked his face around Linette enough to expose one eye. He saw Eddie and with a loud cry burrowed into Linette's skirts.

Eddie backed off, carefully avoiding looking directly at the boy.

Grady waited until Eddie picked up the sack and carried it to the table before he untangled himself from Linette's side and hurried back to the stove, where he squatted to examine the objects that would have to pass as toys until something better could be found or fashioned. Grady made sure to keep his face toward Eddie as if he had to know where the enemy stood.

Linette edged to Eddie's side. "Thank you for being patient with him."

He pulled flour and sugar from the sack as he considered her words. Why should she care, when she had no connection to this child? Yet it made him realize even more how generous his father had been in taking in himself and his mother and giving them his name. He redoubled his vow to live a life that would honor that gift. "He's not a lot different than a scared animal. Here's a slab of bacon and other things Cookie thought you could use. Lots of women wouldn't give an orphaned child a second glance." In his case, his father and mother had married. Eddie was part of the union. But Linette had no connection to this boy. "Why do you?" He kept his voice low so Grady wouldn't hear.

She shifted the supplies around, examining them and lining them up. "We need a shelf for these."

Just when he thought she intended to ignore his question, she faced him.

"I simply cannot walk by someone in need and pretend I don't see them or can't help them." Her eyes flashed some kind of challenge as if she'd had to defend her views before.

"I'm guessing your feelings haven't met with approval."

Her sigh puffed out her cheeks. "According to my parents, ladies don't soil their hands with such matters. They say there are people whose calling is to do such things. People of the church. Not regular people." All the while she talked she held his gaze. Her compassion and conviction poured from her like hot tea.

"You've rescued an orphan boy and a widowed woman. I'd say you've done your share."

Her eyes turned to cold amber. "Are you warning me?"

"Miss Edwards, sometimes practical matters must be considered. And propriety. This cabin won't hold any more charity cases."

"Propriety?" She kept her voice low, but still managed to make the word ring with distaste. "It will never stop me from following my heart and conscience."

Eddie stopped removing items from the sack. "Are you informing me you will have no regard for how you conduct yourself? I warn you, so long as you are under my roof and living with the protection of my good name, I expect you to live in a way that will not bring dishonor to it." Why couldn't Margaret have chosen to follow through on their agreement? She had proven an agreeable companion. Was this all some colossal joke played by the universe? Until this moment, he would have said God had a hand in all the events of his life. Now he wasn't sure. Seems Linette was a stubborn, headstrong woman. If people acted contrary to God's directions, how could they still be under His control?

His jaw ached and he forced it to unlock. He would not let any of these people bring disgrace to the Gardiner name.

Linette regarded him, her face set in hard lines and flat disapproval. "I have always lived in an honorable fashion. I simply refuse to live by silly social expectations, especially if they require I go against the teaching of my Lord and Savior."

He squeezed the back of his neck, feeling the muscles corded like thick rope. "I certainly wouldn't ask that of you. Honoring God is first in life." Right along with honoring his father and mother.

"Good. Then we are agreed." She reached into the sack and pulled out a fry pan and pot. "I'll soon have something for tea."

Eddie didn't feel nearly as satisfied that they understood each other. Somehow he expected she would agree to his terms only if they suited her. How was he going to make sure she didn't turn this into a disaster for him and his family?

She smiled across the table. "Mr. Gardiner, you have nothing to fear from me. I promise I will do all in my power to make this a most pleasant winter. In fact, you might decide you want us to stay."

"Only until it's safe for you to travel."

She ducked her head, but not before he glimpsed the self-assured satisfaction in her expression.

What did she have in mind? Whatever it was, he could tell her she could do nothing to make him change his decision.

Besides, Margaret would reconsider becoming his wife when she heard about the fine house.

He glanced at Cassie, who sat staring at the stove. She had the look of someone lost in her thoughts. The woman was supposed to be Linette's chaperone. As such, shouldn't she be the one preparing the meal? Seems Linette couldn't see when she was being taken advantage of. Allowing a father to thrust a child into her care, allowing a widow woman to sit idle while she did the chores.

If Cassie had been one of the cowboys, he would have whistled and tipped his head toward the work.

How did one order a woman to do her share?

Linette stood at the table, turning the hunk of bacon over and over. He watched her, wondering what her problem was.

She set aside the meat and lifted the towel from the bowl of cooked potatoes Cookie had sent over. She poked them with one finger. Her brow furrowed. Was she unfamiliar with basic cooking? His stomach growled at the thought.

Thanks to Cookie's generosity, there were baking powder biscuits and some cold roast beef. Linette set the latter two out on a plate and put out butter and syrup, along with the tea she had made. She set the table carefully, arranging each piece of silverware as exactly as if she used a ruler. "It's ready," she said, indicating they should sit at the table.

Eddie pulled himself from the wall where he'd been alternately observing the newly arrived occupants of his house and studying the darkening sky out the window. He should be with the men, bringing the cows down from the hills, but the unexpected guests had delayed him and now the sun dipped toward the horizon. It would soon disappear behind the distant mountains.

Heavy clouds hung from the sky. It would be good if the snow held off a few more days. A few more weeks would be even better, but he didn't like to sound greedy.

At Linette's call, Cassie sighed and pushed heavily to her feet. She wasn't as old as Eddie first judged. Life had been hard on her. He suspected a strong woman lay beneath the sharp exterior. Only a fighter would have survived what she'd been through.

The first step Eddie took had Grady scuttling toward the wall. Eddie stopped.

"I'll feed him later," Linette said.

It grated on Eddie's nerves that his presence was unwelcome in his own home. But not nearly as much as it bothered him to be the cause of Grady's fear. "We might as well start out the way we intend to continue. I eat my meals in a civilized fashion. I expect the same from my guests." He made no threatening moves as he squatted to Grady's level. "Grady, this is my house. You're welcome here, but when we eat, we sit together at the table. Think you can do that?"

Grady shook his head and whimpered. His gaze brushed past Eddie, not quite connecting but allowing Eddie to see something in the boy's eyes. Hurt. Insecurity. Rejection. He didn't understand how he knew and recognized it, but he did as surely as he knew his name. This boy was filled with consuming fear and loneliness. He had every reason to feel that way. His own father had turned his back on him.

Eddie's insides trembled and a pain shot through his jaw as he struggled to keep his expression from revealing what he thought of such a man. The boy did not deserve the hurt heaped on him by his father. No one did.

He ached to promise the boy he was safe now. But hurting and fearful animals—and little boys—needed lots of reassurance. "Aren't you hungry?"

Grady glanced toward the table then he studied Eddie hard and solemnly.

Eddie didn't move. Didn't smile. He just waited, letting the child see he meant him no harm. Finally Grady edged away, keeping as much distance between himself and Eddie as possible. He hurried to Linette's side and buried his face in her skirts.

Eddie pushed to his feet. "Grady, you will sit on a chair to eat." Linette's glare seared, while Cassie watched with indifference.

Grady climbed to a chair and sat, giving Eddie a look of defiance. Eddie could almost read his thoughts. *I'm sitting on the outside, but I'm doing what I want on the inside.*

Eddie struggled to keep from laughing.

Linette sat down with a huff of exasperation.

Sobering instantly, he met her gaze. Did she find all rules and conventions to her dislike? "A man is ruler in his own house. Is that not from the scriptures?" At the flash in her eyes he wondered if she would defy the word of God.

The winter looked longer and colder with every passing hour.

Chapter Three

W hy had God made woman to be subject to a man?

Linette knew the verse he referred to. It had mocked her on many occasions. She would never dispute God's word, but some of it was hard to swallow. It made marriage most unappealing. She would avoid it altogether except it provided her only hope of escaping her father's plans.

Eddie waited until she was settled. "I'll say the blessing."

She bowed her head. Although Eddie had insisted on Grady's obedience, he'd at least been gentle with the boy. It wouldn't be hard to be wife to a man who treated her with such kindness and respected her heart's yearnings. But she feared she wanted more than she could hope for. More and more it looked as if she would not find freedom here any more than she had in England. Still, anything was better than marrying a lumpy, lecherous old man.

She waited until everyone had taken a biscuit or several. "I'm afraid I'm not much of a cook," she murmured. "We had a cook at home who refused to let me in the kitchen."

"This is fine."

She'd done nothing but put stuff on the table. If she expected to prove her worth she would have to do much better. "I'm sure I'll manage." If only someone would explain what to do with the supplies. Surely Cassie knew. She sent the woman an imploring look. They had to learn to enjoy each other's company. "This is your second winter on the ranch, isn't it?"

Eddie looked relieved to have something to talk about. "It is."

"Tell us what it's like."

"Unpredictable."

She laughed at his tone—half regretful, half admiring. "How so?"

"It can snow four feet. The temperature can drop out of sight. Then we get a Chinook that melts the snow and makes us all foolishly think the worst is over."

Cassie perked up. "A Chinook? What's that?"

"A warm wind that blasts over the mountains. We can go from shivering under a heavy coat to working in our shirtsleeves all within an hour or less."

"It's a legend then?" Cassie said, sarcasm dripping from each word.

Linette silently prayed Eddie wouldn't be offended. Was she destined to spend her days interceding on Cassie's behalf?

Thankfully Eddie chuckled. "Part legend in that the Indians have all sorts of stories about what it is, but there's nothing remotely imaginary about what happens."

"I can hardly wait," Linette said. "It's going to be exciting to experience a wild Canadian winter."

Eddie's look challenged her before he pushed his plate away to indicate he was done. Did he think she had undertaken this trip solely for the sake of an adventure? She willingly admitted she enjoyed seeing new and exciting things. But no, the impetus behind her bold venture was twofold—escape the specter of a marriage with a man who made her skin crawl, and hopefully, God willing, find a place where she could obey the dictates of her conscience without regard to foolish social expectations.

The kettle steamed again and Linette prepared to do the washing up with the hot water. Cassie turned her chair and pushed it closer to the stove.

Eddie stood and piled up the dirty dishes. "Everyone does his share here." He glanced toward Cassie.

Linette's hands remained suspended over the washbasin. She could manage on her own and didn't mind doing the work, but Eddie gave her a warning look. She ducked her head. Seems he was intent on establishing his rules and she was helpless to do anything but cooperate. Not that she didn't think Cassie should help, but she didn't know how far he meant this rule making to go. She kept her head down as she studied him, measuring him, wondering what would happen if she refused to obey one of his directives. His expression remained patient. On the other hand, how pleasurable to share goals and dreams with such a man.

Slowly it dawned on Cassie that Eddie expected her to help. She pushed her chair back so hard it banged into the table. "Don't see how much help it will be for me to be stuck under Linette's elbow. There's not enough room for one, let alone two."

Linette pulled the basin closer and handed Cassie a towel. She took it silently and dried the few dishes.

Eddie strode outside.

"He's lord and master here, that's for sure," Cassie

grumbled. "I'm sick of men controlling everything. Why don't we pack up and leave?"

"Cassie, where would we go?" She'd gladly leave if she could find an alternative that wouldn't bring her father's wrath about her head. Except—an errant thought surfaced—this was where she wanted to be. She'd dreamed of it for weeks as she prepared to leave home and as she crossed the ocean and the country. She pictured herself sharing life with a man who honored her heart's desire, and the dream refused to die in spite of Eddie's insistence that she go back home. She forced her mind back to Cassie's question. "It's not like there are hundreds of homes around here that would welcome us."

"What about that ranch where those men were going? They seemed like nice gentlemen."

"They were very polite but no doubt would expect to rule their home as well."

"I'm sure we could throw ourselves on their mercy."

Linette grabbed Cassie by the shoulders. "I don't intend to beg any man to keep me." She'd prove her worth to Eddie. She'd make him want her to stay. "Wherever I go, whatever happens, I will do my share. In return, I will expect freedom to make a few decisions on my own."

Cassie shook Linette's hands off. "Mr. Gardiner told you he expects obedience."

"Surely a woman can please a man and still be allowed to express her opinion and choices."

Cassie rocked her head back and forth. "He could make life miserable for us."

"I pray it won't be so."

"You were prepared to marry him."

"I thought I knew a bit about him from Margaret's

letters." Now she wasn't so sure. In fact, nothing seemed so simple anymore.

Cassie plucked at her sleeve. "He could take advantage of us if he wants. Both of us. Look at how small this place is. We have no hope of escaping him."

Linette smiled. "The closeness is our protection. If you feel threatened, you only have to call out. But I think we have nothing to fear from him. Does he not strike you as a man of strong morals?" He seemed intent on doing things the right way. Just how far that went, they would no doubt see in the following weeks as they shared this tiny cabin.

Eddie strode through the door with a length of lumber and a hammer in hand.

Cassie watched with undisguised wariness as he fastened a shelf across one side of the room.

"This should serve as a pantry for now."

"Thank you." Linette truly appreciated his efforts. She hoped it meant he intended to make the best of the situation—a thought that buoyed her heart.

Now that she'd finished the clean-up, Linette called Grady to her and washed him in preparation for the night. "Cassie, do you want to put Grady to bed?"

Cassie jerked her gaze away from studying Eddie, relief filling her eyes. "I'll lie down with him." Linette understood she was grateful for escape from the close quarters.

Linette soon had the shelf neatly organized with their kitchen supplies. Cassie and Grady were only a few steps away in the bedroom, but suddenly she was alone with Eddie. Neither of them spoke and the quietness crowded every corner of the room.

"Tell me about Grady."

His question shattered the stillness and made her

nerves twitch. Then she drew in a deep breath, grateful he had initiated conversation. "You mean besides the fact he is an orphan?"

"He has a father, so technically he is not an orphan. No other relatives?"

Was he hoping he could send the child away? "Apparently not."

"And what if the father changes his mind and wants him back?"

"It would be wonderful if he did. I pray he will."

"In the meantime, you have his care, but who is his legal guardian?"

"I am."

"By whose authority?"

"His father signed the papers naming me such."

Eddie quirked an eyebrow, perhaps in disbelief. "It surprises me he cared enough to do so."

"He didn't. I asked him to do it."

Both his eyebrows rose and Lincttc allowed herself a little smugness at having surprised him.

"You seem to have thought this through."

"You might be surprised at how carefully I consider my choices."

His pause filled the air with quivcring tension. "And yet you still do them."

She ignored the slight sarcasm.

"Cassie has no family she could appeal to?"

"What is this? Trying to find alternate arrangements for your guests?"

He looked at her with annoyance. "No need to be rude. I'm only trying to learn as much as I can."

For a moment she silently challenged him. But he was right. The man deserved to be treated better. "I'm sorry. I didn't mean to be rude. To answer your question,

Cassie has no family she's willing to admit to. I know she complains a lot and Grady is still afraid of everything, but I promise I will do my best to—"

"I'm not trying to get rid of you. I said you're welcome until spring. Rest assured, I won't withdraw my word."

She wondered when the deadline had shifted from improved weather to spring but wasn't about to question God's good favor. "It's good to know I can count on it." There was so much more she wanted to say. How much she'd enjoyed seeing the vast plains of the Northwest. How she'd felt free for the first time in her life. How she didn't mind the crowded conditions of the cabin because it felt cozy. How she couldn't keep from wanting to help those in distress. Instead, she turned the conversation to less controversial topics. "You said you met Kootenai Brown. He sounds like an interesting man. Tell me about him."

Eddie relaxed, stretching his legs out and angling back in the chair. "Kootenai Brown has been in the western territories for twenty years or more. In that time, he has established quite a reputation, if one were to believe all the stories told about him. Soldier, gold miner, police constable, wolfer, whiskey trader. Tales say that he was captured by Sitting Bull and escaped. Another says he murdered a man in Fort Benton. Still another claims he was shot in the back by a Blackfoot arrow, pulled it out himself and treated the wound with turpentine."

Linette watched Eddie as he spun tale after tale of a man larger than life. Some of the stories were undoubtedly exaggerated. Eddie's eyes flashed with humor as he talked. His mouth gentled and his voice carried a rich timbre. And as she listened, she came to a firm conviction. "I can't go back."

Eddie blinked and seemed to pull his thoughts toward her words. "Are you really Linette Edwards?"

Her chin came up and her eyes stung with defiant challenge. "Of course I am Linette Edwards. Why would you doubt it? Who do you think I am?"

He took his time answering. "You aren't dressed like the daughter of wealthy man."

She laughed. She'd managed to confound him and it pleased her to no end. "I traded my fine dresses for practical ones at Fort Benton."

He didn't seem to care that his eyes revealed doubt.

She smiled. "I'm grateful for the few months I'll be able to enjoy this vast country."

The door rattled as if a person sought entrance.

She turned. "Is someone there?"

Eddie chuckled. "You might have cause to hate the country before the winter is out. That, Miss Edwards, is the wind knocking at the door."

He looked a totally different man when he relaxed and smiled. Handsome, kindly and appealing. She caught her thoughts and pushed them into submission. Yet one lingered long enough to be heard. Sharing his company throughout the winter might be pleasant enough.

His smile deepened and his eyes darkened.

She ducked away, pretending to examine an imaginary spot on her skirt.

"Hear the snow against the window?" he asked.

Glad to leave the awkward moment, she turned toward the window. Wet white flakes plopped against the glass with a definite *platt* sound.

"Come have a look." Eddie pulled himself into action with the grace of a young kitten.

She followed him to the door. When he slipped a coat over his shoulders, she did the same. As they stepped out into the night air, she was glad she'd traded her gold locket for the heavy coat even though it was too large. She pulled it tight around her neck and waited for her eyes to adjust to the darkness. Large flakes of snow, driven by the wind, stuck to the side of the cabin. She lifted her face and let flakes land on her cheeks. Cold and refreshing. She put out her tongue and laughed at how the snow tasted.

Eddie chuckled.

She closed her mouth and swallowed. "It's so clean and fresh."

"If it keeps up all night, it will be deep and dangerous."

"But we are safe and warm."

"My cattle aren't."

"I'm sorry. I didn't mean to be selfish. What will happen to them?"

"The wind will drive them, hopefully, into a place of shelter. Then we'll have to find them and push them out."

"Why can't you leave them there?"

"We can if the snow isn't deep, but if it is, cattle can't dig through it. They'll starve. We've been moving them down, but this snow is earlier than expected."

"Then I will pray you'll be able to get your cows to a safe place."

"I will pray the same."

It made her feel as if he valued her offer. It made her feel as if they were partners in some small way. Linette wished she could see him better and gauge if he felt even a fraction of the same connection.

"It's cold. We better go inside."

His words were her answer. He obviously did not wish to prolong the moment.

Eddie rolled up in his buffalo robe and got comfortable on the floor. He'd slept on the ground many times, often out in the cold. In comparison, this was warm and pleasant. If the temperature dropped too low, he would put more wood on the fire during the night.

He lay on his back listening to the women murmur. He could make out enough to follow their conversation.

"Where did you go?" Cassie's voice carried its perennial sharpness.

"Just outside the door."

"What for? You two got secrets?"

Eddie groaned. Cassie seemed bent on seeing evil and inconvenience at every turn. He wondered if Linette would scold her.

But Linette laughed softly. "I wanted to see the snow."

"You're twenty years old. Surely you've seen snow before."

"Not like this. It was so quiet you could hear each flake hit the ground. And the wind sighed as if carrying the snow had become too much of an effort."

Eddie clasped his hands under his head and listened unashamedly. Linette made it sound magical. Perhaps it was. He hadn't put it into words, but there was something about the country. Maybe its newness. How many times did he wonder if he was the first white man to set foot on a certain spot?

"I told Eddie I would pray his cows are safe."

Eddie. She said his name as if it was as special as the new-falling snow. Yet face-to-face, he was Mr. Gardiner, all formal and stiff. But then, that was proper.

Somehow *proper* didn't sound as pleasant as *Eddie*.

"Who cares about cows?" Cassie obviously didn't. "I don't know how I'm going to endure this for an entire winter."

Linette chuckled again.

Eddie smiled just hearing her.

"Cassie, my friend, you don't have to endure. You can enjoy."

Cassie snorted so loud Grady whimpered. When she spoke again, Eddie couldn't catch her whispered words. He strained to hear Linette's response.

"God gives us each day to enjoy."

Cassie made a sound so full of doubt that Eddie choked back a chuckle.

Linette spoke into the darkness. "I had a nurse who taught me many scripture verses. One in Psalm 118 says, 'This is the day the Lord hath made… Let us rejoice and be glad in it.' She said it's a choice. An act of our will to rejoice. And she would sing the verse." Linette softly sang a song putting the words of the verse to music, repeating it several times.

She'd had a privileged upbringing. Despite Mr. Edwards's dubious background, he'd expect his daughter to be treated as aristocracy. Eddie would have to be careful. He wouldn't give her father a chance to ruin the Gardiner good name.

Cassie didn't say anything. Perhaps she'd fallen asleep, comforted by the lullaby of the song.

Eddie turned to his side and listened to Linette sing. Even after the voices in the other room had grown quiet, the lyrics played over and over in his head. He fell asleep to the tune.

He woke next morning, started a fire and put the coffee to boil. It had settled in to snow seriously. He wanted to head out and look for his cows, but doing so would be foolhardy in this weather. He had good men, experienced cowboys. They knew enough to circle the cows and keep them from drifting. He didn't need to be there helping them. Yet it was his responsibility—and his alone—to insure the herd was safe. The future of the ranch depended on it. But he was stuck here, away from the action, doing nothing to protect his investment. Or more accurately, his father's investment.

Noises from the next room informed him the others were up. He slowly turned from the window and poured a cup of coffee. He'd make sure the guests were safe. Later, he'd head out to the barn. At least he could check on the stock that was there.

The three other occupants of the storm-wrapped cabin stepped into view. Cassie's expression was enough to stop a train and send the occupants dashing for safety. Grady fussed for no reason. But Linette smiled and hummed. He immediately recognized the tune. It was the same one playing over and over in his head. "'This is the day that the Lord hath made… Let us rejoice and be glad in it.'" She seemed intent on enjoying the day. She went immediately to the window. "It's beautiful. Snow covers everything like piles of whipped cream."

She turned, and her smile flattened and she frowned. "I'm sorry. This is not what you need, is it?"

"I would have preferred to have the cows closer before this hit."

She nodded, looked thoughtful a moment longer then turned to the others with a beaming smile. "Cassie,

Grady, look. There's snow everywhere." She lifted Grady to the window to look out.

He laughed. "I play in it?"

Eddie stared at the boy. It was the first time he'd heard anything but a cry from his lips.

"I don't think—" Linette looked at Eddie. "It doesn't look safe out there."

"Not while it's coming down so hard." He lowered his gaze to Grady. "You'll have to wait for a little while."

In his excitement over the snow, Grady had forgotten Eddie. Now he clung to Linette's neck. His lips quivered.

Eddie sighed inwardly. He couldn't bear the idea of more fussing and crying. "If you don't cry I'll take you to see the horses as soon as it's safe. But only big boys can come."

Grady swallowed hard and blinked half a dozen times. "I not cry."

"Good boy. Now climb up to the table and let's see what Linette can find to feed us."

Grady edged around Eddie and sat as far away as the small space would allow.

Linette hadn't moved from the window. She stared at Eddie, her eyes wide.

Had he done something wrong? Did she think he was out of place telling Grady to stop crying? Or—he stifled a groan—had he offended her by calling her by her Christian name? "I'm sorry. I meant Miss Edwards."

"No, Linette is fine. Much more comfortable."

Were her words rushed and airy? He jerked his gaze away in self-disgust. Less than twenty-four hours with two women and a child in his little cabin and he was already getting fanciful. He needed the company of some cows and cowboys.

But first, breakfast.

Linette again pulled the bowl of potatoes toward her and turned the slab of bacon over and over.

Eddie grabbed the butcher knife. "I'll slice us off some pieces. You can fry them up."

"Thank you." She avoided meeting his eyes.

"I take it you've never seen bacon before."

"I'm unfamiliar with the term and the format."

He chuckled. She had a unique way of admitting she didn't have a clue. "It's the same as rashers in England."

Understanding lightened her eyes. "You mean—" She pointed to the chunk of meat and watched with keen interest as he carved off thin slices. "That's what rashers look like before they're all crispy?"

He dropped the pieces into the hot fry pan. "They'll soon be something you recognize."

She stared at the sizzling pan. A heavy sigh left her lungs. "I told you I wasn't a good cook, but I assure you I won't have to be shown twice. In no time at all I'll be creating culinary delights to warm your heart."

A man needed a good feed, especially after working out in the cold. "I could continue to take my meals over at the cookhouse."

Linette's brow furrowed. "Are you suggesting I can't manage? I'll learn. You'll see. Just give me a chance." She sucked in air and opened her mouth to start again.

"Okay. Okay." He held up his palm toward her to stop any further argument. "I'll see how things go." Besides, he could well imagine Cookie's protests if he left the ladies alone and sought his meals with the rest of the crew. No, sir, he didn't need to get a tongue-lashing from that direction. "Maybe Cookie will help you."

Her shoulders sank several inches in relief and she let out a noisy gust. "Thank you. You won't be sorry."

He kept any contrary opinion to himself, but he'd been nothing but sorry since she'd landed on his ranch. He expected he'd be sorry until the day she left.

As he waited for her to prepare breakfast he went to the window and scratched a peephole in the frost. Slim and Roper hustled toward the cookhouse. They slid their attention toward the cabin, saw him peeking through the foggy glass and nodded as if they only wanted to say good-morning when he knew they burned up with curiosity.

"Um." Linette sounded mildly worried. "Is it supposed to smoke like this?"

He spun around. The fry pan smoked like a smoldering fire. "It's too hot. Pull it to the side."

She reached for it without any protection on her hands.

"Wait. Don't touch it."

But her palm touched the hot handle and she jerked back with a gasp.

At that moment the pan caught fire.

Cassie jerked to her feet and pulled Grady after her as she retreated to the far corner, casting desperate looks at the door—their only escape route.

Linette danced about. "What do I do?" She grabbed a towel and flapped it.

"Stop. You're only making it worse. Get out of the way." He crossed the room in three strides, grabbed a nearby lid and clamped it over the pan. He snatched the towel from her hands, clutched the hot fry pan and dashed for the door. He jerked it open and tossed the sizzling pan into the snowbank. It melted down a good eight inches.

He tossed the towel to the table and grabbed her wrist. "Let me see that." He turned her palm upward.

The base of her fingers was red and already forming blisters. "Put snow on it."

She seemed incapable of moving, so he pulled her to the door, grabbed a handful of snow and plastered the burnt area.

"Oh, that feels good."

He grabbed her by the shoulders. "Are you trying to burn the place down?"

She glowered back. "You could have told me this might happen."

"Told you?" He sputtered and slowed his breathing. "You said you were prepared to be a pioneer housewife. But you can't even fry bacon."

"I most certainly can and will." She marched past him and back to the house, grabbed the hunk of bacon and whacked off pieces, unmindful of the pain the burns surely gave.

Grady whimpered. Cassie pulled him close. "Shush, child."

Linette gave the boy a tight smile. "Everything is fine, Grady. Don't worry."

Eddie watched her butcher the meat. "You'll have a great time trying to fry those."

"I'll fry them." *Whack. Whack.*

"Three days from now perhaps."

She paused. "Why do you say that?"

"Because you're cutting them too thick."

"Fine." She slowed down and methodically sliced narrow strips.

He went to retrieve the fry pan, scrubbing as much of the charcoal from it as he could with snow. "Practically ruined a perfectly good pot," he muttered.

"What did you say?" she asked.

"Not a blame thing." He took the burnt pot inside

and poured boiling water into it then set to scrubbing it clean.

"I can do that," she protested.

Somehow he doubted she was a fraction as capable as she tried to make him believe.

"I will make a great pioneer wife." She spit the words out like hot pebbles.

"I've yet to see any evidence supporting that claim." He held up his hand to silence her arguments. "It's a moot point. I don't need or want a pioneer wife."

"You don't know what you're missing."

"And yet I don't seem to mind." He again returned to the window and stared out. Spring was a distant promise. If the sun came out and stayed. If a Chinook took away the snow. If the stagecoach headed back to Fort Benton or even Edendale, Miss Edwards and her entourage would be on it.

But the snow continued to fall, shutting him in the tiny cabin with Miss Edwards and her entourage.

A few minutes later, she announced breakfast was ready.

Acrid smoke still clung to the air, drowning out any enticing aroma, but still she served up a passable meal. He'd had worse. A lot worse. Some from his own hands.

Afterward, Cassie favored him with a defiant look as she helped Linette clean up.

Life had gone from simple to challenging since Linette thrust herself into his home. He shifted his chair toward the stove and pulled out a newspaper that had come in yesterday's package of mail. Linette and Cassie worked in silence and Grady huddled at the corner of the table, darting regular glances toward Eddie. The skin on the back of Eddie's neck itched. He refused to scratch it, but like the presence of the others in the room, it would not go away. The walls of the cabin pushed at his thoughts. "I'm going to check on the stock."

Grady nudged Linette and indicated he wanted to whisper in her ear.

She bent to hear his words. Her gaze slipped toward Eddie as she answered the boy. "Not yet."

She straightened and returned her attention to the dishes.

Whatever Grady said had something to do with him. "What is it?"

"Nothing," Linette replied.

He waited. He would not be ignored or dismissed in his own house.

Linette lifted one shoulder. "He wanted to know if you were taking him to see the horses." She smiled down at Grady. "It's still snowing heavily."

Eddie studied the boy. The air around him vibrated with expectation—whether in anticipation of seeing the horses or fear of being told no, Eddie couldn't be sure. Seemed the boy had every reason to expect rejection. "Grady, as soon as it's decent out I'll take you to the barn and you can visit the horses. It's a deal." He held out his hand. Perhaps the boy would trust him enough to shake, but Grady shrank back against Linette.

Eddie lowered his hand. "Well, then." He grabbed his coat and ventured out into the cold. It would take time. Trust didn't happen all at once.

The heavy wet snow reached his ankles. It would be even deeper farther up the mountains. If the men hadn't been able to hold the herd… He refused to think of a disaster. Yet how many stories had he heard of cows driven by the wind, trapped in a box canyon, found dead in the spring?

He stomped through the snow. Things were different here than back in England. The elements were more challenging, but his father would not accept that some things were out of Eddie's control. Gardiners didn't let the elements get the best of them. Gardiners conquered challenges. And his father had sent Eddie West to do exactly that. He expected regular reports at their London home informing him Eddie had dutifully fulfilled those expectations. Eddie was determined he would live up to his father's faith in him and maybe prove himself worthy of the Gardiner name.

He flung the barn door open and stepped inside. Several of the horses nickered a greeting. He breathed in the sweet smell of hay, the pungent odor of horseflesh and sighed. He was at home here. For a few minutes he could forget his problems—the cattle needing to be brought down from the mountains and the people claiming shelter in his cabin.

But both threatened his peace of mind.

Chapter Four

Silence filled the room after Eddie left, as if everyone held their breath to see if he would return. When it appeared he wouldn't, they waited for the feeling of his presence to depart.

Grady slowly unraveled himself from Linette's skirts and edged toward the pieces of wood and rocks Eddie had given him. He sat down and sorted them. Soon he played happily, talking to himself. Perhaps before long, Linette thought, the time would come when Grady would again be a happy little boy.

Cassie grunted. Discontent seemed her constant companion.

Linette strove to keep it from affecting her own thoughts, which had been caught in a maelstrom since she practically set the place on fire. Eddie had saved them from a disaster, but the incident had done little to further her quest to prove he needed her.

"I can't imagine how we are going to survive a winter crammed together like this," Cassie said.

Linette shook off her worries and looked about. "It's really quite comfortable." She could point out that Eddie had the most reason to feel displaced, but Cassie was still too buried in her own grief to see past it. "Let's fix it up a little." Hopefully Eddie wouldn't mind.

"About the only thing that could improve this place is a fire."

"Don't even say that." Linette shuddered. "We came too close to knowing what it would be like." Thankfully, Eddie had reacted calmly when the pan caught fire. She pressed the back of her burned hand. He had taken care of her in a gentle way that brought a strange tightening in her throat. Even now there was a little jump in her heart rate at the memory. She dismissed her errant thoughts and emotions. She wanted only one thing: a businesslike marriage. No emotional involvement that would rob her of her ability to make choices and decisions on her own. "Where would we live? Out in the cold?"

"There's the big house."

Yes, there was the big house. Somehow she doubted Eddie would invite them to share it with him.

"Seems strange to me that he doesn't suggest we all live there."

"It's obviously not finished." She looked out the window toward the big structure. Snow obscured it, but she remembered the stark bareness of the windows. He'd built it for a special woman. He still hoped Margaret would change her mind and grace his big house with her refined presence. She wouldn't tell him Margaret had been relieved to let Linette take her place. It had been her idea, not Linette's as he seemed to think. She shrugged. God had given her a few months in which to prove her worth to Eddie and she meant to make the most of every minute. "I'm happy for a warm place out of the elements. Come help me." She led the way to the bedroom and knelt before one trunk. "I brought some belongings from home."

Cassie sank to the edge of the bed. "I expected things to be different."

Linette had, too. "We'll make the best of it." She pulled out two pictures and a quilt Tilly and the maids had made for her. "These will brighten the place."

Cassie trailed after her as they returned to the main room. Eddie had left the hammer and nails behind and she used those to hang the pictures. She draped the quilt over one chair. "Isn't that better?"

Cassie shrugged.

Linette refused to let the woman's indifference dampen her resolve. Brightening up the place was step number one in her plan to make Eddie see her as a beneficial addition to his life. "Cassie, you must know how to prepare meals."

"You just take the food and cook it."

"Cassie, I don't know whether to fry it, bake it or boil it. I didn't even know what to do with the bacon besides burn it to charcoal."

The other woman shrugged. "You do now."

Linette wanted to shake her. "Cassie, if I don't prove myself capable, Eddie will have no reason to ask me to stay." She fought the tightness in her jaw that made it difficult to speak. "I simply cannot return to London and marry Lyle Williamson. Will you help me or not?"

Cassie again shrugged. "I guess I could tell you whether to boil, bake or fry something."

"Good." She'd hoped for more enthusiasm, but she'd take what she could get."What can I make for lunch?"

Cassie walked to the shelf, pulled down a number of items and plunked them on the table. "Corn bread, beans and syrup." Crossing her arms across her chest, she stepped back and nodded toward the table.

"Great." One step at a time. With Cassie's help— no matter how reluctant—Linette would conquer this challenge. "Now tell me how to make corn bread and cook the beans."

The men joined Eddie in the barn. He sent two to care for the breeding stock he had in the wintering pens. Slim and Roper hung back.

"The ladies settled okay, boss?" Slim's voice was bland as if he was making idle conversation.

"Seems so." Eddie acted as if he didn't know the men were burning up with curiosity. Had they seen the smoking fry pan he'd tossed into the snowbank? Even if they hadn't, they must have smelled the blackened bacon left behind. He tucked away a smile at Linette's incompetence. It tickled him to think of her practically setting the place on fire in her determination to prove herself a pioneer woman. Seems she'd be better off trying for the position of manor wife. His smile died a sudden death as he realized where his thoughts had gone. No Edwards' woman belonged in the big house.

Roper paused from putting hay in the mangers and scratched his head. "They here to stay?"

"Only for the winter."

"Yeah? Then what?"

"Back to wherever they came from." Eddie jabbed his fork after some horse apples.

"Country could use some fine women." Slim hovered over a gate, seemingly interested in one of its hinges.

"Suppose so but not at my expense."

"Huh." Both men grunted out the sound.

The three of them returned to their chores. Silences

were common when they worked, but this one carried a thousand unasked questions. Eddie paused. "I'll finish up here if you two want to go back to the bunkhouse or up to the cookhouse."

"Yeah, boss."

They sauntered out, none too anxious to be sent elsewhere. They closed the door against the snow. Silence filled the room for a moment then Eddie chuckled. They'd hoped for more information. His smile flattened. What could he tell them? That Cassie hated life and Grady hated men? On top of it, Linette couldn't cook. His stomach burned. There was an old trapper's cabin up along the river. Crude. Probably full of bedbugs. You could throw a cat through the cracks between the logs and last time he'd seen it, a corner of the roof had been ripped back. Likely by curious bears. But it held all the appeal of the finest stopping house. Maybe when the storm let up he'd hole up there for the winter.

Except he had a duty and responsibility making sure the cattle were safe and the ranch ran efficiently. He couldn't walk away.

His stomach growled. He shoveled out the rest of the pens, swept the tack room, tidied the harnesses, noted those that needed mending and generally lingered until the growing demands of his stomach made it impossible to continue hiding in the barn. Even cold potatoes would taste good.

He tromped back through the deepening snow, paused outside the door to accustom himself to the intruders before he stepped inside.

The aroma of beans, hot bread of some sort and coffee caused his mouth to flood with saliva. Had Linette suddenly learned how to cook?

He glanced about. Why did the place seem warm and

welcoming? Something was different, but he couldn't quite pinpoint what it was.

"I'm hungry." He hadn't meant to sound so desperate, but it was too late to pull back his hasty words.

"Dinner is ready." Linette stood at the end of the table, her hands clasped together at her waist. "There's hot water in the kettle."

He washed up then took his place at the table where the others waited. Linette still stood. He raised an eyebrow. "Shall I say the blessing?"

"Of course." She dropped to the chair and bowed her head.

Eddie studied her a moment. Did she seem tense? Had she smiled since he stepped into the house? He couldn't remember. And why did it matter? Except it did. A man liked to find peace in his home. And as he'd said to Cookie, Linette had a pleasant smile. He forced himself to add the comment he'd tacked on for Cookie. Matched by a stubborn attitude. He bowed his head and scraped together a sense of gratitude so he could pray genuine words of thanks.

As soon as he said "Amen," Linette passed him a pan of corn bread. He dug out a generous portion, doused it with beans and syrup and lifted a forkful toward his mouth, when he realized Linette watched him. He lowered the fork. "Is something wrong?"

She laughed a little. "No, just waiting to see if you like the food."

He filled his mouth, chewed once then nodded. "It's good."

She sank deeper into her chair. The corners of her mouth lifted as if her smile came from somewhere deep in her heart.

But the second chew revised his opinion. The beans

were hard pellets. He crunched bravely, hoping he wouldn't break a tooth.

She concentrated on chewing. "Are the beans supposed to be this hard?" She looked to Cassie for an answer.

Cassie shrugged. "Guess they should have cooked longer."

Eddie eyed the generous portion of beans on his plate. But after another heroic mouthful he scraped them to one side. "Cook them overnight. They'll be fine in the morning."

Suddenly the corn bread and syrup seemed far from adequate. If this kept up he'd have no choice but to throw himself on Cookie's mercy.

"I'll do better." Linette's words rang with determination. "Like I said, I'm a fast learner." Her gaze caught and held his, silently reminding him of other things she'd said. *A long time till spring. He might grow to appreciate her company.*

The words taunted him. Mocked him. He pushed from the table. Snow still fell heavily, but he must find something to do elsewhere. He grabbed his coat and left the cabin to trudge through the deepening snow to the barn. Apart from sweeping the floor again, there was nothing to do.

He considered going to the bunkhouse where the men would be gathered around the stove fixing their boots or at the table playing cards. They would welcome him, but it encroached on their spare time. He longed to go to the cookhouse and fill up on Cookie's baking, but she wouldn't give him a moment's peace. She'd demand to know why he wasn't entertaining those fine ladies while he had the chance. Even if he repeated a thousand times over that he wasn't interested in whether or not they were fine women and that he was starving, she'd never hear a word contrary to her opinion.

He stepped outside, pulled his woolen scarf around his neck and headed for the wintering pens.

Snow swirled about him, clinging to his eyelashes. The herd pressed against the wooden fences, seeking shelter. They stirred at his approach. The men had put out sufficient feed. All he accomplished by poking around was to unsettle the animals.

He retraced his steps toward the buildings. The house on the hill was barely discernible. If it didn't mean starting a fire to warm the place, he would go there even though it required marching through snow up to his knees.

His steps slowed. There was only one place for him. Back at the cabin. He squinted as he realized there was something he needed to do. No time like the present.

He reached the cabin door, stomped snow from his boots and shook it from his hat before he stepped indoors.

The room radiated warmth. He glanced about. Yes, there was a fire blazing in the small stove, but it was more. He still couldn't put his finger on it.

Cassie sat before the stove with yarn and knitting needles. Linette stood at the table chopping something and dropping the pieces into a cooking pot. He sniffed. Onions maybe.

Grady played under the table. He'd fashioned a fence of kindling and arranged the rocks and bits of wood like animals in a pen.

He chuckled. "Grady, that's how I used to play."

Grady shrank back trying to get out of sight.

Eddie didn't take offense. The child would need time to learn Eddie intended to be his friend.

Linette grabbed a cup from the shelf. "Coffee? Something to eat?"

"Coffee sounds good. Thanks."

She filled the cup and sat it before him.

"No one else is having coffee?" he asked.

Linette and Cassie exchanged glances. Cassie ducked her head, suddenly very interested in her knitting. Linette grabbed a carrot and butchered the thing, scooting the pieces into the pot. "We've had tea already, but I assumed you preferred coffee."

"Having no doubt read about the huge pots of coffee the cowboys drink while on cattle drives." His words, softly spoken, sounded dry and humorless even to himself.

Cassie snorted. "I'll venture a guess she knows more about cowboys than you."

Linette's gaze grew dark. "Of course I don't. But I did learn a lot." She looked past Eddie. If he didn't miss his guess, she looked past the walls of this cabin. "If I were a man I'd join a cattle drive." Slowly, as if realizing Eddie stared at her, she brought her attention back to the room. "Can I offer you a tea biscuit?"

"Thanks." He hoped she had a large plateful. "I kind of like tea especially on a cold wintry day."

"Why didn't you say so?" She bustled to the stove and shook the kettle, then poured in more water and moved it to the center of the stove. "I can make you tea, if you prefer it."

"Coffee will do this time. But in future wait for me and we'll have tea together." Now, why had he said that? It wasn't as if he planned to stop his work every afternoon to join them for a cup of tea and a friendly chat. No, sir. He intended to stay as far away from this place as humanly possible.

The women again exchanged looks. He couldn't begin to guess what silent signal they sent each other. Maybe they preferred to have their tea without his company.

"Unless that interferes with your plans?"

"Of course not. I'd be glad to make tea for you."

He noticed Linette did not include Cassie in her welcome. But it didn't matter. It was his house; he was the host, they the guests. Something they all needed to remember.

He savored his coffee and the biscuits. He had come indoors with a task in mind. Oh, yeah. A letter to Margaret. He pulled the writing things from the bookshelf and arranged them where they wouldn't extend into Linette's working space and get soiled. "I'm going to write Margaret. If she knows about the house I've built she'll change her mind." He bent his head and began. The first part was easy.

Dear Margaret,

How are you? I was disappointed that Miss Edwards came and not you.

I blame myself, because I planned a surprise for you. I see now that I should have told you.

He stopped writing and stared at the tabletop. How did he put his dreams and hopes into a few words and expect anyone to understand?

He'd seen men with a favorite horse share silent communication. If it were possible between man and beast, surely it was possible between a man and a woman. He and Margaret had corresponded for almost two years, and before he left London they had talked about the future. He trusted it formed a basis for understanding the message behind the words he intended to put on paper. He resumed writing.

It is true I now live in a small cabin. Hardly big enough for the four people now crowded in here for the winter. But on the hill is the surprise I planned to have ready for you before we wed. A big house. It is as fine as any house in the West. No, finer. There are six bedrooms besides the main bedroom, which has two large dressing rooms plus a nursery, so it's really a little suite in one wing of the house.

He filled a page of unsatisfying description.

I fear I am portraying this poorly. I will ask Miss Edwards to give you her own description.

The feelings filling his heart would not form as words on the page. He stared at the pen in his hand. What did he really want to say?

Margaret, my dear. I have no intention of marrying Miss Edwards. I will send her back to her home as soon as the weather permits. I hope news of the house I have built will persuade you to reconsider and come in the spring.

He blotted the ink and waited for it to dry then folded the pages and addressed the envelope. He set the letter on top of the bookshelf in plain view. A reminder to Miss Edwards of his intention.

As soon as the weather permitted, he would give Linette a tour of the house then request she write to Margaret with a full report.

He pulled out the magazines and newspapers from yesterday's mail and returned to his chair to read. The room radiated warmth, something on the stove simmered. So far the meals had been a disappointment, but the aroma gave him hope supper might be better.

Cassie's knitting needles clicked in a steady rhythm. Underneath the table, Grady resumed play, murmuring to his toys and occasionally raising his voice as he ordered one of the pretend animals to stop or turn. Linette stirred the pot and hummed.

Eddie thought of the big house and Margaret's presence. Would she fill it with a similar sense of home and contentment? Or would they live parallel lives like so many married couples did? He only had to get through the winter to find out.

Later, they shared a tasty soup full of vegetables. The meat proved to be a little chewy but he managed. It beat starving.

Dishes finished, Cassie took Grady to bed. Linette followed shortly afterward.

For some reason he'd expected her to linger as she had last night. Not that he needed company. Of course not. He was grateful for a chance to be alone in his own house. He had plenty of reading to do. But he kept pausing to listen. He didn't hear a word and soon abandoned reading the newspapers. He unrolled his furs. As he bent to put out the lamp a flicker of color on the wall caught his eye. He straightened, lifted the lamp to a painting, ornately framed. Bluebells, yellow gorse, orange poppies and other flowers in wild abandon filled the canvas.

As he stared, winter disappeared and he imagined strolling through the spring fields of England. The warm moist air bathed his face. The scents of the flowers filled his nostrils.

Another painting hung next to the flowers. The hill country with undulating blue hills in the background and lush green pastures dotted with white sheep in the foreground. In the middle to the left, a cluster of farm buildings. To the right a large manor house. Although the buildings should have dominated the scene they instead became a mere mention in it…a flicker of interest. All that mattered was the land, the hills, the grass.

He stared for a long time, as his heart drank in things he couldn't name. The artist had captured the life of the land and given it a voice.

He held the lamp closer and leaned over to see the name. There were only two initials. L.E. Linette Edwards? He drew back. Had she painted these? He looked at them again—the field of wildflowers and the pastoral scene. They both reached out to him, as if each brushstroke had the ability to talk.

He shook his head and stepped back slowly. These paintings did something to the room.

He turned and another patch of brightness caught his attention. A quilt of cheerful colors hung over one chair. When had it appeared?

He blew out the lamp and crawled into his bedroll.

Had Linette painted these pictures? Who was she?

He dismissed every vestige of curiosity. It didn't matter that her paintings spoke to him. She was not the sort of woman who belonged in his home.

Or his heart.

Chapter Five

The snow fell all the next day. It piled up deeper and deeper, especially at the sides of the little cabin, like dollops of cream that had been scooped there by a huge spoon. Linette made numerous trips to the window to measure the snow with her eyes and to mentally exclaim over its beauty. The way it mounded and drifted in the wind, creating sharp edges and subtle shadows. At first, she had voiced her pleasure. "It's unbelievably beautiful."

Eddie shot her a disgusted look. "It's too early. I can't imagine how many animals we'll lose."

After that she kept her happy comments to herself and learned to take turns at the window with Eddie, who grew more and more glum, sighing heavily as he turned from the view. Then, as if searching for something he couldn't find, he poked through the bookshelf, picked up objects and put them back. After a few moments, he returned to the window. He was understandably concerned about the herd.

Linette watched with a degree of caution. Would his worries make him harsh? *Lord, keep his cows safe. Help him trust You.*

She wanted to tell him of her prayer but feared he would not find it comforting. But to his credit, his actions did not escalate and something inside her relaxed. He was a man not only noble, but self-controlled. The winter might be pleasant enough after all. And provide ample opportunity for her to prove her worth to him.

He jerked toward the door and donned his coat. "I have to see to things outside." He ducked out into the storm.

She rushed to the window, but already the snow blocked his view. "I hope he'll be safe," she murmured. She shivered. A person could get lost in the snowstorm. She'd read about such disasters. What if he met with misfortune?

"I guess he knows what he's doing," Cassie said and resumed her knitting.

"I suppose you're right." But she couldn't see any other building from the window. How could he know where he was going? She had to find something to do to keep her worries at bay. The floor in front of the door was soiled. She prepared hot water and got down on her hands and knees to scrub it. Wouldn't he be impressed with her attention to the needs of the house—small though it was?

She finished and sat back on her heels to admire the job. The floor shone with cleanliness. A fine job indeed.

The door banged open and Eddie entered. As he stepped, his right foot skidded toward her. He windmilled his arms. His left foot went sideways. He flayed madly, but his feet continued their mad journey and he landed on his bottom with a thud that shuddered up Linette's neck.

Her breath whooshed out. She'd done this. Unintentionally but by her hand nevertheless. "I'm sorry."

He rested inches from the basin of water and looked up at her with a mixture of surprise and shock.

For a moment, time stopped as they considered each other. Again she felt an unfamiliar twinge in the region of her heart. Then his eyes burned like a smoldering fire. "Have you decided that if I won't marry you you'll kill me?"

She swallowed hard then tipped her chin. "No, sir."

"Why else would you ice the floor before the door?"

How was she to know the water would freeze rather than dry? Though if she wasn't so keen on proving how much he needed her she would no doubt have realized it. So far all her good intentions had served to give him more reason to reject her. "I don't want you dead, because unless I marry you my father will force me to return."

He sat up slowly. "Were you this vexatious to your father?"

"I fear so."

He rolled his eyes. "In that case he should pay me to take you off his hands."

"Indeed, if you recall I did offer you my dowry." She rose.

"I doubt your dowry could be enough. No matter how generous it might be." He gingerly got to his feet and rubbed his right hip.

She wanted to offer a hand but hesitated for fear he would jerk back and perhaps fall again. "Are you okay?"

"I'll live."

If she wasn't mistaken he sucked back a groan.

How could everything she tried turn into a disaster? She pulled in air, along with a hefty dose of courage and determination. She would learn. She would get better. He would soon view her as an asset to his life.

Unbidden, a deep-throated longing rose within her. She wanted to belong here.

But only as a partner, she reminded herself.

For the rest of the afternoon, she avoided meeting his gaze because every time she did, some stubborn, wayward thought reared its head pointing out that perhaps she had developed a foolish, romantic view of him while reading his letters. Over and over, she reiterated that she only wanted a way out of her constraining life in England and the marriage her father had arranged. Nothing more than a marriage of convenience.

The following morning she stepped from the bedroom and blinked at the sun streaming through the window. "It's stopped snowing."

Eddie cradled a cup of coffee as he stared out the window. "I need to get going. Can we have breakfast as soon as possible?"

"Certainly." She'd pried a few more details from Cassie about cooking and served up a decent-enough breakfast—no fire outside the stove, no raw meat and no hard beans. But did he notice or comment? No, indeed. His neglect enabled her to focus on her goal—a businesslike marriage.

He barely finished before he donned his coat. "I have to check on things." And he was gone.

She released air from her tense lungs and contemplated Cassie and Grady. who both relaxed visibly. "We'll get used to each other."

Cassie grunted. "I can't wait to get out of here." She stared out the window. "Maybe one of those miracle-working Chinooks will melt the snow. and the stagecoach will head back to Fort Benton. If it does I intend to be on it."

"Well, I don't." Linette fixed the woman with a challenging look. "Where do you plan to go?"

Cassie shrugged. "I expect I can be a housekeeper for someone at the fort."

"How would that be better than here?"

Cassie's defiance deflated. "Like I say, a woman has few opportunities in life."

Linette examined the contents of the pantry shelf wondering what to make for the noon meal. "Cassie, we make our own opportunities."

"Like your father is allowing you to do? At least George made an effort to take my feelings into consideration. Trouble was, he never thought my opinions held any weight."

Linette didn't reply, though she more than half agreed that men too seldom thought women had an opinion of any worth. She pulled down a sack and opened it to investigate the contents. Oats. Tilly had taught her how to cook porridge. A breakfast she could handle successfully. She brought her attention back to Cassie. "There's always something we can do to improve our circumstances."

Cassie laughed. "Like ice the floor so a man tumbles at your feet?"

Linette met her gaze, saw the first flash of true amusement the woman had ever revealed. "I wish it were that easy. He did fall though, didn't he?" She chuckled.

Cassie giggled. "Like a tree cut down by an ax."

They laughed until they both wiped their eyes.

She hadn't meant to create a booby trap for him. He might have been hurt. Linette tried to sober, but every time she did she'd look at Cassie and start to laugh again.

The door rattled open and her amusement fled as Eddie stepped inside. He gave them a curious look, having no doubt heard them laughing.

Cassie gave her knitting her full attention.

Grady, who had been watching them with amazement, ducked behind the table.

Eddie shook his head as if to say he wasn't interested and crossed to scoop up the roll of furs he slept on each night. "I'm going to find the cows."

"You're going overnight? Where will you sleep?"

"I've spent many a night on the ground."

"But the snow? The cold?" Her heart beat a rapid drumbeat against her ribs. She'd barely stepped from the cabin and apart from the first day when she'd met two of the cowboys, she knew no one else. She and her companions would be alone. Isolated. That was her only reason for the worry that clawed at her throat. Not, she firmly informed her wayward brain, not that she already missed Eddie and he hadn't even left.

"I thought you'd read about the cowboys. Didn't any of your books mention sleeping out in the cold?"

She'd read about how men pushed away the snow to dry ground or dug shelters in a drift, but they were nameless heroes. "What if something happens to you?" She barely managed to keep her voice calm.

He faced her. Met her gaze. She didn't care if he saw her concern. It was honest, sincere. With supreme effort she banked her worry.

"I have to check on the animals."

She nodded. "I know. I promised to pray for their safety and I have."

The air settled heavily between them, full of her unfulfilled dreams, her aching longings, her nervous worry. *In God I trust.* No need for her to be anxious.

She jerked her gaze away to look at the bright window. "I pray God will keep you safe as well."

"He has in the past. But don't worry yourself. If something happens to me the men and Cookie will see you are taken care of. They'll make sure you get back to your father."

Her eyes burned. She was concerned about his safety, but he wouldn't let an opportunity pass to remind her of his intention to send her back. She gave him a look laden with every ounce of anger and denial flooding through her. "I'm quite capable of managing on my own." Never mind her temporary flight down a fear-filled path. Put it down to the unfamiliar circumstances. And thinking of Eddie being out in the wintry weather. After all, he was her means of escape from her father.

"I'm sure you are, Miss Edwards." He filled her name with resignation then ducked out of the house before she could respond.

She jerked about. "Oh, that man."

A few minutes later she heard the thud of horses' hooves riding away.

Cassie reported from her station at the window. "Eddie and three others."

Linette reached the window in time to see the snow kicked up by the departing riders. She tried to remember exactly how many men were on the place. Had he left at least one behind? Surely someone had to take care of the stock on the ranch. Would that person also check on the occupants of the cabin or were they completely on their own? The cookhouse stood across the roadway. She assured herself Cookie was there. Wasn't she? Perhaps she had left to visit someone while the men were away. Would it have hurt Eddie to give her a little reassurance?

Unable to soothe her pounding heart, she spun on her heels. Her father would be expecting a letter soon, and if he didn't receive it. . .

She shuddered. She would not let him drag her home. Any more than she would let Eddie send her back.

She yanked paper, pen and ink from the shelf. But what could she say? If her father thought Eddie didn't intend to marry her he would send someone after her, not giving any leeway for the weather. If he ordered it, he expected a man could overcome simple obstacles like snow and cold. Yet she wouldn't—couldn't—lie, and say they'd proceeded with wedding plans. In the end, she reported she'd arrived safely and didn't offer to send proof of a wedding because she couldn't.

Two days passed. She'd not seen another soul apart from the occupants of the house. With each hour Linette's insides twisted tighter. Had Eddie abandoned them to starve and freeze? She eyed the shelf. How long would those supplies last? He'd directed her to the wood in the attached shed, but they used an alarming amount in a short time.

"Still think he's going to marry you?" Cassie asked. "If you ask me, he's left us to manage on our own for the winter. I guess we'll see if you're as good at pioneering as you think."

Cassie's words served to jolt Linette from her worry. "Cookie is across the way." Although she'd seen no evidence of it. To divert herself, she pulled out one of Grady's shirts and mended a torn seam. With each jab of the needle, annoyance at Eddie mounted. If her father heard how he'd treated her—

Heaven help them all if he did. She'd pay as dearly as

Eddie. The thought only served to anger her more. She'd come in good faith. Eddie could at least allow her that.

Cassie stared out the window, as she often did. She never commented on the beauty, never saw any blessing in their situation. Linette knew she saw few blessings in her life.

Right now Linette didn't see a whole lot more. She'd forgotten to trust God. She calmed her breathing, slowed the speed of her needle.

"Someone rode into the yard." Cassie said it with resignation rather than the curiosity and anticipation Linette felt as she sprang to the window.

A man—a cowboy—with a snow-crusted buffalo-hide coat slouched low in the saddle. Eddie followed, sitting tall on his horse, his buffalo coat equally coated with snow. The others did not appear. Perhaps they'd stayed with the cattle.

He was back. Relief melted her muscles and she clutched the logs of the wall to hold her up.

He certainly looked regal. Born to rule.

He rode closer to the cabin. Despite his upright posture, his face seemed drawn. No doubt he was worn out by riding in the cold. She'd make certain he had a hot drink when he returned to the cabin. He rode by without glancing in her direction.

Hmmph. Her relief twisted into frustration. Was he too high and mighty to take note of the newcomers in his cabin? To give a thought to their comfort and security?

The pair rode to the barn.

She watched until they were out of sight. Only then did she realize she held her breath, and let it out with a gusty sound.

Cassie left Linette's side. "I expect it's bad news."

Linette strained for another glimpse. "Why do you say that?"

"Hasn't Eddie been expecting it? How many times has he told us how cows can die in deep snow? How they can't find anything to eat? Stupid animals. Buffalo are built for this land, but what happened to them? People shot them for their hides."

Linette kept her face toward the window. Buffalo coats certainly looked good hanging from the shoulders of a cowboy. "It's natural Eddie should worry. His responsibility is a heavy load."

If only he'd allow her to share the weight of his responsibility, lighten his load in any way she could.

Lord, show me how to help him.

"He's coming." She spun away and hurried to the table. She didn't want him to think she'd been staring after him. She barely found her way to a chair and picked up a shirt to mend before he flung the door open and stepped inside.

"They're safe."

Linette nodded. Her anger fled and she grinned at him. "Glad to hear it."

Their gazes connected and held. A strange feeling of accord trembled in her heart. Then Cassie made an impatient noise and diverted her gaze from Eddie's dark eyes.

He hurried to explain. "The boys had the animals all gathered and when they sensed the snow coming, got them into the shelter of a wooded area. Ward says they even had some grazing." He rubbed his hands together and looked thoroughly pleased

"I prayed God would keep them safe and He did," Linette gently pointed out.

"So you did. Do you want me to thank you?" His voice carried a hint of teasing.

"Would it hurt you?"

He tipped his head back and laughed.

His amusement danced across her nerves until she could hardly remember what they'd been discussing. She ducked her head and returned to the mending in order to get her thoughts sorted out. In her hurry, she jabbed her finger and found the pain erased everything else from her mind. She sucked her fingertip and tried to be annoyed that he'd caused her to be so careless. Except it rather pleased her to know he felt comfortable enough to tease her.

He stopped laughing, though he grinned so wickedly she had several errant thoughts of further enjoyment. She tried to remember that she didn't want to feel anything toward him. But he had a smile that made her forget everything else.

"Thank you for praying," he murmured, his voice thick with amusement. "Me and the boys…and the cows…appreciate your help."

Cassie rolled her eyes. "So what happens now to these wonderful cows of yours?"

"The boys will hold them there until the snow melts then ease them down. A Chinook is already blowing in. Can you feel it?"

"The wind?" Linette turned toward the window and listened. The door rattled. A sound sighed around the cabin.

"Yup. You'll soon be throwing open the door to let in some warmer air."

The room did seem warmer. Or was it only her churning emotions? She drew in a deep breath and settled her tremulous feelings. "A Chinook. How exciting."

Already melted snow dripped from the eaves and she caught sight of a puddle on the road.

"It certainly makes a mournful noise." Cassie hugged her arms around her and looked about as pleased as if stung by a hornet.

Linette laughed. "Seems you have to take the bad with the good. I try to overlook the bad so I can enjoy the good."

The look Cassie shot at her held the power to curdle Linette's breakfast if Linette had a mind to let it. She didn't.

Eddie rubbed his hands together and considered the view from the window, looking as pleased as if he had personally invented sunshine. His pleasure drew her to his side.

"'Net?" Grady whispered. She turned from the window to answer Grady's insistent tug at her arm. She bent to hear his question. "I go see horses now?"

She glanced toward Eddie and met his brown eyes.

He smiled. "This change in weather makes a person want to go out and play, doesn't it, Grady?"

Grady pressed to Linette's side but nodded agreement.

The change in the weather must be the cause of her emotions swinging so wildly from worry to fear to… pleasure? Of course she was happy Eddie had returned safely. He was her means of escaping Lyle Williamson.

"We'll give it time to melt more of the snow and then I'll take you. You just be patient."

Grady nodded again and Linette's heart crowded her ribs at the way Eddie smiled at the boy. Grady needed to know not all men would look at him and dismiss him as a nuisance the way his father had. Eddie's gaze had softened as he smiled at the boy. For a moment his eyes held hers in a strong grip, as if silently promising her something she could not identify…

She managed to divert her attention to something beyond his shoulder. This was to be a marriage of convenience. Nothing more. But something inside her had shifted as she realized he was a man of his word. What he said, he would do. They could all take comfort in the fact.

Except his word to her had been that she was safe here for the winter and then he would send her back to her father.

And to Lyle Williamson with his pudgy hands and leering eyes.

She tucked in her chin and pulled herself tall and straight. Somehow between now and spring Eddie would change his mind.

From the corner of her eye she saw Eddie watching her.

She allowed herself a steady glance at him, saw what looked like concern in his eyes.

Then he blinked. "I'll take you up to the big house before it gets muddy. Then you can tell Margaret about it."

It wasn't an invitation. It was an order. Just as the "tell Margaret about it" was an order. However, she didn't care. She'd stared at the house for two days and her curiosity had built with each passing hour. She couldn't wait to see it up close. If her prayers were answered, her plan fulfilled, the house would be her home.

"I'd like to see it." She reached for her coat.

"I come?" Grady whispered.

Linette looked at Eddie for his approval.

He shook his head. "The hill will be slippery. Best you stay here with Mrs. Godfrey this time, Grady." He held the door open for Linette.

She stepped out. The wind tore at her. She pulled her collar tight and laughed as the bottom of her coat whipped about her ankles.

"Hang on to your coat." Eddie bent into the wind and headed across the yard.

She pushed after him, the wet snow heavy on her boots. Lifting her head, she sucked in air laden with promise. God had kept Eddie's cows safe. He was faithful. She trusted Him to continue to provide the ways and means for her to avoid marriage to her father's choice.

Eddie paused at the bottom of the hill. "I don't have a proper trail up to the house yet. Think you can manage the slope?"

Snow covered whatever path had been there. In most places the snow was sticky as it melted. "I'll be fine." She put a foot forward, following in Eddie's footprints, and discovered the ground was slippery where the snow had melted. She went down on one knee.

"Here." He held out his hand.

She grabbed it and straightened, tipping her head back to meet his gaze. "Thank you." Something flickered in his eyes as if seeing her for the first time. *See me,* she silently begged. *Give me a chance.*

His grasp was firm, his hand strong and reassuring. His gaze, however, warned he had only one plan in mind and that plan did not include Linette staying permanently. He turned and resumed his climb.

They reached the top and she looked back. "Oh, my. No wonder you picked this spot." She looked down on the ranch buildings, on the snow-covered river wandering through the land and past red-painted buildings, past the ridge of dark green pine trees to a white-topped mountain, purple in the distance. Strong and powerful. "I could never get tired of this view."

"I can see the whole ranch at a glance from here." He paused. "Not all the land, of course. Our lease is thousands of acres. It takes several days to ride it. Some areas are practically inaccessible on horseback." For a moment, they both took in the view.

Her breathing was ragged from the climb. His came loud and clear, matching her own. They breathed in and out in unison. She admired the landscape and knew he did as well, though he might be seeing his cows and his responsibilities while she saw the strength and beauty of God's creation. Her hope and faith drew sustenance and renewal from the sight.

They exchanged a glance of understanding then he turned away. "I'll show you the house." His brisk tone reminded her of his expectations—see the house, report on its fineness to Margaret.

The feeling of sharing something special ended with his words.

"It isn't finished yet." He sounded almost apologetic.

She couldn't imagine why. "It's a big house. No doubt it's required a great deal of work."

"Two stories." He pointed. "A balcony off the main bedroom." A stone chimney dominated the roof. Bay windows were capped by the round balcony he referred to. "Servants' quarters at the back."

Did he intentionally emphasize the word *servants* as if to remind her he didn't need or want a pioneer wife?

She would not acknowledge the possibility.

They climbed the steps to double doors and he threw them open to a large foyer. She could see through to another set of double doors at the far end with glass panes allowing light to flood through. Wide stairs rose to the second floor and curved toward a landing. Doors opened off the foyer to various rooms. Disappointment twisted through her.

"It's like…" A manor house.

"The plans were drawn up in London, a replica of the manor house on the Gardiner estate."

Linette shook her head. "This is the West. Full of possibility for change. Why would you want to replicate the old ways?"

His look was rife with disbelief. "The Gardiners are proud of their heritage."

The Gardiners? "What about you?"

"I'm a Gardiner." He seemed to think that said it all. He slid back the pocket doors to the right. "Our dining room. Those doors lead to the kitchen." He pointed to a wooden door in the far corner.

"Very convenient." Oak panels covered the walls. She could almost see a long table with heavy chairs surrounding it. But she didn't like what she saw. The room was so official and stiff. "Is there some other place for family meals?"

He led her to another pair of pocket doors and silently slid them back to reveal a smaller room filled with sunlight. The bay windows she'd admired from the outside made the room almost circular. She could easily imagine matching wing chairs in green brocade before the windows, a basket of sewing nearby and a book opened for reading. At her feet, a circular rug in burgundy and green. She stepped toward the curve of the windows and looked out at the mountains. "This is a lovely room. I expect you can see the sunset from here."

He stood at her side. "You can. It's spectacular at times. I'll bring you up some evening so you can see for yourself."

She wanted to thank him for his offer, but after

a glance at the hard lines in his face she guessed he wished he hadn't spoken the words.

Again she had the peculiar feeling they breathed the same air, felt the same draw to something outside themselves, something big, inviting and exciting. Wishful thinking on her part. He would certainly deny the notion vehemently if she mentioned it.

The cattle in the wintering pens down below shuffled, sending up a cloud of steam.

"Come along. I'll show you the rest of the house so you can give Margaret a complete description."

She sighed. Of course, he was only thinking of the impossible hope of persuading Margaret to reconsider. Though a tiny doubt poked at her brain, perhaps once she learned of this manor house Margaret might indeed change her mind. Heaviness caught at Linette's limbs, so it took a great deal of effort to follow him.

He showed her the rooms on the other side of the foyer—the big parlor, a den, and the library with empty shelves. "Do you have enough books to fill these?"

"They're in crates waiting to be shipped come spring."

Come spring. Seemed everything hinged on that season.

He led her across the hall to the kitchen, stark and empty. A door from the kitchen led to small bedrooms. "For the servants." He turned from the area and led her up the wide, curving staircase with a flawless wooden banister that gleamed as if he'd spent hours polishing it.

Upstairs, to the left of the landing, he opened the door to a huge bedroom. A door with the upper half in glass gave her a view of the balcony. "Oh, what a lovely place to sit and read." She could see herself ensconced in a wicker chair, the sun warm on her face as she read her Bible and prayed. "Or draw."

"I saw the initials L.E. on those paintings in the cabin. Did you do them?"

She wished she hadn't mentioned her little hobby. "It's a pleasant way to spend a few hours."

"They're good."

Her cheeks burning with pleasure, she spun about to face him. "You think so? Really?"

"They have…" He paused, his gaze steady and unblinking. "Heart." His eyes slid away as if he was embarrassed by his comment.

She swallowed hard. "That's the nicest thing anyone has ever said about my painting. Father considers it an occupation suitable for a female. In other words, a waste of time." But he encouraged it. Found it preferable to some of the other pursuits she chose, like speaking to the people she saw on the street, or handing out coins to beggars. Which was the only reason he'd allowed her to study with one of the finest art teachers in the city.

Eddie met her look again. "The world would be a poorer place without the art of great men and women."

Surprise flared in her heart. She floundered in the depths of his gaze, got lost in his look, his words, his approval.

He jerked away, freeing her to find balance and sanity. "There's more." He crossed the room and opened the door. "The nursery."

"Ah." Thinking of babies while standing next to the man she had planned to marry filled her with hot embarrassment. But she could not stop from dreaming of little boys and girls playing noisily, happily, in this beautiful room.

She noticed three smaller rooms branching off the larger area.

"Bedrooms for children and a nurse," Eddie murmured and moved away quickly, leading her across the hall and opening the doors to a water closet and four generous bedrooms.

The size of the place awed and inspired her. She could see so many possibilities. "This is wonderful. I can see using this wing to help others. The ill. The brokenhearted."

He spun about and faced her. Any sense of connection, promise or hope fled in the anger wreathing his face. "This house is for the Gardiners. These rooms are for family." He waved toward the main suite. "My wife and children." He waved his other arm down the hallway. "These rooms are for my parents and grandfather, should they choose to visit. Or other family members and friends of the family. For company when I entertain." He indicated she precede him down the stairs. "Once Margaret learns how fine the house is, she will change her mind about coming West."

Linette's heart lay wounded and heavy. She'd momentarily imagined the house as hers. Why had she so foolishly revealed her thoughts to him?

She glanced to her right as she reached the bottom of the stairs and fought the truth crashing in upon her. She could see he wasn't thinking pioneer wife, but rather, lady of the manor. She sucked in cold air and stiffened her resolve. She could be that, too. She'd been raised to be such. Taught to show interest in only ladylike activities, pretending no interest in the real things of life. But the idea sent shivers up and down her arms. She wanted more. She wanted to participate in life, enjoy shouldering a challenge. She wanted to be part of building a new world where women could be more than objects in a fine home.

Most of all, however, she wanted to avoid marrying Lyle Williamson and being subjected to some of the obscene things he had whispered in her ear on their last encounter.

She had only one recourse. Pray.

How foolish of her to see Eddie as her future husband before she'd even met him and given him a chance to say yea or nay. Though, in fairness to herself, she'd thought his letter meant he said yes. She wouldn't give up her dream. Not yet. With God all things were possible.

They stepped out into a warm and promising wind that caressed her face. She turned and smiled at Eddie. "I enjoyed seeing your house. It's beautiful."

The remnants of his anger fled, replaced by a look of pride. "Be sure you tell Margaret that."

She exhaled loudly. "Of course." She'd also be sure to mention the deep snow and moaning wind. Perhaps, too, the long distance to the nearest town, or what passed as a town out on the frontier. Oh, and not to forget the fact that there were only three females on the place and two of those would be leaving if Eddie insisted on sending her back to England.

Not that she had any intention of going. As she'd said the first day, there was many a slip between the cup and the lip.

Chapter Six

Eddie took Linette back to the cabin, mumbled something about returning for lunch then strode toward the wintering pens as if he had a fire to douse. Her eagerness and approval of the big house had warmed his heart, teased him into letting his guard down. For just a few minutes, he'd enjoyed her enthusiasm, seeing the place through fresh eyes, and he felt as if he'd accomplished his goal of building a house to meet his father's expectations. And then she'd said how she pictured the house—as a refuge for the ill and hurting.

He'd never heard such nonsense. He wasn't opposed to helping others. Needy people were more than welcome on the ranch, but a home was a shelter for the family.

Margaret would never have such foolish ideas. She was a refined lady. She would never sell her fashionable gowns for pioneer dresses. Or wear an over-big man's coat. She was…

He tried to bring her face to remembrance, but all he pictured was pale brown hair, direct brown eyes and a very determined expression. Linette's face! Not the one he wanted to keep in mind.

He loped onward and reached the pens where the red, white-faced cattle chowed down on the hay Roper and Slim had tossed out for them. The steam of their warm breath disappeared in the wind. Snow melted in the corrals, creating soft, mushy footing. Some of the cows jerked away at his approach, instantly alert. The younger heifers crowded around him, curious as only the young can be.

"Boss?" Slim called out.

"Just checking them over."

"Good breeding stock. You done right by bringing these in."

"Yup." His father had balked at the idea, but Eddie knew crossbreeding them with the hardier Texas stock would give him the best of both breeds.

He mucked about the yards, passing time as much as checking on things. As the sun reached its zenith, he reluctantly returned to the cabin for lunch, determined to think of nothing but his responsibilities.

He gritted his teeth. Only until spring. He could endure anything if he made up his mind to, and he had. He sat down. Linette dished up stew and kept up a steady commentary on the weather and the mountains.

Cassie grunted her displeasure. "I hate the wind. It tears at my thoughts until I feel like screaming."

Linette chuckled. "Maybe you should go outside and let it sweep your thoughts clean."

Cassie mumbled something about staying indoors until spring.

"Don't you want to see the mountains?" Linette asked in a tone that suggested of course she would. When Cassie didn't answer, Linette continued, undeterred by the lack of response. "I told Cassie about your big house," she told Eddie.

"Too bad it wasn't finished so we wouldn't have to crowd into this place," Cassie muttered.

Grady watched Eddie. Every time Eddie met his gaze, the boy jerked away. But not before Eddie caught a glimpse of stark fear. Eddie longed to ease the boy's apprehension. "Clean up your plate." He addressed Grady. "And I'll take you to see the horses."

The boy ducked his head and scraped his plate clean.

Eddie pushed from the table, thanked the women for the meal that was finally satisfying and reached for his coat. "Get your coat, Grady."

The boy hung back at Linette's side. "'Net go."

Linette shot Eddie a look of apology then touched Grady's face and turned him toward her. "You can go by yourself, Grady. Mr. Gardiner won't hurt you."

But he only pressed himself closer to Linette.

"Looks like you'll have to come along, too." Eddie couldn't keep the reluctant note out of his voice. Bad enough the woman filled his cabin. After her visit, he feared he'd feel her presence every time he went to the big house. Now it seemed he'd be forced to have her invade the barn, too. How was he to get her face out of his mind if he couldn't get away from her?

"You're welcome to come, too, Cassie." Perhaps Cassie's presence would make the whole outing less nerve-racking.

Cassie shuddered. "No, thanks." She smiled tightly at Linette. "I'll do the dishes. So you go along."

Linette sprang into action, putting warm clothes on Grady then pulling on her own coat.

Eddie's nerves grew tauter each second as he thought of her walking at his side. Only because he feared for his safety, he silently insisted. Not because he wondered how she would see the ranch. Would she recognize its beauty? See the work he'd done? "I'm hoping you haven't any plan to do me bodily harm while we're out there." He gave a mirthless chuckle in the hopes of making her think he only teased.

She slowly faced him. "I admit I've made some mistakes. I hoped you'd put it down to inexperience."

He'd been trying to guard his own thoughts but had stumbled into bad behavior. "I apologize."

"As I said, I am a fast learner. You won't see me make the same mistake twice." She pulled on a knitted mitten and indicated she was ready.

He opened the door. "It won't change what happens when winter is over."

"Sooner or later you will change your mind." She met his gaze briefly. Long enough for him to see the hot determination in her eyes.

Her continued refusal to accept his answer made his teeth ache. But rather than continue this pointless discussion, he stepped outdoors. With relief he realized she'd successfully enabled him to consider her company with nothing more than reluctant acceptance.

Linette lifted her face to the sun and sighed. She turned full circle, pausing to look long and hard at the mountains. "Beautiful."

"The great Rockies are something to see all right." He constantly sought the view of the mountains when he was outside. The sight of them filled him with both calmness and hope. Something he needed now as never before. Having a woman show up and demand to become his wife had an unsettling effect on his normally steady thoughts.

"Reminds me of a verse," Linette said. "'I will lift mine eyes unto the hills, from whence cometh my help.

My help cometh from the Lord, who made heaven and earth.'"

"Did your nurse teach you that?"

A thoughtful look came to her face. "You heard?"

He banged the heel of his hand to his forehead. "I didn't mean to let you know."

Her eyes widened and she swallowed hard as she seemed to recall what else had been said. "I hope you aren't offended by Cassie's complaining."

"I figure it's just a bad habit and nothing to do with me other than I'm handy for the moment."

She laughed. The sun caught in her eyes.

He jerked away. She was the most disconcerting female he'd ever had the misfortune of encountering. It was not yet November. Spring seemed an eternity away.

If Linette didn't give him permanent stomach problems with her cooking or maim him with her "helpfulness," she would certainly do her utmost to upset his carefully planned life with her quiet determination that he would sooner or later want to marry her.

She'd already upset his equilibrium. How would he survive? He would. Because he was a Gardiner.

Linette caught the hint of confusion in Eddie's eyes before he turned away, and she smiled. Maybe he was beginning to see her for what she was and what she could offer him as a wife.

She shaded her eyes and studied the surroundings. They stood in the center of the roadway with buildings on either side. "It's like a little town." A neat row of red buildings stood next to the cabin. To their left were a long, low building, a big red barn and a collection of corrals. The trail angled to the right where a bridge traversed the stream. Beyond that were more buildings and corrals. She could see cattle munching on feed in the pens around those more distant structures.

"Purposely designed that way for efficiency," Eddie said with a degree of pride. "Storehouses on the right. The bunkhouse to your left, close to the cookhouse." He led her past those buildings. Two men jerked open the bunkhouse door and crowded through the opening.

"Hello, boss," one called.

"Boys."

She thought Eddie intended to pass them, but he slowly ground to a halt. "You can expect to be an object of curiosity around here."

She chuckled. "It's mutual."

He shook his head. "Don't encourage them."

"Why not? Are they dangerous?"

He faced her squarely. "I wouldn't have a dangerous man on the place. But they pretend to be hard when inside they have the same hopes and dreams and desires as everyone else. It would be a mistake to take their feelings lightly."

His warning was clear as the air around them. "I don't flirt, if that's what you mean."

He studied her with unyielding eyes.

If he looked hard enough he would find truth and sincerity. He'd see her for what she was, what she could offer. *Please see me.*

"You admit you're desperate to marry. Don't toy with these men."

Before she could sputter a protest, he called, "Boys, come and meet my guests."

She wasn't desperate. At least not to marry anyone. Her father wouldn't hesitate to ignore a legal marriage if it didn't meet his purposes. Which meant marrying someone who would bring advantage to the Edwards name. Someone who met her own high standards. She quickly enumerated them—kind, noble, trustworthy, a man who would see her as a valued addition not only to his home but his life.

The two men jogged over, abused Stetsons clutched to their chests.

Eddie made formal introductions.

Blue Lyons had pale red hair and a matching mustache. His gray eyes were somber. He nodded and backed away, obviously embarrassed in the presence of a young woman.

Linette, wanting to make him feel comfortable, said it was an honor to meet the cowboys.

Blue's face grew even ruddier.

Grady shrank against her side, as uncomfortable as Blue.

Ward Walker was shorter than Eddie but solid built. He had black hair and shockingly blue eyes that smiled along with his wide mouth. He held out a hand to Grady, but when he saw how the boy retreated, he grinned. "Don't mean to scare you, young fella." He straightened to face Linette. "Pleased to meet you, ma'am. And what do you think of the country?"

"I've only just arrived, so I haven't had a chance to see much of it, but I'm looking forward to doing so."

"I'd venture to say you saw a lot of it from the stagecoach."

"For the comfort of others, the curtains remained drawn while traveling. But I saw enough. The land seems wild and free."

"And you liked that?"

"I like the idea of beginning over."

"Yes, ma'am."

She didn't blame him for sounding a little confused.

She hadn't answered his question. Before she could say she liked the wildness of the land, Eddie spoke.

"Boys, I want you to take supplies up to those bringing the cattle down."

"Yes, boss." They jogged away.

Grady yanked at Linette's hand. "Horses?" he whispered.

"We'll find some in the barn." Eddie led them toward the solid-looking structure.

They stepped inside. It took seconds for Linette's eyes to adjust to the dim interior. But the smells hit her immediately. Warm horseflesh, fresh hay, dust and new wood.

A horse neighed as if greeting them. "Grady, do you want to say hello to Banjo?"

Linette giggled. "You named a horse Banjo?"

"What's wrong with that?" Eddie's voice carried an injured tone.

"Absolutely nothing, I'm sure." She couldn't contain a snicker. "But how did you choose such a name?"

Eddie kept his expression serious, but his eyes twinkled. "When I first got him he was all strung out like a—"

"Banjo." She whooped at the idea.

The horse nickered.

Eddie leaned closer and whispered, "He knows we're talking about him."

Almost as if they were coconspirators, Linette thought, the idea dancing across the surface of her brain with unexpected joy.

"You better say hello."

Glad to be diverted from her foolishness, she moved toward the big black horse, with Grady clutching her skirts. "Hello, Banjo."

Grady relaxed slightly, interested in the horse.

Here was a chance to help Grady learn to trust Eddie. It would make life easier for everyone if he stopped shivering and withdrawing every time he saw the man. Or any man. "Grady, have a look at Mr. Gardiner's horse." She urged him forward.

He took one step, still hanging on to her coat.

The horse looked over the top of his pen and nickered.

"I touch him?" Grady whispered.

"You certainly can," Eddie answered. "Let me lift you up so you can pet his head." He grabbed the boy around the waist, but Grady screamed and kicked.

Eddie set him down abruptly and stepped back. Banjo snorted and spun away. Throughout the barn, horses whinnied and stomped.

Linette squatted and held Grady. "Hush. You're scaring all the horses."

Grady clung to her, burrowing his face against her neck. He stopped screaming but sobbed and shivered.

"I'm sorry," she whispered, not sure if she apologized more to Grady or Eddie. She held Grady until he calmed then straightened, allowing him to cling to her. Her heart poured out grief and concern at his heart-wrenching sobs.

"I think we better return to the cabin," she murmured.

They walked in silence toward the house. Grady's behavior troubled Eddie. Why should the boy be so frightened of him? Being rejected by his father didn't seem enough reason for such a reaction. Would Linette know if something else had happened to upset the boy?

They stepped into the cabin. Cassie looked at Grady. "What happened? Why is he crying?"

Grady straightened his face. "I not crying."

Eddie glanced at the cookhouse. "I don't know if this is a good time, but if I don't introduce you to Cookie, she'll nail my hide to the wall."

Linette's gaze darted toward the cookhouse and she shuddered. "She sounds like a curmudgeon."

Knowing Linette would be pleasantly surprised, Eddie only said, "You'll have to judge for yourself. Does everyone want to go over?"

"I'd love to have tea." Cassie grabbed her coat.

The four of them crossed the yard to the cookhouse.

Linette hung back as they approached the door, clinging to Grady as if the boy could protect her.

Eddie carefully kept his face expressionless as he opened the door. "Cookie, I brought company."

Cookie swept across the floor. "Why, this must be the young woman who came to—"

He broke in before Cookie said anything about marrying. "She's visiting for the winter. May I present Miss Linette Edwards and Mrs. Godfrey. Linette, this is Cookie—Miz Liza Mc—"

"Never mind the Miz stuff. Just call me Cookie." She wrapped Linette in a bear hug and banged on her back. "So good to see you, gal. You don't know how good it is. Welcome, welcome." Every word was accompanied by another smack that jarred Linette's whole body.

"Cookie, you might let her go before you break something."

"Well, I guess I plumb forgot myself." She let Linette escape.

"You'll recover in a few minutes," Eddie said. Cookie's greeting seemed like justice.

Linette gasped and sent him a hard look.

"Hey, don't blame me. She's like that with everyone. Cookie, how many times have I told you to have a little respect for breakable bones."

"Ah, pshaw." Cookie flicked a towel at his leg. It connected and stung. He knew there would be a welt. Cookie didn't even bother to give him a second look.

She turned and wrapped Cassie in a likewise-crunching hug.

Cassie gasped for breath when Cookie released her to turn to the boy clinging to Linette. "And who is this little man?"

"Grady Farris."

Cookie squatted to eye level with Grady. "And aren't you a handsome young fella. How old are you?"

Grady held up four fingers.

"Why, I'd say that's old enough to join us for tea, right, boss?"

Eddie waited, expecting Grady to disappear into the folds of Linette's coat, but he beamed at Cookie. His eyes glistened like sun off the snow. He looked sweet and innocent, not drawn and fearful. Seems he didn't object to the friendship of women. "I'll leave you ladies here while I get to work." He retreated.

Cookie made it to the door with a speed that seemed impossible with her big body. "Not before you have tea." She grabbed his arm and dragged him back to the center of the room.

He glanced at Linette, saw her amusement and jerked away to face Cookie as a bolt of something he could only think of as admiration flickered through his brain. "A little respect here." He struggled to contain his grin. Cookie didn't need to know he wasn't serious.

Cookie dropped his arm. "Sorry, boss." She neither looked nor sounded repentant. "Coffee?"

Eddie glanced longingly at the door but nodded. "Sounds good."

Cookie laughed heartily. "That's more like it."

So they sat at the long table. Linette made sure to position herself between Eddie and Grady.

Cookie poured their drinks then she put a platter of fresh cinnamon buns before them. "Eat hearty," she instructed.

Linette took a bite of the bun and sighed. "These are delicious. They practically melt in my mouth."

Cookie beamed. "Nice to have someone appreciate my cooking. The men—" she slid an accusing glance at Eddie "– wolf it down without comment."

"Isn't enjoyment the highest form of praise?" he asked. He consumed two rolls and two cups of coffee.

The door jarred open and Bertie strode in, his arms full of supplies from the storehouse.

Eddie made introductions again. Bertie reached out to shake hands with Grady but pulled back when Grady buried his face in Linette's sleeve. Bertie shifted direction and took Linette's hand as he asked about the trip.

Eddie rose. Cookie and Bertie could entertain the ladies. "Thank you, Cookie. Now I have a ranch to run." Eddie hurried for the door before Cookie could tackle him.

Cookie roared with laughter. Just before the door closed behind him, Cookie spoke to Bertie. "There'll be a wedding before the winter is out. Mark my words."

Eddie bolted as if he could outrun his churning thoughts.

Let Bertie and Cookie fall in love with Linette if they so desired. He didn't have a mind to do so. Sure, she was cheerful. But also stubborn and independent. Even worse, she got all prickly at the idea of acting like a proper lady.

No. He anticipated sharing life with a woman who welcomed the chance to be the lady of his big house, a woman who would bring to this wild country the sort of life that had taken centuries to establish in England. A woman who would do his family name honor.

The sound of the door slamming crashed through Linette's mind. Her face warmed. Eddie had not been pleased by Cookie's prediction. Not that it robbed her of hope. She trusted the Lord to help her. In the meantime, she would enjoy learning about life in the West.

Bertie sat across from them and Grady shrank to Linette's side. She placed a reassuring hand on his quivering shoulder. His reaction to Eddie's touch worried her. How would they spend a winter together in tiny quarters if Grady screamed at his touch and retreated at his presence? The poor man would feel unwelcome in his own house. That would not serve any of them well. Besides, it seemed unnatural and unhealthy for the boy to be so afraid of men.

She turned her attention back to the conversation around the table. Cassie spoke more freely and friendly with Cookie than Linette had heard her speak with anyone to this point. Turned out both of them had once lived in the same area of Ontario and even had some mutual acquaintances.

"So you and your man were planning to head west?"

"I didn't want to go, but that's what George wanted. He sold everything and quit a good job. Now we have nothing." She swallowed hard and corrected herself. "I have nothing. Not even a home." She ducked her head but not before Linette caught a glimpse of tears.

Cassie hadn't shared her husband's dreams. No wonder she was annoyed that men made the decisions. "You have a home here."

"For the winter. Then what?"

"Whatever the Lord has in store for both of us. And Grady."

Even if returning to England wasn't a dreadful prospect, she wanted to stay here. Foolish it might be, but she still saw Eddie as ideal, saw him through her earlier reactions while reading the letters he'd written to Margaret. His words of hope and faith in the new land, his description of the mountains, his references to his family and his duty as an obedient son had all served to give her a vision of a man who was strong and noble.

Her opinion of him hadn't changed in the slightest despite his resistance and continued denial of her plan. He simply needed time to get used to it and see how ideal she was as a rancher's wife.

Cookie chuckled. "Could be you'll both find what I've found with Bertie. I wouldn't trade that man for ten thousand acres of the best rangeland in this here country." She leaned closer to her husband. "He thinks the world of me, too."

"That I do, my love." Bertie patted his wife's generous arm.

Linette wasn't interested in that kind of marriage. Love, she feared, would eliminate her right to make choices and follow the dictates of her heart.

Cookie pushed to her feet. "Most of the men are out, but I still need to make a meal for those hanging around. Excuse me while I tend to my duties. Feel free to stay and keep me company."

Grady's head had been nodding for several minutes. "One little man is ready for a nap," Linette said.

"It doesn't take two of us to put him down. I think I'll stay and visit with Cookie."

Linette was glad if Cassie found something to make her happy and she prepared to leave. Cookie accompanied her to the door. "If you need anything, don't hesitate to say so."

Linette glanced past Cookie to the cinnamon buns under the tea towels. "I wouldn't mind learning to bake like you do."

"It's easy as falling off a log. I'll gladly show you." Cookie laughed and made to slap Linette on the shoulder. She thought better of it and dropped her hand.

Chapter Seven

Eddie needed fresh air and hard work. He saddled Banjo. Remembering Linette's amusement at the name of his horse, he chuckled. Guess it *was* funny if you stopped to think about it. Linette had certainly considered it a joke.

Enough of thinking of her. He shifted his thoughts toward little Grady and the way he'd reacted when Eddie touched him. "I can't believe that boy screamed. I'm not such a bad guy, am I, old friend?" He'd seen how Grady shrank back from Ward and every other man on the place, so had to believe it wasn't personal. "I wonder what happened to make him so afraid of men." He remembered that Grady's mother crossed the ocean to meet her husband. How long since the man had left? "I suppose it could be that the boy hasn't spent much time around men." But the screaming when Eddie touched him seemed extreme. "They've upset my quiet little life," he muttered to Banjo as he led him from the barn. "I'm not happy about it, either." He swung into the saddle and headed down the trail to join his men.

Ward and Blue were already gone, but they led pack-horses. Eddie would soon overtake them.

The more he thought about Grady, the more he wondered if it wasn't more than not seeing many men. He scrubbed at the back of his neck. Had some man done something cruel to Grady? Or perhaps Grady had witnessed a man hurting his mother. He tried to think what Linette had said about the pair. She'd met them on the boat. Had they been in cabins or steerage?

He decided he would ask more questions though he wasn't sure how it would change anything. He'd seen frightened animals. Sometimes you could simply walk into their world and strong-arm them into capitulation. Other times, you had to give them space and let them figure out you were safe to be around. He kind of figured he would have to give Grady space. He chuckled, causing Banjo to perk his ears in curiosity. "You wouldn't understand, but it's going to be a little hard to give the boy room when the place is only three hundred square feet."

Banjo tossed his head as if comprehending every word his master said.

Eddie laughed. He saw the boys ahead and flicked the reins to hurry Banjo toward them.

Ward waited for Eddie to fall in at his side. "Hey, boss. Miss Edwards is a right pretty gal."

"Guess so." He thought her coloring a little uncertain. And she was on the small size. He'd thought Cookie would crush her in her enthusiasm. Again, he thought it a form of justice at the hands of another for a woman who had forced her way into his peaceful life and turned it topsy-turvy.

"Boss, I don't want to speak out of place…"

"Go ahead. Speak your mind."

"Well, Cookie said she came out to get married but you're not interested. That so?"

He knew his life was open to examination by everyone on the ranch. He was being asked if he had an interest in Linette. He had none other than to see she got back safely to her father as soon as spring arrived. Back to an arranged marriage with a man that brought a twist of disgust and fear to Linette's mouth.

He squeezed his fists about the reins. Even if Linette was too small, dressed poorly and had ideas of helping misfortunates, she didn't deserve that.

He turned to Ward. "I expect my intended will change her mind and join me in the spring."

"Then I guess any of us can court Miss Linette." Ward grinned widely.

"Suit yourself." Things might be looking up. If Ward had an interest in Linette then it would make her presence in his life less intrusive. He smiled as he rode on ahead, though his smile didn't go any deeper than his face. Why should he feel it necessary to take care of Linette? She sure wouldn't welcome such a sentiment.

He saw the cows ambling along, being moseyed toward the winter pasture. The crew moved them at a slow pace, letting them find the easiest path, giving them time to graze, but still keeping them headed in the right direction.

He checked the horizon. No threatening clouds. They might not get any more snow for a few days, but he knew better than to count on it. Last year he'd lost several hundred head in the heavy snow. His father had no idea what the country was like. He saw only the numbers and losses. His reprimand, given in a letter, had been strongly worded.

Eddie didn't intend to repeat his mistake.

He spoke to each of the men, assured them more supplies were coming with Ward and Blue. Satisfied that the men had the herd under control, he headed back to the ranch.

Darkness engulfed him by the time he reined in at the barn. He led Banjo inside, unsaddled him, brushed him thoroughly, filled a manger with hay and left the barn. Many times he had returned home after dark, to an empty, cold cabin. Now a light beckoned from the window, drawing him irrevocably to its welcome. He paused outside the door, but when he heard Linette's laugh, eagerly he reached for the handle. He stopped, turned and looked at the big house. Linette laughed again and he forgot the unfinished manor on the hill and stepped into the light.

Linette stood in the middle of the room, a blindfold on her eyes as she tried to catch Grady, who giggled and jumped away. "You're too quick for me, Grady."

Grady saw Eddie and fear wreathed his face. He ran to Linette and clung to her skirts.

Linette slowly removed her blindfold. "You're back."

It seemed unnecessary to respond, but he nodded as he pulled off his heavy coat. He took his time hanging it on a hook. His silly, unexplainable eagerness at seeing the cabin lit up and stepping into its warmth had been snatched away by Grady's fear.

Linette edged Grady to Cassie's side and slipped over to Eddie. "I'm sorry he's so frightened. I wish it weren't so."

"But it is." Eddie knew he sounded weary and he was. He wanted to relax before the warmth of the stove and enjoy the evening. But Grady's fear palpitated through the room.

"Have you eaten?"

He shook his head.

"We waited for you."

The smell of venison stew enabled him to push aside the problem of Grady's fear. "It smells good."

At Linette's signal they gathered around the table and Eddie said the blessing.

"It's good," he said after he had tasted the food.

"Thanks to Cookie, who has been kind enough to teach me. Cassie has discovered she and Cookie are from the same town."

Cassie smiled. "I know her sister."

Eddie had never seen the woman smile. It took ten years off her face. Seemed she might find the winter pleasant enough because of Cookie's company. He shifted his gaze to Grady who pressed as close to Linette as he could. Now, if only the boy would shed his fearfulness.

Cassie helped Linette do the dishes without any prodding then took Grady to bed as she'd done the previous nights.

He pulled his chair closer to the stove and propped his feet on the wood box. "How do you know Margaret?"

"Margaret and I met at a tea given by Viola Williamson."

"You say that name with a curl of your lip. Is she a distasteful woman?"

She flashed him a grin. "She's a very nice woman. A distant relative. And sister to Lyle Williamson, the man my father wants me to marry."

"Ah. I see."

"Viola gives the best teas. In the summer she puts up linen shelters and serves cold lemonade and sweet cold tea. She invites young ladies and their mothers. There is music and plays and games. Margaret and I got matched up for charades. Then we were seated together at tea."

"What did you like about her?"

Linette ducked her head as if embarrassed. "She told me about you and let me read your letters."

He'd often regretted his inability to put down words of affection, but now he was grateful he hadn't. Knowing Linette had read his letters left him feeling exposed. Why had Margaret shared them? It didn't seem as if she put proper value on their relationship. Or perhaps her parents regretted their agreement to let her move so far away. Had they influenced Margaret's decision?

But surely, once they knew of the big house and his plans to live a genteel life such as Margaret was accustomed to, they would realize it wasn't a mistake to let her go. "Did you write Margaret and tell her about the house?"

Her gaze caught his in silent challenge before she gave a tight smile. "It's done and waiting to be posted." She nodded to the letter on the shelf beside his own.

Had she written as he wished?

She sighed as she read his unasked question. "If it's a fine house she seeks, I told her she'd find it here."

Somehow she managed to make it sound as if it would be a poor excuse for marriage. Perhaps. But didn't most women put a great deal of stock in what a man could provide? Seemed Linette didn't. He decided to change the subject. "How did you meet Grady's mother?"

She tipped her head and looked troubled. "I wandered about the ship, exploring everything and meeting as many people as I could. It was the first time I'd had a chance to converse with such a cross section of people. Dorothy Farris was on the lower decks. She appealed to me to help her."

"Because she was ill?"

Linette lowered her head. "It was more than that."

"Someone was bothering her?"

Linette nodded. "Her only companion was Grady and he wasn't much protection."

"Do you think Grady knew what was going on? Perhaps felt threatened by it?"

Linette still looked at her lap. "Once I found him outside a cabin crying for his mother. When I asked, he said she was inside. The door was locked and a man ordered me away when I knocked."

Eddie's jaw protested as he chomped down on his molars. It was as he suspected, though he couldn't guess how much Grady had faced. Threats? Physical abuse? More? He didn't want to imagine anything done to the boy, but something had made Grady fearful beyond reason. "It might explain why he is afraid of men."

"I suppose so. The poor child."

The air shimmered with embarrassment at the subject they discussed. Her cheeks flared like a summer rose of palest pink.

He stood to stir the fire and put on more wood.

"I thought I saw bruises on his face a couple of times, as if he'd been struck, and I know his mother didn't do it."

Eddie groaned. He suspected there were bruises Linette hadn't seen and, even worse, damage to little Grady's soul.

"I don't know how to help him," she whispered.

Eddie didn't know, either. "About all I can think of is to encourage him to see men as his friends."

"I guess the more time he spends around you the better then."

He snorted. "Considering his reaction, that might prove a challenge."

"It's a shame he is so frightened of you."

"Yes, but what are we to do about it?"

Her gaze bored into him. He couldn't imagine what he'd said to bring that burning look to her eyes. Then she banked the fire. "Give him time, I suppose."

"I will bid you good-night." She scurried away and a few minutes later crawled into bed with Cassie, Grady between them. He moaned a little at the disturbance. What had the poor child seen or experienced? The subject of what Dorothy Farris had done—or rather, endured—was not a topic proper ladies took part in. But Eddie needed to understand Grady's fear.

Eddie had asked what they could do about it. He'd made them partners. It meant her plans were succeeding.

"What were you two talking about?" Cassie whispered.

"How I met Margaret. And what awful things Grady might have seen on the boat."

"What things do you mean?"

Linette edged closer and whispered as softly as she could. "His mother was afraid of one of the other passengers. I think he was being inappropriate."

"You think he was—" Cassie didn't finish. One didn't even mention the shameful things that went on in secret. "Where was Grady?"

"Once I found him locked out of a cabin, but I can't say about any other time. Like I told Eddie, I saw bruises on Grady more than once."

Cassie let out a short sigh. "Poor little mite. Sometimes life is so unfair."

Linette couldn't argue with her.

She whispered good-night to Cassie and turned over, but she didn't sleep right away. Miserable thoughts of

Grady's past tangled with joyous thoughts of success in proving her worth to Eddie. But the latter held little importance alongside Grady's needs.

Next morning, she rose with a plan in mind. Over breakfast, she put it into action. "Would you object to Grady and me wandering around the ranch?" she asked Eddie. She hoped her eyes told him she had an ulterior motive for her request—to help Grady grow comfortable around the men.

His steady look searched beyond the surface.

Finally he nodded and she believed he understood her silent message. "I've no objection. I'll be out in the yards today."

He headed for the door. Not until it closed behind him did Grady jump down from the chair to play.

"Cookie has invited me to visit anytime I like," Cassie said. "So while you venture around the place, I'll go over there."

"I'll go with you and discuss what I can make for dinner before I take Grady for a walk." Cassie looked relieved to think Linette might not bother her as much about meal preparation anymore.

It took only a few minutes to tidy the little house and then Cassie, Linette and Grady crossed to the cookhouse. Linette spent a pleasant hour planning meals. Cookie invited her back in the afternoon to help bake cakes.

The sun was warm overhead, the snow melting and a breeze drifting down from the mountains when Linette took Grady outside.

"You can run and run here," she said to Grady.

Squealing, Grady raced down the trail toward the barn. Eddie lounged against the fence watching. Grady, unaware of Eddie's presence, turned at the corner of the corrals and raced back. Several horses nickered at his laughter.

Linette caught him and turned him about. "Let's say hello to the horses."

They edged toward the fence. She lifted Grady to the top rail so he could touch the horses that came for attention. He laughed as they snorted a greeting.

Suddenly he noticed Eddie in the pen and drew back.

Eddie pretended not to notice the boy as he scooped up droppings with a pitchfork.

"It's okay," Linette soothed. "Do you think the horses would be ready to play if they were afraid of Mr. Gardiner?"

"He not hurt horses?"

"No. And he won't hurt little boys, either."

Grady wasn't convinced and wanted down. He took Linette's hand and pulled her away from the corrals.

Eddie eased closer. "Take him along the road toward the other buildings across the creek. You'll come to the wintering pens and pigsty. Some of the men are working down there. I've instructed them to ignore the boy until he's ready to make friends."

"Thank you." How thoughtful and kind he was. He would be an excellent partner in assisting her to help others. She wanted to say so, but Grady tugged at her, wanting to escape.

Once Grady felt he was far enough away to be safe, he slowed his pace to examine every detail—the rocks beside the trail, the leaf that blew across the path, the raven flying overhead with a raucous call that made him laugh.

The wooden bridge was solidly built over a frozen stream sheltered by bare-limbed trees. On the span they paused to admire the view. A pig squealed and Grady looked up at Linette, his mouth a surprised *O*.

She chuckled. "Do you want to see some piggies?"

His blue eyes bright with excitement, he nodded and raced across the bridge. He noticed a man near the pigsty and ground to a halt. Slowly he backed toward Linette.

She knelt beside him. "Grady, not all men are frightening. Most are very nice people who would like to be your friend. Mr. Gardiner especially wants to be your friend. You need to give him a chance."

Grady shuddered and clung to her side.

She recognized the person by the pigs as Ward Walker. "You remember that man from yesterday. He works for Mr. Gardiner. Mr. Gardiner would never let a bad man live here, so you can be friends with him, too."

Ward touched the brim of his hat. "Ma'am." But he said nothing more and turned to fiddle with a gate.

Linette stood up. "Can we get close to the pigs?"

"Right up to the fence," Ward said as he continued his work, though Linette wondered if he actually did anything productive. Warmth wrapped about her heart as she realized Eddie had coached them all to be present for Grady but give him the space he needed. Again, she admired Eddie's kindness. Just think of the things they could do together, helping those in distress. It filled her heart with such joy she wanted to laugh out loud.

Grady kept his eyes on Ward until he got close enough to see the pigs nosing around in the feed trough, snorting and pushing. Fascinated, he watched and forgot about Ward even when the man walked past him, heading toward the larger pens where a number of cows milled about.

She let Grady watch the pigs for a long time. Then

she interrupted him. "We have to go back so I can make dinner."

"I stay?"

"Do you want to stay with Mr. Walker?" Ward moseyed along the path.

Grady jerked back as he noticed the man. "I go with you."

Linette smiled an apology at Ward as they walked away. "One day, young man, you will realize these men can be your friends."

"Not make me?"

She stopped to face the child. "Of course not. You can't force someone to be friends. It comes when you realize they are good people who care about you."

"Not hurt me?"

Had there been others besides the man on the ship? "Grady, who hurt you?"

He looked past her, his gaze seeking the distance. She guessed he was seeing something in his past. When she called his name, he blinked. "Grady hungry."

"Then let's go make dinner." It had been a little glimpse into what had happened to the boy. She could hardly wait to tell Eddie about their walk and Grady's little confession. They could work together to help Grady learn to trust men. Another step toward showing Eddie how they could be a team.

Remembering his reaction to a similar statement in the big house, she decided she wouldn't speak of it in those terms.

Chapter Eight

After lunch, Eddie climbed the hill to the house and stepped into the quiet interior. With some hard work, the place would be ready for occupancy by spring. A fine house for a fine lady. He grabbed a length of oak trim, measured it and cut it. Tension he hadn't been aware of eased away. There was satisfaction and peace in the work.

A few hours later, his growling stomach and the growing darkness forced him to stop. He set his tools to one side. He'd return next morning and spend the day working.

As he made his way down the hill, the light from the cabin beckoned. Beyond the doors lay something he wasn't used to—warmth, welcome, a hot meal…

Inside, the smell of cinnamon and ginger greeted him. As did Linette's smile.

He paused, caught between the unfamiliar welcome and a resistance filled with the voice of his father and his promise to Margaret. Turning to hang his coat and hat on the hook behind the door, he pushed his thoughts back into proper order. "Food smells good."

"Once again Cookie has been kind enough to offer

me some instruction. Under her supervision I made ginger cookies."

"Ah. That explains the cinnamon smell as I stepped in the door."

"Cookie said they were your favorite." Her voice strummed a bass chord in his heart.

Their gazes collided, caught for a moment, just long enough for him to feel a flash of something unfamiliar before her gaze darted away.

Linette passed around potatoes, carrots, fried pork chops and canned applesauce. Later, when the plates were cleaned, she served tea with cookies still warm from the oven.

He pushed back from the table. "Excellent meal."

Linette grinned. "Thank you, sir. I told you, I'm a fast learner."

He recalled what had accompanied her statement of being a fast learner—a promise he'd beg her to stay before the winter was over.

His pleasure in the meal faded. The interior of the cabin seemed less welcoming.

Cassie took Grady to the bedroom shortly after the meal. Linette didn't linger more than a few minutes before following them.

He finally relaxed. Life in the cabin could be pleasant enough if she would be content simply to pass the time while waiting for traveling weather.

Before he fell asleep he came up with a plan to divert Linette's single-mindedness.

The next morning was Sunday. Linette wondered if Eddie did anything to honor the day.

"We have a simple worship service in the cookhouse," Eddie explained. "Nothing fancy, but it's the best we can do."

Linette liked the idea just fine. "It sounds perfect. I tried to guess how you managed to make Sundays special with no church out here. I read one story about a missionary who held services wherever he went. Didn't matter if it was in a tent, a sod shack or even in the open air. Wouldn't that be special, worshipping God in His own cathedral?" She went to the window to glimpse the mountain peaks to the west. "No church built by man could rival the majesty of God's creation." She turned to Eddie, saw him watching her with surprise, and—dare she hope—a hint of appreciation. "Wouldn't you agree, Eddie?"

"I think," Eddie said slowly and softly, "He gave us the great outdoors to enjoy and to make us realize how small we are and how mighty He is. Then we would acknowledge our dependence on Him. We'd see how great is His grace that He considers us with such favor. Perhaps that is the kind of worship He desires."

Linette stared, darted a look at Cassie and saw from the expression on her face that Eddie's eloquence had surprised her as much as it had Linette. She couldn't find a response as her thoughts lifted Heavenward, carried on the wings of his words. "I like the way you put it."

Eddie shifted from foot to foot and shrugged. "Let's get over to the cookhouse."

Linette held his gaze a moment longer, feeling again, as she had several times in the past few days, a sense of connection. He would no doubt deny it, but they shared the same awe at God's creation visible around them in the form of mountains, streams and even storms. They shared the same need to establish new roots in a new world.

He broke eye contact first to look out the window. "The men are already filing in."

It took her a moment to pull herself back to the here and now. How could she so easily forget that Eddie didn't want to use the new world to do new things? She followed the direction of his gaze in time to see a man disappear into the cookhouse. "Come on, Grady." She held her hand out to the child, but he backed away, retreating under the table. So long as she remained next to Eddie, the boy would not come to her. Sighing her frustration, she moved across the room and called Grady again.

Darting frightened glances in Eddie's direction, he scrambled to her side and clutched her hand with both of his.

"Grady, Mr. Gardiner is not going to hurt you."

He whimpered.

Eddie grabbed his Stetson and jammed it on his head. "Not to worry. It takes time to put aside fears." He stepped out the door and held it for the others. Grady shivered against Linette as they slipped past Eddie.

Eddie fell in at her other side, casually keeping two feet away so as to not further frighten Grady. They crossed the yard and entered the warmth of the cookhouse. The benches had been placed on one side of the table; Bertie faced them from the other side, a Bible tucked under his arm. Cookie sat on a chair at his side.

She rose as they entered. "Grady, boy. Come sit with me."

Grady saw all the men and pressed closer to Linette's side. She pushed forward to an empty place on the back bench, carefully putting herself between Grady and the others. Cassie settled on the end of the bench on Grady's other side.

Linette looked about. Eddie had not followed her. Instead, he sat on the far corner of the bench in front.

Someone sat beside Linette. "Morning, ma'am."

She turned. Ward Walker, all slicked up and polished for the day. "Good morning." Her gaze slipped toward Eddie.

He nodded and smiled, not a bit disturbed by this arrangement. Rather, he seemed pleased.

Her head buzzed with a thousand protests all as troublesome as a swarm of insects. She wasn't prepared to be so easily dismissed. She signaled her warning with her eyes but he turned away as Cookie cleared her throat.

"Shall we begin?"

Linette gave her attention to the pair at the front.

Bertie opened the service with a prayer. Cookie, with more enthusiasm than skill, led them in singing three familiar hymns then Bertie read a passage about the prodigal son. He closed the Bible. "I once wandered far from God eating of the husks of life. It took hitting bottom for me to turn around and look for God. He was there waiting all the time. Folks, He always is. No matter what we need, He can supply." He spoke several more minutes, then closed with a prayer.

The cowboys shifted, as if uncertain what they should do next with two visiting ladies in their presence. Cookie rose to the occasion. "I'll make tea for you all. Stay and visit. Make the ladies feel welcome."

Cassie hurried to help Cookie, but was shooed away. "Go visit. Enjoy yourself."

Roper edged forward and asked Cassie how she enjoyed the country.

Linette didn't catch her answer as Ward asked at her side, "Miss Edwards, are you liking the country?"

"Like I said before, I love it." She sought Eddie, found him standing across the room, grinning.

More protests buzzed loudly in her brain.

"Not too wild for you?"

Good manners forbade her from walking away from Ward and telling Eddie exactly what she thought of his enjoyment of her situation. "Not at all.'"

"I have some land north of here. Intend to have my own place just as soon as I can get me a few head of cows. It ain't much. Not fancy like this. But it's mine."

Linette nodded, sensing the man's enthusiasm. "It sounds great. I wish you every success. When will you take up residence?"

"Not for a while. Ain't had no cause to make the move. Maybe that will change now." Did he sound hopeful? Had Eddie said something to encourage the man?

She glared at Eddie with a burning look.

He flicked a glance her way and then turned his back to her.

Oh! The man was impossible beyond description. Did he think she would simply substitute another man for him? It wasn't possible. She recalled Eddie had said something very similar about her substituting for Margaret.

"Come on," Ward said. "Let's get tea and cookies."

Later, after they'd returned to the cabin and eaten a simple lunch, Linette tried to think how best to inform Eddie that she wouldn't be diverted from her purpose and that she had no intention of wasting her time with a cowboy, though no doubt Ward was a very nice man. Just not a man her father would accept as her husband.

But before she found a chance, a knock came on the door.

"Company." Eddie didn't sound a bit surprised. He opened the door. "Come on in, boys."

Ward and Roper stepped inside.

Eddie's smile practically broke his face in half. "Thought you ladies could stand some visitors for a change. So I'll leave you to visit while I take care of some business." He grabbed his coat and ducked out, leaving four awkward adults behind.

Linette's thoughts raged. How dare he assume she would welcome this any more than would Cassie, who set aside her knitting with such vehemence Linette wouldn't have been surprised to hear something rip. Thankfully, Grady had fallen asleep in the bedroom so didn't have to endure this…this invasion.

"Ladies, if this is awkward…" Ward twisted his hat.

Linette pushed aside her anger. It wasn't their fault. "Of course not. Come on in. We'd love to hear about your ranch—" she indicated Ward "—and about your plan in life," she said, indicating Roper.

They edged toward the table and each pulled out a chair and sat down. Cassie, her face revealing anything but welcome, shifted her chair to face them.

Linette filled the kettle. How did one entertain a pair of cowboys on a Sunday afternoon? From what she'd read, they played cards or chewed the fat, which meant they sat around spinning yarns. Well, she had no problem learning more about the country.

"What brings the two of you to northwest Canada?" she asked the men.

They talked easily about the cattle drives they'd been on and the country they'd seen.

"Working for Eddie is good," Ward said. "He's a fair boss and the both of us have year-round work."

Roper nodded. "What about you ladies? Where have you come from and why here?"

Linette turned to tend to the tea. How much did the pair know? Did they know she'd come with plans to marry Eddie to escape her father's arrangement? But she had no intention of confessing so. "I want a life where women are allowed to follow their hearts."

Both men looked at her, confusion in their eyes.

Ward spoke slowly. "Where does your heart want to go?"

Where, indeed? So many things filled her thoughts. Escape, for sure. Freedom to tend to those who were hurting and in need. Those were the motivations she gave to Cassie and Eddie. But hidden deep inside lay a secret reason. She saw in Eddie something she'd admired from the first letter Margaret read. She had no words for the feeling. She only knew it was there.

She realized the others waited for her answer and she gave a little chuckle. "I'm not sure how to answer other than to say I grew tired of the restrictions society places on women in England and hoped to find new opportunities here."

A moment of silence greeted her response then Roper turned to Cassie. "Mrs. Godfrey, what brought you to the West?"

Cassie considered the man for a moment then sighed. "A boat, a train and a stagecoach."

Linette laughed along with the others. She knew Cassie meant to be dismissive but had instead been funny. Something warm flickered through the other woman's eyes at their amusement.

They visited until Grady called from the bedroom. "'Net?"

Linette excused herself and went to the boy. "Come out and visit."

He shook his head and clung to her hand. "I scared."

She sat on the bed and pulled him onto her lap. "Grady, I don't know what's happened to you to make you so fearful, but you are safe now. I won't let anything bad happen to you. Eddie won't let anything bad happen to you. Cassie won't let anything bad happen to you. Nor will Cookie, or Bertie or any of the cowboys on the ranch." She said it with total confidence, knowing her words were backed up by Eddie's character. "You can trust me on this."

Grady snuggled close.

"Do you think I'll take good care of you?"

He nodded.

She asked the same question with Cassie's name.

Again a nod.

Then with Eddie's.

Grady shivered. "He big."

"Yes, he's strong. That means he can take care of you really well."

Grady shook his head. "He big. He strong."

Linette closed her eyes. Had a man used his strength, his power, to hurt Grady or perhaps his mother? How could she explain strength as a good thing? "Grady, if you needed something big and heavy carried, would you ask me or Eddie to help?"

He didn't answer.

She wrapped him closer. "You'd ask Eddie because he could do it and I couldn't. Sometimes we need strong people to help us."

He considered her words then sat up. "I not move anything big."

She laughed. "You know that's not what I mean, you little scamp." She rose to her feet with the boy. "Now, come along and say hello."

He jerked his hand free. "I stay here. Okay?" His eyes pleaded.

"Fine." She couldn't force him to forget his fears. *Please, God, heal his little heart.* She returned to the other room. "Sorry."

Cassie gave her a worried look. "Where's Grady?"

"He prefers to stay in the bedroom."

Roper stood. "We'll be on our way."

Ward scrambled to his feet as well.

Roper paused at the door. "The boss said the boy was afraid of men. Sorry to hear that. But we won't be doing anything to feed that fear. Thank you for a pleasant afternoon." He donned his hat and stepped outside.

Ward grabbed his Stetson and smiled at the ladies. "'Twas a very pleasant afternoon. Thank you." He shifted his attention to Linette. "Perhaps you'd like to see my ranch someday." He twisted his hat round and round in his hands. "Think you might see lots of opportunities there."

"Perhaps." She closed the door behind him and leaned on it.

Cassie grinned at her. "I expect he'd marry you at the drop of a hat."

"Perhaps." Her predicament couldn't be so easily solved, and if Eddie thought otherwise, he would soon learn differently.

The next morning she wakened and listened. Eddie moved about in the other room. He lifted the lid on the stove and added wood. He moved to the table. Was he reading? Perhaps writing another letter? Would he beg Margaret to join him? A great ache filled Linette until she was forced to clamp her teeth together to keep from moaning.

She'd dreamed she'd be valued as a pioneer wife, able to share the work of building a new life in the West.

Lord, help my plan to succeed. Help Eddie see me as a woman to share this life as a partner, a helpmate.

She hurried to make breakfast. As soon as Eddie finished, he announced, "I'll be working on the house most of the day."

Linette allowed herself only a small smile. This was exactly what she'd hoped for.

"I go see piggies?" Grady asked.

She wanted to rush ahead with her own plans but couldn't ignore the child's wishes. "As soon as we clean up."

Cassie scurried about helping, more eager than Linette had seen her before. "I told Cookie I would help her this morning," she explained. "I so enjoy talking about where we used to live." She paused, a faraway expression on her face.

Linette studied her. Seems Cassie preferred living in the past to facing the present, whereas Linette felt just the opposite. There was nothing in her past she wanted to return to except to keep in touch with her family. Especially her brother. When they were younger she'd enjoyed following him around and imitating some of his activities. She'd ridden a horse astride, raced a wagon down the road, done a number of adventuresome things with him until their father and mother discovered the nurse wasn't supervising closely enough to suit them.

A new nurse, given the task of seeing Linette turned into a lady, put an end to her fun.

She shook away the memories and regrets.

She'd expected marriage to Eddie to change all that, give her back what she'd lost. She stiffened her spine. She wasn't about to give up hope.

Linette took Grady for a walk while Cassie hurried over to visit Cookie.

Grady skipped ahead murmuring to himself. She caught up to him, hoping she might learn something from listening to him, but she couldn't make out his words. He ground to a halt. She stopped and glanced about to see why he'd grown so quiet.

Her attention on the child, she hadn't noticed Eddie leaning against the fence, his arms crossed, one foot resting on the tip of his cowboy boot. He appeared relaxed, yet she felt his alertness as clearly as if it had found wings and flew before her face.

The sun flashed in his eyes. His steady watchfulness never faltered. Hadn't he said he was going to the big house? Had he changed his mind? What did he want? And why did her heart pound against her ribs at the sight of him?

His gaze lowered to Grady and he slowly stepped away from the fence and bent to pick up a rope. He moved to the middle of the pen and began to circle the rope over his head in a wide loop. With great ease and grace, he danced the loop down to the ground and up again. Then he lowered it over his body, hopped out of the circle and swung it over his head.

Grady, as fascinated as Linette, moved closer to watch, mesmerized by the twirl of rope.

Eddie continued the show for several minutes. Then casually, he let the rope fall to the ground, gathered it into neat coils and hung it over his shoulder. He turned, touched the brim of his hat. "See ya." He headed for the barn.

Neither Grady nor Linette moved.

Slowly she drew in a breath. She suspected he'd put on the show for Grady but allowed herself to hope a part of him was trying to impress her, too. The thought filled her with hope that he had begun to view her differently.

"What did you think of that, Grady?"

He stepped away from the fence. "Can I see piggies now?"

She laughed as she took his hand and headed toward the bridge. "You aren't about to give in easily, are you?"

No more than she was.

Eddie stood in the house and stared at the piece of wood in his hands. Why had he put on that little show with his rope earlier? For Grady, of course. He wanted the boy to be curious about him, maybe get up enough courage to talk to him. But he kept wondering what Linette thought of his roping skills.

Not that her opinion mattered one little bit.

He turned back to the task at hand—measuring and cutting the wood trim. The finishing details took time but he was determined to do them right. Margaret deserved the best. The house was much smaller than either of them was accustomed to in England, but it was still a beautiful house. Margaret could entertain important people and fine ladies.

Never mind that fine ladies and gentlemen were few and far between in the territory.

An errant thought blasted through his mind. The kind of people Linette favored as occupants of the house were everywhere, even here. Widows like Cassie. Orphaned or abandoned children like Grady. Even some of his cowboys. Quiet, good men with a background of hurt.

"Hello. Can I come in?"

He jerked toward the sound. Was he imagining Linette called?

The main door closed with a gentle thud. "Hello?" Her voice sounded closer.

What was she doing here? He had struggled for the past hour to erase her presence from the house and picture Margaret there instead. Now she would undo all his hard work. "In here," he called. He intended to finish the family dining room first. As Linette said, the view over the ranch, the coziness of the quarters, made it one of the nicest rooms in the house.

She stepped into sight and rubbed her hands together. "I thought you might be able to use another pair of hands."

"I have half a dozen men I can call for assistance if I want help."

She ignored his dismissive tone. "It seems they are busy elsewhere."

He considered her. Would she leave if he asked or simply disregard him if it didn't suit her? No wonder her father felt he had to marry her off to someone who would control her. Best he keep that opinion to himself. "You know anything about carpentry?"

She tipped her head and looked thoughtful, though he didn't miss the teasing twinkle in her eyes. "I know the difference between a nail and a hammer. Does that count?"

He intended to be disapproving, discouraging, insisting he didn't need her hanging about getting in the way and distracting him. Instead, he laughed. "That's valuable information, I'm sure. Certain to be a great help."

She recognized the teasing in his words and chuckled. "You can never tell."

He held her gaze, feeling her smile, and something more. A challenge. Never one to pass up a challenge, he nodded. "Let's see how useful you can be. I was about to nail this trim into place." He indicated the window frame he was finishing. "Hold the end in place."

She clamored to the window, but instead of attending to the task, she stared out the window and sighed. "I could never get tired of this view."

He joined her to enjoy the sight. Slim and Roper jogged past the buildings.

"How was your visit yesterday?" He'd sent Ward and Roper in the hopes of giving Linette other prey to stalk.

"It was very pleasant."

He waited, hoping for some indication as to how she felt, but she gave him nothing. "Boys are headed for town. Carrying the letters to Margaret." Margaret would soon know the truth about the house he'd built for her.

Linette didn't speak. He felt her silence as solidly as the hardwood in his grasp. What did she think as she watched the men walk away? Was she accepting that her stay here was temporary?

"Let's get to work." She grabbed the end of the window trim and eased it into place. She eyeballed the other end. "You got a level?"

He blinked. For someone who barely knew a hammer from a nail, it was an informed question. "Let me check it." He did and she adjusted the end with ease.

"How do you know about levels and hammers? It hardly seems…"

"Ladylike? My parents couldn't agree more. You going to tack this in place or leave me holding it for the rest of the day?"

Feeling a little as if he'd been tardy about his work, he reached around her to nail it. In order to get the end he had to press close to her. Close enough to feel warmth from her body, breathe in the smell of cinnamon and more. A scent completely unlike those he'd grown used to. If he'd had a free hand he would have smacked himself. Of course she didn't smell like cows or cowboys. More like flowers and home.

He chomped down on his teeth and drove in the necessary nails. He obviously needed a long hard ride or a good dose of salts to cure his foolishness. "You can let it go now." He placed each nail carefully and stepped back to study his work. It looked satisfactory.

Now to keep his mind focused on the task. It was easy. All he had to do was turn to the right and grab the next piece of wood. Instead, he turned right and met Linette's gaze. He should thank her. But his tongue refused to move.

She grinned, her eyes dancing with amusement. "I learned a tiny bit about carpentry when I helped one of the servants build a shed." Her humor fled, replaced with a mixture of regret and determination.

He'd seen that look before. Knew it signaled a decision on her part to dig in her heels and fight for what she wanted.

"When my father learned what I was up to, the poor man lost his job. I've always regretted that."

Slowly, she turned full circle to study the room then returned to face him. "Did you do all this work yourself?"

"I had the boys help."

"How did you learn?"

"I worked on the estate."

Her eyes darkened. "Aren't rich boys supposed to play the wastrel?"

He shrugged. "Some, I suppose. Others are encouraged to be useful."

"Unlike daughters who are expected to be only ornamental."

"I never thought of it that way."

"You have sisters. Are they allowed to be useful? Or even to have a choice about what they want?"

"I've never considered it." He'd been too busy trying to prove he could do all that was expected of him.

"No, of course you didn't." She sighed deeply, as if chasing away dark thoughts. "Tell me about your sisters."

Glad to be free of the direction she'd headed with talk of how women were treated, he smiled. "Jayne is almost twenty." He and Jayne had been good friends. Mostly, if he had to venture a guess, because they were the two oldest and Jayne was sensible and intelligent. He paused to consider the younger ones. Seems they were in the nursery or under the watchful eye of a governess, so he didn't feel he knew them as well as he knew Jayne. "It's hard to think of them getting older. I haven't seen them in such a long time. Bess must be seventeen now and Anne, fourteen."

"But who are they? What do they like?"

He chuckled. "I seem to remember them clustering about each other giggling."

She wrinkled her nose. "You make them sound like silly ninnies. I'm sure they're not."

He'd never given it much study, but now that he did, he realized his father tended to dismiss them. Yet he and Jayne had shared some insightful conversations before he left. "Jayne and I were closest growing up. She liked studying languages. She's promised to a young man. They haven't set a date yet. I think Jayne would like it to be soon, but Oliver seems to have other ideas."

Linette nodded. "And Bess?"

"She has a beau, too, but Father forbids her to see him."

"Why?"

"He's the son of the groom."

"And that says it all. Not good enough for a Gardiner."

"She wouldn't be happy living the life he could offer and he lacks the education to be worked into the family business."

"So she has no choice in the matter?" Her voice dripped disapproval.

"I think my parents know what is best for her." Intending to forestall the impending argument, he continued, "Anne is our baby. She's been spoiled, I expect. She has only to smile prettily and everyone gives her what she wants. If that fails, a little pout will work." Remembering the girls, he chuckled.

Linette laughed, too.

Talking about his sisters had filled him with missing them.

"Maybe they'll visit someday, though I know Jayne will never leave her beloved Oliver."

"Never is a long time." She looked pensive as if missing her family, too.

That was good, he assured himself. Maybe she'd be ready and willing to return after a few months away. Exactly what he wanted. So why did he consider patting her shoulder and saying it got easier with time? He turned, picked up a piece of wood and cut it to fit.

She held the piece in place without needing instructions. And she talked.

"Austin is my only brother. He's a year older than me. We were best of friends until Father took him into the business. Then we hardly saw each other. And when we did, Austin felt duty bound to agree with Father's opinions."

Eddie heard the sour note in her tone. "Did he agree with your father's plans for you?" Seemed to him if the situation was as intolerable as Linette believed, her brother should have intervened.

When the board was in place, Linette stepped back. She tugged at her earlobe. "I think Austin felt sorry for me, but like he said, neither of us had much choice about what we would do with our lives." She sighed heavily. "I think Austin would have preferred to farm rather than work in an office, but Father wouldn't hear of it." She shrugged. "Guess it proves men aren't always able to make free choices, either."

He nodded. "We all have duties and obligations." He returned his attention to the project at hand and cut the next piece of trim.

Linette sprang forward to help. "Mort—that's the man who let me help construct the outbuilding for storing grain—he said it needed to be solid and tight to keep the grain dry. He said a man's character is revealed by the quality of his work. 'Course, he didn't say the same about a woman's work, but I expect it's true." She held a piece of wood in place. When it was secured, she stepped back. "I'd say Mort was right. For instance, I can tell much about you by what I see here."

He paused to study her, filled with curiosity. "Is that a fact?" Not that her approval or assessment mattered. Still, he couldn't keep from asking, "What do you see?"

She went to the windows. "Remember you said the world needed art and artists to see the beauty of the world? I think the fact you set the house here so these windows provide a view of the mountains reveals that you have an artist's soul." She practically choked back the word. "I mean eye."

He tucked a smile behind his heart. It felt rather nice to think he had an artist's soul—or eye—but he wasn't about to let his thoughts wander down a trail he didn't want to take. "I laid it out this way so I could see the ranch operations."

"If that's all that mattered, why not over there, behind the cookhouse?" She pointed to the hill she meant then turned and caught his gaze, holding it in a demanding, challenging look.

He wouldn't admit he'd looked at several building sites and chosen this one for the precise reason she'd given—the marvelous view of the mountains. Any more than he'd confess—even to himself—how it pleased him to have her recognize his motive.

She turned to study the room. "I know you'll say you only followed plans drawn up in London when you built this place, but…" She went to a corner hidden behind a door and examined the baseboards. "Did you place these?"

He admitted he had.

"Perfect fit. I see you are careful even on things no one might see or notice. That tells me you are honorable and have integrity."

He tried to laugh off her comments. "Or that I'm certain my father would notice any mistakes and point them out."

She again drilled him with her demanding gaze. "Can you say that's your reason?"

The word *yes* came automatically to his mind, then he reconsidered and discovered a truth he'd been unaware of. "Only partially. I would do the best job I could regardless of who saw it. After all, God sees and expects us to do our best."

She grinned. "I knew it." Suddenly she sobered. "Did you know it, too?" Not waiting for an answer, she pointed to the patch of sun pooling at the foot of the windows. "It's almost lunchtime. I'll have it ready in a few minutes." She looked about at what they'd accomplished. "Not bad. Not bad at all." Then she scurried away.

He watched out the window as she trotted down the hill. She paused at the doorway of the cabin to glance in his direction. She must have seen him still there, for she lifted her hand in a quick wave. He didn't turn away until the cabin door closed behind her.

Then he slapped his forehead. She'd done it again. Intruded on his plans, his world.

How long before he heard back from Margaret?

Perhaps he'd get Ward to help with the carpentry, then if Linette insisted on coming up the hill, she could get to know Ward better.

Chapter Nine

Linette hummed as she and Cassie cleaned up after lunch.

"You're mighty pleased with yourself," Cassie said, sounding curious as much as anything.

"I spent the morning helping Eddie in the big house. I think he is beginning to accept me."

Cassie let out an impatient sigh. "Accept you or just your help?"

"Either way, it's a start. He'll soon see I'm suited for ranch living. If you stay with Grady for his nap, I'll help him this afternoon, too."

Cassie picked up her knitting. The afghan was steadily growing large.

"You never did tell me who you are knitting that for."

"For myself. I have no one else, if you care to recall."

"I'm sorry. Perhaps you'll find someone out here. Roper seemed rather interested. I think he's half in love with you already."

"I'll marry again if I can." She jabbed her needle through a stitch. "A woman needs protection of a man. But it won't be for love. No value in that."

Linette didn't answer, but she couldn't argue. Love

had no place in the lives of those she knew. Certainly her mother and father seemed to tolerate rather than love each other. Mother ventured no farther than her sewing room and her lady friends. Father's time and attention were devoted to enlarging his holdings and amassing more money. Her aunt was the only woman she knew who spoke freely of loving her husband and, as far as Linette could see, it made her aunt far too pliable and ready to jump at every little suggestion her uncle made. Linette had no desire for such a life.

"I'll stay with Grady if you still have a mind to traipse up the hill, but it seems to me he's a man who knows what he wants."

"And it isn't me? Is that what you're saying?"

Cassie lowered her knitting and met Linette's gaze. "The man was quite clear on the matter."

Linette pulled on her coat before she faced Cassie again. "I have until spring to change his mind and I intend to make the most of my time. I'll be back later."

"No rush. I can manage Grady. Maybe we'll go over and see Cookie."

Linette took her time climbing the hill. She'd seen the flash of surprise darkening Eddie's eyes when she'd said he had integrity. He'd surely looked at her with more interest than he'd previously revealed. She'd shown herself capable of working at his side. Surely he was learning her value…an asset to help him build a new life here. She would not think of the letters even now starting their journey to Margaret. She could imagine what Eddie had said, likely they were words of love urging her to join him.

But if Margaret changed her mind… Her heart dipped toward her toes. She had until spring. She prayed it would be long enough.

* * *

"Boys, turn the tailenders into the pen then head for the cookhouse." Only the weak and young cattle were brought to the ranch. The rest were in nearby pastures where he could keep an eye on them. "Cookie is sure to have some hot coffee and fresh bread." Eddie's gaze went unbidden to the little log cabin across from the cookhouse as Slim and Roper urged the animals toward their winter home. He'd left only three days ago, before the weather had taken a turn for the worse, but it seemed months since he'd last stepped into the comforting warmth of the little house and he looked forward to it with unusual eagerness. "I think we've all earned a warm bed and hot meal."

"Yeah, boss. And now you can stop worrying about your cows." No doubt Slim spoke for all the cowboys.

"Now we can watch them and feed them," he corrected. "I'm not prepared to let them fend for themselves if the snow keeps coming." It had started snowing soon after they left and continued intermittently while they were gone. He'd worried about the occupants of the little cabin but assured himself they'd be safe and sound. Still, he couldn't wait to see for himself. "I'm grateful we got them down before it got any nastier."

The men rode after the cows and Eddie reined toward the barn, glancing at the cabin again.

A movement on the hill beyond caught his attention. A handful of Indians slid past, only the sound of muted horses' hooves and the whisper of a travois broke the silence. No doubt they were headed to join other Indians in their wintering grounds to the south. He hoped they'd have sufficient supplies.

He watched until they slipped out of sight. Seeing the

Indians had given him an idea on how to teach Grady to trust him.

He continued toward the barn where he took his time taking care of Banjo, brushing him thoroughly, feeding him a scoop of oats, cleaning his saddle.

The cold bit into his lungs as he stepped out into the bright sun. Sparkling crystals filled the air. He turned toward the cabin. Something dark disappeared around the corner of the cabin. He crept toward the spot and edged along the wall until he could peek around the corner. Linette. His breath whooshed out. Not an intruder or wolf.

But what was she doing? It looked as if she planned to bury something in the snowbank.

"Linette?"

She dropped whatever it was she held and spun around, her eyes wide. "You didn't take long enough."

"You think I should stay out in the cold?"

She darted a glance to the brown blob at her feet.

"What is that?" he asked.

"Nothing."

"Don't look like nothin' to me." He squinted at it. "Looks like—"

She stepped forward and tried to hide the lump. "It's nothing."

He crossed his arms and leaned back on his heels. "Uh-huh." He waited.

She shifted back and forth. Couldn't meet his gaze. "Oh, very well. You might as well know the truth." She stepped aside and stared at the lump. "It's supposed to be bread, but it won't rise." Her voice quivered. "It's the second time this has happened." She dropped to her knees and scooped a hollow in the snow. "You weren't supposed to see it." She dug the hole deeper and shoved the lump into it.

"Bread, huh?" He purposely kept his voice flat though amusement trickled through him.

"Cookie said it was simple." She pushed snow over the hole and pounded it. Hard. Every slap made Eddie blink. "Simple for her. Not for me."

Did her voice catch?

She planted her hands on the packed snow and leaned forward. What was she doing? Praying? He couldn't think how praying would salvage the dough. Her shoulders twitched. She sniffed.

"Linette?" He took one hesitant step forward. "Are you crying?"

"No." But the word ended on a sob.

He fell to his knees at her side. "It's only flour and water." Or whatever went into the mysteries of making bread. "Nothing to be upset about."

Her sobs ended. She faced him, stubborn determination hardening the bones in her face. A tear clung to her lashes. "You don't understand."

He patted her shoulder. "It's only bread," he soothed.

"My father was right." Her words choked with pain and defeat. "I'm only good for sitting and painting."

Her father had certainly bruised her heart. The agony in her voice drove arrows through his heart. He wanted to reach inside and yank them free, end the pain. Both his and hers. "I like your paintings."

A tear made a silvery trail down her cheek.

He'd said the wrong thing. But what was the right thing? "Linette, you can learn to bake bread."

She looked beyond him.

"Look how far you've come. And I don't mean simply crossing the ocean and most of Canada, though that's admirable in itself. I mean from a young society woman to a pioneer." She flicked a glance at him. Did he imagine she showed interest? "You can build a fire in the stove. You have learned how to make corn bread and how to fry bacon. Remember your first reaction to a slab of pork?" He chuckled, earning him a surprised look. "You've come a long way." He meant much more than her culinary abilities. He quieted, took a deep breath and released the words he deemed safe, though they were but a sliver of all he felt. "I admire your spunk and courage. I admire your spirit." She'd make a good pioneer wife.

Too bad that wasn't what he wanted or needed.

She grew still then she wiped tears from her face. Determination darkened her eyes. "I refuse to give up."

He sat back on his heels to study her.

A riot of emotions raced across her face. Her determination seemed to weaken, grow fragile, and then she scrambled to her feet. "I did succeed in making cookies. Care to try some with tea?"

He bolted to his feet and followed her to the cabin, grateful the moment ended before he'd tossed all his good intentions to the wind and decided a pioneer wife would suit him just fine.

Grady glanced up as Eddie entered. His eyes widened and he stiffened but then sank back to playing with his growing collection of rocks and bits of wood plus a handful of carved animals several of the men had crafted for the boy.

At least he hadn't withdrawn under the table and didn't cling to Linette's skirts. A notebook lay open on the table. Linette closed it and set it aside as she put out tea and cookies.

A little later, he noticed her notebook on the shelf.

He'd seen enough to guess she wasn't writing. "Were you drawing something?"

She grew still and seemed to consider her answer. "I'm afraid I feel the need to capture life in my sketch-book."

He wondered why she seemed so apologetic. He certainly didn't object to the activity, but perhaps she wondered if he might. "What did you capture today?"

She picked up the book and opened it to reveal a simple pencil drawing of the interior of the cabin. It should have been crude, even barren, but the few lines portrayed warmth and charm.

"You make it look appealing."

Her eyes lit with humor. "Isn't it?"

He chuckled, beguiled by her smile. "Not many would see it as so."

"I guess it's all in the eyes…and heart…of the beholder."

He considered her statement, uncertain how to respond. Did she see everything this way? He answered his question. She did. Except the man her father meant for her to marry. "Perhaps you see things through an artist's eyes." He realized he'd used the same words she used to describe his choice of where to build the house and wondered if she'd notice.

Her smile deepened, her eyes darkened and he guessed she did notice. For a moment, he allowed himself to share a tenuous feeling of connection.

Behind him Cassie sighed and stopped his useless thoughts from wandering further. "Linette sees through rose-tinted glasses. She's always saying everything will turn out fine."

Linette chuckled. "Those aren't my words. They're

God's. He says, 'All things work together for good to those who love God.'"

Suddenly Eddie was filled with curiosity as to how she viewed everything. "Did you do drawings of your trip?"

"Certainly."

"Would you mind showing them to me?"

"So long as you don't mock my immature efforts."

"I'd never mock." He sat at the table, across the corner from her, and she opened the first page. "This is our ship." He saw steaming smokestacks and a captain with a steaming cigar.

He laughed. "I think you're mocking the man."

"Only a little." She bent her head over the sketchbook and turned the pages.

There were drawings of the ship's dining room, caricatures of many of the passengers that made him chuckle. A young woman who might have been pretty except for her thinness and the strain in her eyes.

"Who is that?"

Linette sucked in a sigh. "I'd forgotten this. Grady, come here."

The boy played near Cassie—about as far away from Eddie as he could get in the small room. He got to his feet, shot a fearful look at Eddie and remained motionless.

Eddie prepared to move away but Linette shook her head.

"Give him a chance." She spoke to Grady again. "Come and see the picture I drew of your mother."

Grady sidled up to Linette's far side. When he saw the picture a sob choked from him. "Mama." He touched the picture gently. "Mama's gone?"

"Yes, honey." Linette pulled him to her side and

pressed a kiss to his blond head. "Mama's gone but you're safe with us."

"I have her picture?"

"Tell you what. I'll make a copy for your very own and keep this one safe. Okay?"

He nodded, touched the picture again and moved away.

Eddie felt the boy's pain like a spear to his heart and wished Grady would allow him to hug him. Instead, he sat motionless as Grady again settled on the floor with his playthings and carefully kept his back to them.

Cassie, bless her heart, patted his head and squeezed his shoulder.

Linette turned a page in her book and Eddie brought his attention back to the sketches. He looked at her pictures of the train, the stagecoach, then the mountains. He stared at the different ways she portrayed them—distant and pale, close and majestic, sometimes harsh, sometimes gentle.

"I never stopped to think the mountains have so many moods and yet, as I look at your drawing, I see they do."

"I can't wait to see them in their spring finery."

He couldn't, either.

And then there were two side-by-side sketches of the big house. One seemed to breathe warmth and welcome; the other looked cold and imperious. He stared at the pictures. "Why the difference?"

"A house has moods, too." Linette closed the book. "That's all." She took the pencils and sketch pad to the bedroom. She'd stay hidden there except there wasn't any point in hiding. She could only hope Eddie hadn't seen what the pictures of the big house meant. Bad enough he'd discovered her trying to hide the evidence of failed bread making. She smiled. It had provoked him into saying he admired her. *Thank You, God.* He might not have been so approving if he'd understood the drawings of the house. The formal one revealed the house as a manor house ruled by an aristocratic woman. The other showed the house as a home and sanctuary—a place of welcome to all.

It would not benefit her plan for him to guess she saw the second with her at the window. Thankfully she hadn't drawn herself there nor drawn Margaret in the window of the first.

She pressed her palms to her chest. He was learning to appreciate her. Surely that was a step toward her goal. Buoyed by the thought, she returned to the main room, paused to study each of her paintings as if she'd never seen them before, then moved to the window. Unable to look at the big house without being reminded of her foolish drawings, she moved to the pantry shelf and needlessly tidied the contents. Then she shifted to the bookcase.

"You're welcome to any of the books there," Eddie said. "In fact, anything there."

"Thank you." She'd been curious about the items on the shelves but out of respect for his privacy, she'd only glanced at them. Now she pulled out a box that she'd wondered about. "Do you mind?"

"Not at all." Both her words and his smile were inviting and she tried hard and without success to ignore the sudden racing of her heart.

She lifted the lid to reveal a beautiful hand-carved chess set.

"Do you play?" he asked.

"I love the game."

"Any objections to playing right now?"

"Not unless you have objections to losing."

He laughed. "I think you'd better give me a chance to see if you can beat me."

"Prepare to be challenged."

They set up the game and she soon learned they were pretty evenly skilled. She won the first game but only, she guessed, because he underestimated her. He didn't expect her to be his equal. A lesson he would do well to apply to more than a chess game.

He won the next match.

Grady shoved aside his playthings. "I'm hungry."

Linette bolted to her feet. "Is it that late already?" She served a simple meal of creamed peas and boiled eggs on toast.

"My nurse used to make this every Sunday," he told her. "It was my favorite meal."

"Mine, too." Linette's smile came from a warm spot deep within. She couldn't break free of his look as they silently shared enjoyment of a favorite childhood meal.

"Comfort food," he said with a chuckle that landed in her heart with a happy sound.

She laughed, feeling for certain they'd made progress during the past few hours.

Then Grady's hand slipped as he tried to cut his toast and she turned to help him.

They laughed often as they ate the simple meal and finished with bread and jam. Even Grady laughed when Linette and Eddie reached for the jar of jam at the same time and sent it skidding to the edge of the table. Only Eddie's quick reflexes prevented it from falling to the floor.

Later that evening, Linette couldn't force herself to head for bed as soon as Cassie and Grady left. She wondered if Eddie felt the same way, as he appeared to be prepared to sit by the fire and visit. She counted it as further evidence of progress in gaining his acceptance.

"I saw some Indians pass earlier today," he said. "Moving to their winter camp. I wonder why they aren't with the others."

"Others?" She kept every emotion out of her voice, but the stories she'd heard about Indians tensed her muscles.

"The larger bunch went by a few weeks ago. Usually they travel together."

He didn't seem concerned with their presence. Nor had she been alarmed at the few she'd encountered in her travels. "There was an Indian lad in Edendale. Would he be part of this group?"

"Probably."

"He was sick, probably with hunger."

"The boy? Was he alone?"

"The storekeeper said he'd been hired by a freighter who no longer had need of him." She doubted she managed to keep the anger out of her voice. "The boy looked like he hadn't been allowed a decent meal in a long time. I asked why he hadn't been given food."

Eddie dropped his chair to all fours and stared at her. "You said this to the storekeeper?"

Linette snorted. "No, I saw the freighter and confronted him. Asked him if he starved his mules and expected them to serve him well."

Eddie's eyes widened. "Took kindly to that, did he?"

She chuckled. "I expect if I was a man he would have used his fists to give his opinion. As it was, he settled for directing a stream of brown spit to one side and telling me in very colorful language to mind my own business."

Eddie sighed deeply and shook his head. "Some

might have not been so generous. Out here a man considers his business to be his own."

"I guess you know by now that I don't turn my back on someone in need. In my mind, people are equal. Doesn't matter their station in life or their race." She silently challenged him with her words. "Would you turn your back on someone in need?"

A grin began at the edges of his mouth and drew his lips wider. "I allowed you and Cassie and the boy to stay, didn't I?" His eyes reflected his amusement, but something more. Something that allowed her to think he didn't regret his decision, didn't see it as a hardship.

Her heart tipped sideways and poured out a bolt of hot hope. "Why would the Indian boy trust himself to the man? Why would he give up his freedom?"

Eddie studied her a moment before he answered. "He won't likely trust so easily again, will he?"

"I expect not. It's a hard lesson to learn."

"'Spect so. What happened to the lad?"

"I got him a hot meal and arranged a ride on top of the stagecoach so he could join his family."

Eddie held her gaze for a moment more. "Can't say I'm surprised." He pushed to his feet, signaling an end to the evening. Then he seemed to think of something and sat again and leaned back, tipping his chair to the back legs. "Who taught you to play chess?"

"My brother, Austin, and I learned under his tutor."

"You've mentioned your brother several times. You must miss him."

"I miss him dreadfully. We used to spend a lot of time together until—" She didn't want to ruin the day by mentioning how her freedom had been curtailed.

He grinned. "Until your father learned that you weren't acting like a proper lady."

She relaxed. So long as he saw the humor in the situation and didn't judge her as unsuitable because of her activities. "Yes, and then he joined Father in the business. Pushing numbers across a page is how he described it. Father saw to it that Austin had little time for frivolous activities unless they were with a proper young woman."

"Has he found one?"

"Sorry?" She wasn't sure what he meant.

"A proper young woman."

She laughed merrily. "If you saw what Father considers suitable young women—" She shuddered. "Poor Austin. I wish he could come to Canada and live an adventure."

"What's to stop him?"

It was a strange question from a man who lived to fulfill family obligations. Might it provide an opportunity for her to point out how stifling obligations were? "I suppose he feels duty bound to do as Father dictates."

Eddie nodded.

She'd planted the thought that a person might wish to be free of obligations. It was enough for now.

"I'm heading out in the morning to hunt some game."

"I will bid you good-night. Thank you for playing chess with me."

"It is I who should thank you for giving me an opportunity to play with a worthy opponent." His smile seemed like a blessing and she ducked into the bedroom with hope and joy warming her insides.

He'd soon realize how much they had in common and see that duty wasn't reason enough to marry Margaret.

But what did she offer? A marriage of convenience? Though what was wrong with that? Convenient sounded very close to comfortable…or even wanted.

* * *

Eddie was gone when Linette rose the next morning. After breakfast, Cassie took Grady with her to visit Cookie, leaving her by herself in the cabin.

A little later, a scratching sound came at the door. Linette listened. It came again. She tensed and rose slowly. For the first time she was apprehensive that she was alone. Very alone. Though she hoped a scream would bring people from every direction. With that assurance, her nerves steadied. She set aside the shawl she was crocheting as a Christmas gift for Cassie and went to the door and cracked it open. "Why, hello." It was the boy she'd helped in Edendale. And beside him a woman who looked about ready to faint.

"Remember me? Little Bear." The boy patted his chest to indicate it was his name. "My mother, Bright Moon," he murmured with silent appeal.

Linette helped the woman inside and to the nearest chair, where she unwrapped the bundle in her arms to reveal a baby. A very new baby.

Little Bear stepped to her side. "Baby brother."

"Where is your father? The rest of your people?"

The boy struggled with English but managed to explain his mother had been too weak to keep up with the others and his father had gone looking for food.

"You did right to bring her here." Within minutes she had hot sweet tea for the woman. She spread syrup on several biscuits and handed a plateful to both the woman and her son. They ate slowly, savoring each bite. The woman nodded toward the furs in the corner that Eddie slept on.

Linette understood her silent appeal and spread the furs. The woman lay down, cradled the baby to her breasts, which likely had little to offer by way of nourishment. Both baby and mother soon fell asleep. The boy sat cross-legged at their side, his gaze never leaving them.

Linette filled a pot with meat and vegetables. She didn't know how long the little trio planned to stay, but when they left they would go with full stomachs and a jar of stew.

The woman slept until the baby's weak mewling woke her. She nursed the baby, her eyes dark with worry and fear.

Linette offered food. "You need to eat."

The boy translated.

The mother nodded and squeezed Linette's hand in gratitude. The boy accepted food as well but stood at the window as if he felt the need to keep watch. As they ate, Linette filled a jar.

She glanced up at the sound of several horses riding hard. The boy jerked from the window and murmured something to his mother. They scurried to the door.

"Wait," Linette called. "Take this."

The boy grabbed the jar and bent his head in thanks. They slipped silently away. Apart from the unfolded furs on the floor and the used dishes on the table, she could almost believe they hadn't been there.

Outside, the men were making a racket.

She went to the step to see what the cause was. Three ranch hands she recognized had a fourth man tied—an Indian. Ward held a rifle at the man's back.

She grabbed her coat and headed to the fray. "What's going on here?"

"We caught this Injun trying to steal one of Eddie's cows," the young man, Cal, said.

The suspected thief was most likely the father of the two boys and husband of the woman she'd just helped.

"There's only one way to deal with a rustler," Slim said, his expression indicating he would not give an inch on frontier justice.

Cookie, Bertie and Cassie stepped from the cookhouse, Grady behind them. Several more men came from the barn.

"Where's Eddie?" Bertie asked.

Ward answered. "Out hunting wild game. Even he doesn't butcher a young cow."

Linette trotted closer, confronting the knot of men. "This is his decision to make. Why not tie the man in the barn and wait for him?"

Ward and Slim exchanged looks.

"Look," she tried again, "I know it's none of my business, but maybe Eddie would like to handle this himself."

Again they silently consulted each other. Ward shrugged. "If you think it best." He sounded less than convinced, but he directed the men to lead their prisoner away.

Linette watched until they were out of sight then hurried to the cabin. Grady had retreated inside and pulled a chair to the window to watch. His eyes were wide with fright. "That a bad man?"

"Maybe he and his family are hungry."

Cassie followed on her heels. "The men weren't happy about your interference. Cookie said they have to act swiftly and justly in order to prevent losing so many head they might as well pack up and go home."

Linette wanted to protest that many a man turned to stealing if he was starving, but she kept her thoughts to herself. There was only one person she had to convince.

She watched out the window for Eddie's return, hoping to speak to him before the men, but he approached the ranch from the other side. Even before he dismounted, his men crowded around him.

She could not leave the man to be hanged or shot. Not when he had a wife and children to feed. She grabbed her coat and hurried toward the barn.

Eddie stepped out before she got there. He saw her and strode in her direction. He grabbed her elbow, turned her aside. "We need to talk."

"I had to stop them from carrying out their plans."

He grunted—a sound full of distress.

"What would you do if your wife and children were starving and a thousand cows grazed close by?"

He led her to the far side of the cabin...the same place they had first confronted each other.

Her heart thudded deep in the pit of her stomach. Despite a few times that offered hope, it was plain things had not changed a great deal in the recent weeks. She had a choice. Give in to the opinion of Eddie and his men, which would no doubt earn her favor in his eyes, or risk disfavor and defend the Indian.

She didn't even hesitate over her choice. "Remember that Indian boy I told you about in Edendale?"

He nodded.

"He showed up on the doorstep this afternoon with his mother who had a newborn baby at her empty breasts. They're all starving to death. I fed them and gave them a jar of stew. How long do you think that will last? How long before the baby dies...before they all die?"

"A thieving man of any race has to be stopped."

"Rather than force the man to steal, give him enough meat for the winter. Isn't that a better way to stop him?"

Eddie looked at her as if she'd lost her mind.

She pressed the matter. "Does not God say He wants

us to show mercy? Hasn't He shown us undeserved mercy?"

Eddie looked past her and sighed deeply. "This is what your father had to deal with?"

She drew up tall. "I told you from the first I will not turn my back on those in need. I've said my piece. I'll let you decide what is fair and right." She turned and walked away, her head high, her heart beating hard.

Lord, give him a heart to show mercy. Spare these poor people.

If Eddie didn't help, the family would starve to death. And she'd have to reconsider her desire to marry him, which left her facing the fact that her father would find her, drag her home and insist she marry according to his wishes.

She shuddered and prayed Eddie would live up to her opinion that he was a noble man who wouldn't turn his back on another in need. She included herself in that statement.

Chapter Ten

What was right and fair?

Eddie stared after her. The woman certainly had definite ideas about the matter. Shouldn't she stay inside the house and let the men decide such things?

He turned toward the big house. She'd never sit quietly indoors and ignore the challenges of creating a new world. She seemed to think her ways would make the new world better. His insides twisted mercilessly. New world. New ways. Those in the old country favored the old ways. And why not? They had worked for centuries. Why not here?

He released a blast of air from his tight lungs. Her interference left him facing a dilemma—show frontier justice or show mercy. Which was right? His heart said one thing, his brain another. He kicked at a lump of snow then crossed to the barn where the cowhands waited. Young Cal swung a rope before the Indian, taunting him with the loop he meant to throw over the rafter above their heads.

Ward and Slim didn't look quite so eager for a hanging and poor Roper looked ready to bring up his lunch.

"Boys, you know that big old steer mixed in with the

breeding stock?" All winter they'd joshed about how good the critter had it just because he refused to leave the yard.

"Yeah, boss." Slim sounded relieved, as if he understood what Eddie had in mind. The others merely looked curious.

"I couldn't find any deer and we're getting real short of meat. I think fresh beef would be great. What do you all think?"

The whole works cheered. "Nothing like well-fed beef," Slim said.

"Yes, sir." Eddie looked about. "Cal, Ward, Slim— butcher that steer. Cut off the back quarter, wrap it in canvas and throw it in the back of the wagon."

"Boss?" Cal didn't want to believe what he'd just heard.

"I think we have plenty enough for sharing. Anyone disagree?" His words were soft, but not one of the boys missed his silent challenge.

"Nope." The three tromped off.

"Let the man go," he said to Roper.

The Indian shook his wrists once then faced Eddie.

Eddie wasn't sure how much of the conversation the man understood. "I'll give you the hindquarter. You don't need to steal from me. If you're in need come and ask for help."

The man nodded slowly as if struggling to comprehend. "Boy right. He say not all white men bad. I go now. Not wait. Family need me."

Eddie nodded. "I'll bring the meat later." He had seen enough signs to guess the Indians camped in a grove of trees a few miles away.

He hummed as he headed for the cabin. Linette would be pleased with his decision.

He stepped into the warm room. Linette glanced up from a tiny garment she was folding and his heart stalled. Baby clothes. How he wanted babies to fill his house…his heart. Babies of his flesh and blood. He drew in air that caught several times on the way in. Did she have a secret she hadn't revealed? A hidden pregnancy?

"I saw the man ride away." Her face beamed with gratitude. "You let him go."

"I told the boys to butcher an animal. I'll take some of it to him."

"I knew you would."

From the other side of the room Cassie snorted. "Bertie says they're a thieving bunch."

Neither Linette nor Eddie even looked at the woman.

"What do you have there?"

"I brought this with me, intending to use it as a pattern if I ever needed it. Well, I think I need it." She held up the tiny sweater. "I want to give it to the baby."

She meant to give it away. Thank goodness. His heart resumed a normal pace. "Do you want me to take it when I deliver the meat?"

Her expression grew thoughtful. Shifted to determination. He knew her answer before it came.

"I want to deliver it in person. Make sure Bright Moon is okay."

"It's not a fit journey for a young woman." He knew the fact wouldn't influence her.

"I thought by now you would realize I will not be controlled by such things. When are you going?"

He hesitated. "What if I forbid you to come along?"

Her look held steady. "Why would you do that?"

"It could be dangerous."

She shook her head, unconvinced, unyielding. "I

crossed the whole country getting here. Is it any more dangerous than that was?"

"I'm wasting time while daylight passes." He turned to leave.

She bolted to her feet. "I'm ready."

Could he hope to trot away and escape her? He snorted. She'd likely trot right after him.

"I'd like to give the mother something, too. But I have nothing except…" She paused. "My coat."

He shook his head in disbelief. "I expect they have lots of furs to wrap themselves in." He would forbid her giving away her coat, but he didn't think she would take kindly to orders from him. "What they need is food. Why don't you take a sack and fill it from the supply shed."

She clapped her hands in delight. "I'll do that."

He remembered a woolen blanket in a box of belongings and said he'd get it as well.

"Thank you for being so generous. You are a good man." She took a sack from the shelf, grabbed her coat and headed for the door where he still stood.

She saw him as good? Or was she simply pleased to get her own way? What did it matter either way? Except it did. "I'll go with you and get the blanket." He stole a glance at her. Her face fairly glowed. She liked helping these people. She didn't seem to care about race or station of life, rich or poor, respected or outcast. The knowledge seeped through the cracks in his heart brought about by the many comments of disapproval over his lifetime, the frequent whispered and hurtful words about his birth, and softened their sharp edges.

Together they marched to the storage shed and selected a container of loose tea, dried apples and raisins. He lifted the lid on the box and pulled out the blanket.

The wagon rumbled past on the way to the cabin. "The beef is ready to go." He took the sack of food to the wagon then they headed up the hill.

It was easy enough to follow the trail the Indians had left. The cold had deepened throughout the day and it was growing late.

"We should perhaps wait until morning," he suggested.

"I'm okay. Besides, I fear that baby will perish if his mother doesn't get adequate nourishment."

Eddie didn't mind pushing on. He was used to the cold but Linette wasn't. She might suffer for it. She'd been pampered and protected all her life. He pulled the buffalo robe tighter about her knees and edged a little closer on the wagon bench to protect her from the chilly air.

She made no protest at his actions.

They smelled the smoke from the Indian camp before they saw the tepee.

Linette gasped. "They'll freeze."

"They've survived centuries doing things their way."

She relaxed. "Of course, you're right."

The Indian man lifted the flap and stepped out to greet them. "Red Fox." He tapped his chest to indicate it was his name.

His son ducked out after him. "Little Bear."

Eddie gave his name and Linette's then accepted an invitation to step into their abode. He'd been inside native tents before, but Linette had not and she glanced about with interest then hurried to the woman resting on the furs.

"How are you feeling?"

Little Bear translated for her. "She say much better. Stew good."

"I brought the baby a gift and Eddie brought some food."

Eddie put the sack on the floor.

Red Fox crossed his arms and stood up proud.

Linette saw that he was about to refuse their offering and spoke again to the woman. "White women give gifts to each other when there is a new baby. This is my gift to you." She indicated the sack.

Little Bear explained what she'd said and the woman nodded.

Linette handed her the baby sweater. "I hope it will help keep him warm."

The woman took the sweater and chuckled softly. She spoke to Little Bear. A quick smile crossed his face before he translated for Linette.

"Mother say thank you and baby now have to live to prove worthy of the gift."

Linette turned to Eddie, a radiant smile on her lips, then spoke to the mother again. "I will pray for him to grow into a strong, noble man."

When her son explained what Linette had said, the woman nodded vigorously, her eyes expressing her appreciation so clearly that no words were necessary.

"Snow come," Red Fox said.

Eddie didn't ask how the quiet man knew, but understood they must hurry. "Let's get the meat unloaded." He and Red Fox slipped outside to do so.

A few minutes later Eddie and Linette were back in the wagon. Red Fox stood at Linette's side. He touched her arm as he spoke to Eddie in words Eddie did not understand.

Red Fox stopped, searched for English words and shook his head. "She good woman. You keep her. Now go. Snow come."

Eddie needed no more urging. The cold had deepened enough to hurt his bones. "Stay close to preserve your body heat," he urged her when they settled on the wagon bench.

Five minutes after they left, snow began to fall in big lazy flakes.

"He knew." Linette sounded pleased that Red Fox had been correct.

"They seem to feel the weather."

She lifted her face to the heavens. "It reminds me of the first day I was here. It snowed then, too."

"Except for the fact we are two months further into winter and it's about twenty degrees colder." He didn't point out that darkness was falling and the wind had picked up. They could be in for a snowstorm. He'd hunkered down against many storms but never with a woman to guard and protect.

"You're worried about us getting home safely."

"I admit I am." Eddie knew they would need divine intervention to make it back, and he didn't mind asking for it. Without closing his eyes or relaxing his grasp on the reins, he prayed aloud, "God, protect us and guide us home."

The snow fell heavier, making it hard to see the tracks they had left only a short time ago. He leaned forward, peering into the swirling snow. A shadow caught his eye. It moved like quicksilver. It wasn't the shadow of a tree. It was a wolf. And likely only one of several.

He didn't say anything. Didn't want to alarm Linette.

"What was that?" She'd noticed.

Not that he was surprised. But he didn't answer.

"There it is again. It's some kind of animal."

He held the reins tightly as the horse grew nervous. He leaned back for the rifle he had behind the seat.

"It's wolves, isn't it? I read about them." Her hard tone informed him she knew enough not to think this was a lark.

He couldn't put his hand on the rifle. Didn't dare loosen his grip on the reins. "My gun is behind you. Can you reach it?"

She shifted away, letting a blast of cold air separate them. "I've got it." She handed it to him but left space between them for him to maneuver.

"I need you to hold the horse. Think you can do that?"

"I can do whatever I put my mind to."

For once he didn't mind her stubborn determination. He showed her how to hold the reins. "Don't let up no matter what."

He cradled the rifle against his shoulder and watched for the slinky shape of a wolf.

A shadow erupted from the darkness. It left the ground, grew larger. The horse whinnied and jerked away.

"Hold him."

"I have him."

The wolf disappeared in the darkness before Eddie could get a shot off. They'd been the animal's intended target. Sweat pooled in Eddie's armpits. He didn't dare miss next time. He had no intention of becoming wolf food. Nor of letting Linette be torn by vicious fangs.

He squinted into the shadows of the trees. Was that a moving shape among the snow-shrouded branches? He cocked his gun and fired. A yelp! Had he shot one of them?

Something thudded in the wagon. He turned in time to see a wolf coming at them from the back.

Linette glanced over her shoulder and gasped.

Eddie didn't have time to reload. Instinct took over and using his rifle as a club, he clouted the animal as hard as he could. The wolf yipped and stumbled back. For a second he faced Eddie, challenging, then he jumped over the side and disappeared.

"Are you okay?" Linette demanded, her voice quivering.

"Yes. Are you?"

"Yes." But the wail in her voice told him just how frightened she'd been.

He reloaded and glanced about. After a few minutes he decided he had succeeded in scaring off their attackers. "I think they're gone." He put the rifle across his knees, ready to use, and took the reins. He had to pry her fingers loose. He gripped the reins with one hand and pulled her close to his side with the other. "You did good."

She clung to him, her fingers knuckling into the lapels of his coat. The grasp seemed to go further, deeper, right into his heart to wrap around it and squeeze from it admiration and something sweeter that he didn't want to identify at the moment.

"We'll soon be home."

She didn't speak.

"You held the horses. You didn't panic." Not once had she screamed. "You make a good pioneer woman."

She gave a thin laugh. "I've been trying to tell you that."

"So you have." His words rumbled in his chest, easing back the tension that had held him for the last few minutes.

She relaxed her grip, but continued to press to his side. "You're a good rancher. You scared off the wolves.

You handled the situation with Red Fox well, showing wisdom and compassion. You're a born leader."

Each word drifted through his mind like a warm summer wind, full of the perfume of affirmation, full of sunshine and blessing. He tightened his arm across her shoulders.

For this moment he would allow himself to bask in her approval. For the rest of the trip he would enjoy sharing the challenges of frontier life with her.

Linette groped from one heartbeat to the next, one breath to the next. Her fear would not subside.

Eddie seemed to think she'd shown courage. But as she'd held the reins, stories she'd read filled her mind— men hurt by wolves, scarred for life. Or worse—torn to pieces. She knew how the animals hunted in packs, diverting attention to one or two animals so the others could surprise their prey. If the horse had bolted and they'd been thrown from the wagon they would have been easy victims. She would not be responsible for such a predicament. She'd held the reins so firmly they'd bitten into her palms.

Now she clung to Eddie's side trying to calm herself. Together they'd evaded the attack. He'd finally seen her as suitable for pioneer life. Her heart should dance with joy, but she felt vulnerable, shaken. As much by the way she found strength and comfort pressed next to his heart as from the threat of being torn to shreds by the wolves.

She sucked in air, pushed her turmoil away and carefully examined her emotions, skipping the terror part, which was understandable and explainable.

He'd said the words she'd longed for. But they didn't satisfy the way she'd expected them to. She wanted his offer to marry her. But she wanted more. No. She shook the thought away. All she wanted or needed was a marriage that would allow her to live in this new country and establish new rules for how a woman could conduct herself.

She pushed upright, pulled the furs around her. "Until we get safely home I'll be keeping a close watch for them to reappear."

"Indeed. So shall I."

She squinted into the deepening darkness, concentrating every thought on the shadows around them.

The wagon clattered down the hill. The barn door opened and four of the men stood with lamplight behind them. Ward reached for the horse. "Beginning to worry about you, boss. Didn't know if we should go looking or not."

"Thanks, boys. It's nice to know I can count on you. We ran into wolves on the way home."

Several talked at once. "How many?" "They attack?" "Where?"

"I'll tell you about it in the morning. I need to get Linette to the house. Ward, send two more men to help watch the herd."

He jumped down from the wagon. When he reached for Linette she couldn't make her limbs move. He lifted her down and carried her to the cabin as Ward took the wagon away to the barn.

Cassie threw open the door. "Is she hurt?"

"I'm fine. I can stand." But her protests sounded weak even to herself.

"She's cold." Eddie carried her to the stove, grabbed a fur from his bedroll and wrapped her tight. "Cassie, is there tea?"

Cassie brought a cup, but it was Eddie who held it to her lips and urged her to drink.

The warm liquid eased down her throat. She hadn't realized how cold she'd grown. Terror had driven away such ordinary concerns. "I'm fine." She reached for the cup with stiff fingers.

He pressed his fingers over hers, holding the cup steady as she took another swallow.

Their eyes caught over the rim and his gentle smile threatened to take the fragile strength from her hands.

"You did well," he said. "Real well."

Before she could reply, Grady crowded close to her side.

Cassie hung over Eddie's shoulder. "What happened?"

Eddie told the story, making it sound even more adventuresome and Linette more heroic than she had been. His gaze flashed back and forth between Cassie and Linette. Each time, she felt something wrench inside her—a strange twist of both hesitancy and eagerness.

She shifted her attention to Grady, whose eyes had grown wide as Eddie retold the events.

"Eddie save you?" He looked at Eddie with new-found awe.

Eddie laughed. "No more than she saved me."

His approval warmed her as much as the tea and the fire and she let the fur slip from her shoulders. "Thank God we made it home safely."

"Amen." Eddie's voice deepened and against her better judgment she glanced at him. The depth of emotion in his eyes stunned her, left her struggling to find equilibrium.

It was only because they had shared a frightening experience. Only that he'd finally admitted she would make a good ranch wife. Only that they were both grateful to be safe and sound.

Later, in bed, Linette could not fall asleep. Each time she almost did, she'd jerk awake with a wolf lunging at her throat.

She heard Eddie moving about in the other room and wondered if he was having the same difficulty.

His arms about her would calm her fears. Would it be appropriate to put on her heavy robe and go to him?

Appropriate or not, she would not do so. She'd proven her courage to him. Now she had to prove it to herself.

She would not seek or desire anything from Eddie but a marriage offer. She would not allow her heart to overrule her head. Nor would she let her emotions turn her into a weak, needy woman.

The next day Eddie and his men hunted wolves. They found one dead where he and Linette had encountered the animals and tracked half a dozen others. The trail headed toward the wintering herd.

Eddie urged his horse to a trot. "If they've attacked the herd—"

There was no need to say more. The men with him kept pace. They met Ward and the others before they reached the herd. Two wolves hung from Ward's saddle.

"What happened?" Eddie asked.

"A pack of them came at us last night. Good thing we were prepared and able to stop them. Got these two. The others slunk away."

"What direction?"

Ward pointed.

"I'll track them. Blue, you come with me. Ward, head back to the ranch." He gave Ward the wolf carcass he'd picked up earlier. "The rest of you keep a sharp eye out for more attacks."

Blue was the steadiest man, the most accurate shot of

those who worked for him, and together they followed the tracks for the better part of two hours.

"Boss, looks like they've left the area."

"For now." There wasn't any point in going farther. "Let's head on home." The shadows had lengthened and covered the feet of the trees. He would be glad to get out of the saddle and have a hot drink. And some food.

They retraced their steps. By the time they reached the barn, darkness had settled in.

Ward knelt outside the barn, working by lantern light. He'd already skinned two of the hides and nailed them to the wall. He worked on the third carcass.

He looked up as Eddie and Blue approached. "Everything okay?"

"The rest of them have hightailed it to the mountains."

"Glad to hear it."

Eddie grunted agreement and led his horse inside. As soon as he took care of the animal he headed for the cabin and flung the door open to warmth and gentle lamplight.

Linette sprang forward. "I was getting worried. Here, let me help you." She assisted him as he unwrapped his woolen scarf and removed his heavy coat.

"I'm fine." Though it felt nice to have someone fuss over him.

Cassie sat by the stove knitting and Grady played at her side.

"You must be cold," Linette said. "Sit by the stove. Have you eaten? I saved soup for you."

Home sweet home. He sat by the warm stove and took the bowl of soup she offered.

She sat at the table watching.

"The wolves seem to have moved on," he said in answer to her silent question. "I killed one last night and Ward killed two later. He's at the barn skinning them."

"So everyone and everything is safe?"

He nodded.

"Thank God."

"Amen to that." He finished the soup and handed the bowl to her as he failed to stifle a yawn.

"I expect you're tired."

"It's been a long day."

"Well, we'll say good-night." The three of them departed to the bedroom and a few minutes later he threw himself on his bedroll and put out the lamp.

Despite his concern about wolves stalking his herd, he felt warm and content. He had almost fallen asleep with a smile on his lips when he recalled what he'd said to himself earlier. Home sweet home.

The thought was very close to what Linette had promised. And that he would be begging her to stay before winter ended. He clamped a lid on such errant ideas.

The big house would be every bit as welcoming. Margaret would take equally good care of him. Or would she assign the task to a servant? He didn't have the energy to think of an answer.

Linette lay on the bed praying her gratitude for Eddie's safe return. Throughout the day, Cookie and Bertie had told tale after tale of disastrous encounters between men and wolves to the point Linette thought she'd run into the cold and bury her head in the snow to block the words.

After they left the cookhouse and returned to the cabin, the minutes ticked by with the reluctance of a boy headed for a whipping.

She spent much of her time staring out the window hoping, praying for a sign of Eddie's safe return.

Cassie watched her. "Aren't you the one always saying God will take care of things? So why are you worried?"

"You heard Cookie and Bertie. He could be hurt. Or killed."

"And then what would you do? Isn't that what's bothering you?"

Linette had jerked around to face Cassie. "Of course. What else would it be?" But deep inside, she wondered if her concern went beyond the marriage she hoped for, planned for.

How absurd. She simply wasn't thinking straight because of the tension. That's all it was. All it could be.

And now he was back safely. Likely sleeping while she lay in the dark reliving each waiting moment.

She made herself think of something else. The shawl she worked on. Her attempts at bread making. What had she done wrong? Were the wolves as big as she imagined?

One way to find out. She'd ask Eddie if she could see the dead animals.

She waited until after breakfast. "I'd like to see the wolves."

Eddie set his cup down with a crash. "They've left for good, I hope. Besides, didn't you see enough of them the other night? One practically leaped at your throat."

She clutched her throat and cast a look at Grady. Thankfully he seemed occupied playing beyond the stove and didn't appear to have heard the comment. "I meant the dead ones."

"Oh." He gulped the last of his coffee. "They've been skinned out."

"I'd still like to see."

"Then come along. I'll take you to the barn."

She scurried into her coat and followed him out the door. Before they reached the barn, she saw Ward admiring the pelts stretched out on the wall.

Her steps slowed. She'd never seen death this close.

Ward stepped to one side as they reached the pen. "These are prime pelts." He brushed the fur beside him. "See for yourself."

She moved closer, pulled off her mitten and stroked the fur. The wolves had beautiful heads. Like a majestic dog. "It's a shame they had to be killed."

An explosive noise came from Eddie and she jerked about to face him. He scowled at her. "Don't be feeling sorry for them. That one—" he indicated the pelt farthest to the right "—tried to kill us." His anger filled the air like a blast of hot air. "I suppose you'd prefer I rescued them. Turned them into pets."

"I meant nothing of the sort. I only admired their beauty." She kept her tone neutral though she wanted badly to answer him in kind.

He scrubbed his chin. "I just can't stop thinking of how close we came—" He shook his head and shifted his attention to something beyond the barn, though she guessed he saw nothing.

"Eddie, we're safe. Everyone is safe. You said so yourself." She pressed her hand to his arm in an attempt to comfort him.

He shrugged, forcing her arm to drop. "Yes. Everyone is safe." He ducked into the barn.

Linette didn't follow. He needed time alone.

Ward cleared his throat. "I know what you mean about killing such noble animals, but sometimes it's necessary."

"I understand." All kinds of things were unpleasant but necessary.

Ward leaned against the wall and tipped his hat back. "Too bad it's snowed again. I'd hoped to take you to see my ranch."

Eddie stepped from the barn. "You could put runners on the wagon and take it in the snow."

Linette shot him a look fit to curl the leather on his boots.

"Boss, you wouldn't mind?"

"Not at all. I think Linette would enjoy it. Wouldn't you?"

"Perhaps another time." She spoke to Ward, keeping her voice as gentle as possible when inside she burned like a raging forest fire. How dare Eddie encourage Ward? "Cookie promised to give me another lesson in baking bread." She turned to Eddie and made no attempt to disguise how she felt. "I am determined to learn that skill." Just as she was determined to convince Eddie she would make a good pioneer wife. For him. Not Ward.

His expression remained stony, as if to inform her nothing she said or did would change his mind.

"Good day to you both." She strode toward the cabin as if hurrying could put out the fire within. But it only fanned it hotter. What was wrong with the man? How could he be so blind? So stubborn? Yes, he'd said she'd make a good pioneer wife, but not for him. For anyone but him. It burned clear to the depths of her marrow to think he continued to reject her.

Chapter Eleven

"Boss, I get the feeling she's still got her hopes pinned on you. She barely sees me." Ward, like Eddie, stared after Linette's departing figure.

Eddie grunted. He'd made a mistake in telling her she'd make a good pioneer wife. He'd given her hope, when he only meant to compliment her. Although, if he was honest, in the heat of the moment, his heart pounding with fear, he'd been glad enough to hold her. No reason she should read more into that than two brave, frightened souls helping each other.

"Take care of—" He didn't finish. Let Ward figure out for himself what to do. He crossed the bridge and went to the wintering pens. With a practiced glance he checked on the animals till he felt satisfied they were in excellent condition. Come spring he'd begin his new breeding program. In the coming years he expected to see the results in healthy, hardy cattle that brought top dollar. Leaning his arms on the top rail of the fence, he relaxed as he watched the cattle eating the hay he'd insisted the men put up during the hot summer months.

His sense of balance returned and he ambled over to the barn, where Slim worked alone on the harnesses.

"Where's Ward?"

"Gone to check on his ranch. Said to tell you he'd be gone for a few days. Hoped it was okay."

"Fine by me." He joined Slim at the workbench. Eddie relaxed further. Ward would not be sending Linette adoring eyes. Until he returned. In the meantime...

Slim wasn't much for talking just to hear his voice, so they worked in companionable silence for the most part.

Far too soon it was time to return to the cabin for dinner. If his stomach wasn't so demanding he would forgo the meal rather than face Linette.

Slim left the barn, paused to look over his shoulder. "Boss, time to eat."

Eddie nodded and strode for the door. He'd faced floods, snowstorms, angry drunks and attacking wolves. No way would he hesitate to walk into his own cabin because he'd offended Linette. Yet his steps lagged as he headed across the yard. He paused with his hand on the doorknob and listened. All quiet. He sucked in air and opened the door.

The aroma of roast beef greeted him. Along with a smile from Linette. He tried to believe the smile reached her eyes. But she turned away quickly. "It's right ready. Grady and Cassie, come to the table."

He shucked off his coat and sat with the others. "A very nice meal," he offered.

"Thank you. Like I promised, I'm a fast learner."

He nodded. If he wasn't mistaken, her voice carried a note of warning. Which he chose to ignore. He'd made himself clear from the beginning and if she refused to listen, well, that was her problem.

He finished his meal and prepared to leave the cabin.

"I'd like to walk with you," she said as she put on her coat.

"You aren't asking, are you?"

"How astute of you to notice."

He looked at Cassie, who poured hot water into the dishpan.

She shrugged.

No sympathy from her.

Linette stepped outside. He closed the door gently behind her. "Where would you like to go?"

She tipped her head toward the big house. "That way is fine."

They passed the cookhouse. She said nothing. They reached the bottom of the hill. She said nothing. They climbed the snow-covered path. Still nothing.

The roast beef sat heavily in his stomach. Whatever she meant to say, he wished she'd get it done with.

They reached the front doors of the house and she stopped, turned slowly and faced him, her eyes burning like hot embers.

"Do not think you can toss me off on some poor unsuspecting cowboy. My father would have no regard for such a marriage. He would send his henchmen to drag me home."

"What about the convent?" He knew before he spoke the words how she'd react.

Her look practically scalded him. "I came West to start a life free of artificial restrictions. I mean to get it."

He leaned closer, not giving her fury any quarter. "Miss Edwards, I told you from the beginning I mean to marry Margaret. So how, pray tell me, do you intend to live this life?"

"I will find a way." She spat the words out like bitter seeds. Then the fight left her. She shifted as if to hide the fact from him and looked at the far mountains.

"Linette." He touched her arm. "You'll make someone a fine wife. A fine pioneer wife."

She blinked, brought her gaze back to him. "Someone like Ward, you mean?"

He began to nod then changed his mind. It was exactly what he meant. But he couldn't say it. He didn't want to upset her further. But something more than concern about her reaction stopped him. He would not give it a name.

"I'm sorry," he murmured. Though for the life of him he couldn't say what he was sorry for. He swung his attention to the house. "Did you want to come in?"

"I don't think so, thanks. I plan to spend the afternoon with Cookie." She sauntered down the hill and into the cookhouse without so much as a backward look.

He jerked about. It wasn't as if it mattered what she thought. Only he hoped— What? What could he hope for? He toured the house, reminding himself of all the plans he and his father had discussed. Tried to forget the eagerness Linette showed for certain rooms. How she meant to use the extra rooms to help those in need. He came to a halt in the room that would be the family parlor. The room where Linette had exclaimed over the view and helped him put up trim. Where she'd pointed out the good job he'd done and likened it to him being an honorable man.

He tossed aside the piece of wood that he held, having no idea when he'd picked it up or why. She saw him as an honorable man but he'd acted like a scoundrel trying to force her into Ward's sphere.

All because she had succeeded in making him confess she was a pioneer woman. And in the confessing, he'd allowed himself to see her working side by side with him, building a new life in a new world.

In effect, he'd punished her for his own wayward thoughts.

He meant to make up for it. But how?

Linette liked pretty things. She liked color. All part of her artistic nature. If he thought the store in Edendale would have artist's paints, he'd ride into town and purchase some for Linette. But so far as he could recall, the shelves had only necessary supplies.

Surely among his books to be shipped there'd be one or more that she'd enjoy. But they wouldn't be arriving until spring.

Except he had a box he'd never opened because he didn't have room or need for anything more in the little cabin. A box his mother had packed to help him set up housekeeping.

Eddie jogged down the hill, past the cookhouse, kept his gaze from the cabin and went to the storage shed. The crate stood in the far corner. He pried the lid up and began to pull out items. Some pretty dishes and an assortment of table linens. No doubt Linette would enjoy the whole lot, but there was hardly room for them in the tiny kitchen. He dug farther. Miniature portraits of his parents. He set those aside. They belonged in the big house, not in the log cabin. He lifted a fine woolen blanket and wondered if the ladies had need of it. When he saw what lay beneath it he laughed. Mother's dancing lady. A porcelain figurine of a woman in a swirling pink gown holding a china rose to her nose.

Eddie held the figurine in his hands. It was one of his mother's most prized possessions. She'd had it since before she married Randolph Gardiner. Why had she sent it with Eddie?

Memories of his mother and other family members filled him with loneliness. Sighing, he turned the dancing lady over. He studied the bottom as if hoping for clues as to why his mother had sent it.

Nothing but the name of the manufacturer.

He sat back on his heels. She'd never said where she got it. He'd always assumed it was a gift from someone. But if from her parents or a friend, wouldn't she have said so?

That left one possibility he'd never considered.

His real father had given her this. He almost dropped the figurine. Who was the man? Eddie would never know because his mother refused to discuss it. She must have endured so much shame and ostracism until Randolph Gardiner married her. His position in society forbade anyone from treating her, or Eddie, poorly.

He owed his father a great deal. There was one way to repay the kindness—fulfill his father's expectations.

Deciding the figurine belonged in the big house next to the likenesses of his mother and father, he set it aside and dug deeper.

A china teapot. Plain brown but so much superior to the tin pot they'd been using. He returned everything else, nailed the lid down again and headed for the cabin.

Since her return to the cabin Linette had renewed her plan to make herself invaluable to Eddie. She'd already tried everything she could think of—learning to make meals, helping at the house. She'd even helped fight off wolves. How much more could she do? Learn to make bread, but she knew it would not influence his thoughts any more than the cookies and biscuits and roast beef had.

The door opened and Linette glanced up. Her heart caught on its next beat.

Eddie! Had he changed his mind?

"I brought you something." He held out a china teapot.

"A Brown Betty teapot!" Cassie sprang to her feet and set the kettle to boil. "Finally. Some decent tea."

Wild hope rushed through Linette. Surely this meant something more than tea without the tinny taste. "Thank you, Eddie. Where did you find it?"

"There's a crate of things out in the shed. Thought I'd poke through it and see if there was anything we could use."

We? He'd been thinking of them. Her hope settled in to stay.

He put the pot on the table and leaned back on his heels, grinning as if all was right with his world.

She smiled back, feeling as if her world returned to balance.

Their look went on and on until Cassie grabbed the teapot from under Linette's elbow. "I am going to enjoy a cup of tea." She paused and gave Linette and Eddie a serious look. "If no one has any objections."

Linette jerked away to stare at the stove. "I'm going to try making bread again. This time I'm going to succeed."

"I'm sure you shall." He sounded so confident she stole another look at him.

His smile faltered. "I was afraid I was rude earlier today, so I—" He pointed toward the teapot and shrugged.

"You brought a gift."

He nodded, then with a wry smile shook his head. "My way of apologizing."

"Apology accepted." Surely her voice didn't quiver, but she feared it did.

"Tea is ready. Who cares for some?" Cassie asked, handing them each a cupful.

The three of them pulled chairs around the stove as Grady played with his growing assortment of toys. No one seemed impatient about supper. Linette certainly wasn't. This bit of kindness and concern filled her heart with hope.

And something more that she wasn't prepared to look at too closely for fear she would be alarmed at what she saw. A growing fondness for the man.

Eddie finished his tea and strode the three steps to the window, peered out then turned. "Linette, would you like to go for a walk?"

She'd been staring at the mixing bowl she'd used for the failed bread dough, wondering what she'd done wrong. She'd asked Cookie to explain the procedure again and still could not understand where she'd veered from the woman's instructions. She gladly pushed the task aside and grabbed her coat to join Eddie.

They walked past the barn, past the wintering pens as he explained the advantages of the cows he'd chosen, the way he fed them and a bunch of things that had never before mattered to Linette but now seemed the most important information on the face of the earth. They climbed the rough trail beyond the pens. He took her hand to guide her over the rocky path. They came to a grove of dark pines where they stood with the sun on their cheeks.

Still hand in hand, they watched a raven rise from the trees, squawking at the intrusion.

"Every time I came up here during the summer, if I sat real quiet, I could watch a deer and twin fawns," he told her. "They tiptoed from the trees to nibble at the grass."

"Maybe I'll get a chance to see them in the spring."

He faced her, an inscrutable expression on his face. Was he imagining her at his side throughout the changing seasons? The thought strengthened her resolve. She would, with God's help, prove her value to Eddie's plans. She intended to tell him so, but before she could say anything, he spoke.

"I need to help the boys repair a fence the bulls broke down, but I thought you might enjoy seeing this place." He dropped her hand and led the way back down the hill then strode off, leaving her at the cabin staring after him.

Why had the walk ended so abruptly? It was as if he regretted taking her there. Or perhaps he regretted taking her hand to assist her? Or…dare she hope he was beginning to see how suited they were to one another and the thought frightened him?

She clung to the notion as she returned to the cabin. Perhaps all her efforts were bearing fruit. A smile curved her mouth. By spring he'd be rejoicing over her presence rather than fighting it.

"I'm going to work on the house," Eddie announced the next day as he pushed from the breakfast table. "I could use a hand measuring the baseboards."

Her heart took off like a horse freed from a pen. Her eyes jerked toward him. He had asked her to accompany him. Surely that meant he had changed his mind about her. She calmed her racing heart. "I could help."

"You might want to bring your sketchbook."

She couldn't force her eyes away. Her father had scoffed at her art as useless. But Eddie seemed to appreciate her drawings. Even his comments made her realize he understood the emotions she tried to capture. Try as she might, she couldn't stop pleasure from blossoming in her heart at his approval.

"The sun is shining. The mountains glisten with fresh snow," he said. "Might make a good picture."

He wanted her to capture the sight? She certainly itched to see the view and draw it. But even more, she anticipated discovering what this change in him meant.

Cassie reached for her coat and handed Grady his. "I'll take the boy with me to see Cookie."

The interruption enabled Linette to break from Eddie's gaze. She sucked in air as if she'd forgotten to breathe. "I'll get my things." She rushed to the bedroom where she kept her supplies, but at the trunk she hesitated. She wanted to prove to Eddie how capable she was. He'd seen her failure at baking bread. Did he also need to see how she wasted her time drawing pictures? Though her skill wasn't entirely wasted. She'd copied the sketch of Dorothy Farris for Grady and been pleased at the boy's pleasure.

But she'd done that in her spare time while Eddie was away. Now she needed to prove she had some practical value on the ranch and she returned to the other room without the sketchbook.

Cassie and Grady had left.

"Couldn't find it?" Eddie asked.

"What?" As if she didn't know what he meant.

"The book you draw in."

She shrugged. "It's only something I do when there's no work to be done."

He pinned her with his dark gaze. "Are you refusing to draw a picture because I requested it?"

She shook her head. "That's not why."

"Then would you mind drawing a picture of the mountains for me?"

To refuse would be churlish. She returned to the bedroom and scooped up the sketchbook and her pencils then followed Eddie up the hill. She went immediately to the window while he built a fire in the round-bellied stove in the room that would serve as the family dining room and parlor. "Oh." The word escaped her. "Beautiful. I can see why you want to capture the sight. But there is no way I could do it justice in black and white." How she itched to pull out her canvases and oils. But she wondered if crowding the cabin would give Eddie the impression she didn't put proper value on the comfort of others.

"My mind can fill in the details." He joined her at the window.

She simply stared at the view as they waited for the fire to drive the cold from the room. Oh, how she loved this room. She wanted to be a part of this house, a part of this ranch, a part of this land. She wanted to be part—

She silently commanded her thoughts to stop. She did not want to be part of this man's affections. She would not give up control of her heart. Not even to belong here. She would, instead, prove her value as a woman who contributed. "I'm ready to get to work."

His gaze went to the sketchbook on the window ledge.

Her gaze went to the stack of wood next to the wall. "I'll give you a hand with those first."

He looked about to argue then nodded. "If you wish."

For two hours she helped him measure, cut and nail the boards in place. While she worked she had no trouble keeping her thoughts in place except when her glance went to the window and she watched the changing face of the magnificent Rockies.

He cut another board, but rather than nail it, he straightened. "I'll be back in a moment."

She stared after him as he disappeared into the kitchen area.

A few minutes later he returned with a wingback chair and put it before the windows.

She gaped at the chair. It was green. Exactly as it had been in her imaginings.

"I'm done until you do what you promised." His words jerked her back to his request.

"I don't recall making any promises." Not out loud to him.

"A drawing of the mountains." He indicated she should sit.

She hesitated but only out of caution. Her insides burned to capture the sight. Giving in to her yearning, she dropped to the chair, pulled her sketch pad to her lap and started to work.

Peripherally she heard Eddie leave the room and return with a second chair matching hers. He parked it close to hers, facing the window, and sat quietly at her side as she worked. But her attention and imagination were on the scene before her. The lines flowed from her mind to the paper. The ruggedness of the mountains, the contrast between the snow and dark green pines, the neatness of the red farm buildings.

After a while her neck ached and she straightened and looked around. "How long have I been drawing?"

Eddie grinned. "More than an hour, I expect."

She groaned. "I didn't mean to waste your time or mine."

"Let's see the finished product." He reached for the sketch pad.

"It's only rough."

He studied it. "This is not a waste of time. May I have it?"

"Of course."

He carefully tore the page from the pad. "I'd like to frame it and hang it in this room." He tried to close the pad. The pages stuck. He turned them one by one. And stopped to stare.

She stifled a groan. She hadn't meant for him to ever see the drawing of him confidently riding his horse.

"This is me. I look like…a cowboy."

She laughed as much from relief as amusement. He hadn't seen anything extraordinary in her depiction of him. But even at the time she'd struggled to see him as only a means to an end—a way to gain escape from her father's plans. Not as a strong, handsome, trustworthy, noble man. She jammed a log in the flood of his admirable qualities rushing to her mind. "Don't you think of yourself as a cowboy? A good cowboy, from what the men say about you."

"I ride because my tasks require it. Sure, I enjoy it, but that's not uppermost in my mind." He glanced about the room. "Just as I enjoy working on this house, but I don't do it for that reason."

She thought she understood his reason—build a house that would win Margaret's favor. The pleasure she'd enjoyed as she sketched fluttered like a dead moth. Did she stand a chance against such devotion? How could she possibly hope to get him to change his mind?

He went on as if talking to himself. "It's a job entrusted to me by my father and I am determined to prove I can handle the responsibility. Prove, I suppose,

I am equal to the task. That my father was right in assigning it to me."

"You feel the need to prove yourself to your father? Yet he must trust you a great deal to send you over here with the responsibility of finding land, purchasing a huge herd of cows and building a house that would make anyone proud."

"It's more of a test than a sign of trust."

She thought it was an odd answer. "What sort of test would that be?"

He made a deep-throated sound. "To see if I'm fit to be a Gardiner."

She shifted so she could study his expression. His smile was mocking, as if he'd said more than he meant to or perhaps regretted sounding so hurt. But the look in his eyes spoke volumes. She knew—just knew—his words revealed a lifetime of doubt and striving. She held his gaze as the knowledge slid sideways into her heart and burned a raw path. "Why do you need to prove such a thing?" Her words scalded her throat.

"Because I am not a Gardiner."

"But your name—it *is* Eddie Gardiner. Yes?"

His smile tipped to one side. His eyes darkened. "I was born before my mother married my father. My real father was not in the picture. My mother has never revealed one detail of how I came to be. She said that part of her life ended when she married Randolph Gardiner and it was up to me to make sure he never regretted taking me as his son." He seemed to do his best to smile widely, but she read in the set of his lips a world of wondering if he'd truly been accepted.

She curled her fingers into her palms to stop herself from reaching for him. Her circumstances were vastly different. She was her father's biological daughter. Never once had she doubted her value in his world. As a commodity. A business advantage. A bargaining chip. She knew she wasn't valued for who she was or what she wanted. This trip to Canada had been her first victory.

Her nails dug into the heels of her hands. Never would she give up the freedom she'd won. Never would she give up the independence she'd struggled so hard to win. But Eddie's unspoken pain beat relentlessly at her thoughts. He ached from not feeling totally accepted. She understood he would not acknowledge it. Never admit anything more than a commitment to live up to Mr. Gardiner's expectations. "I expect he is pleased with how well you've done." She glanced around the room to silently emphasize his success.

He shrugged. His gesture seemed to indicate more defeat than indifference. He glanced about the room and then turned to look out the window. "Father does not understand how different things are out here. How I must make decisions based on the circumstances of the moment. Anything I do that differs from his plans is under suspicion."

She turned the idea over in her mind, finding that it scratched at her insides. "How much has he planned for you?"

His laugh was short. "Every detail he could think of, because he doesn't believe I can handle decisions on my own."

"Does that include the woman you will marry?"

He refused to meet her look, instead stared steadily out the window.

"Ah. You don't think I'd pass inspection?" Somehow that didn't surprise her. Her father could be abrasive and had offended any number of people in his quest to claw his way to the top. Though she wasn't sure what he hoped was at the top or even where the top was.

Eddie sighed heavily.

She guessed he felt a need to earn the favor he never felt he qualified for. She glanced about the room she had grown to love. "Did he design the house?"

"Certainly. Though I made a few changes to better suit the setting."

"Like what?"

His grin was genuine. His eyes lit from within as if he spoke from a secret, joy-filled spot.

Her insides mellowed knowing she'd distracted him from worrying about his father's expectations.

"This room. According to the plans, it should face the other direction, but that would have been a mistake, don't you think?"

"Indeed. As I'm sure he would agree if he ever saw this view."

Eddie sobered. "I hope so." He studied the sketches before him as if they held some dark secret. "I have been entrusted with a job. I intend to do my best. I aim to honor my father for giving me his name and a family. I pray it will honor and please God as well."

She waited, but he didn't look up from his contemplation of the drawings. His commitment to his family and God was noble and honorable. "I think your father would be proud of all you've done."

He stared at her drawing of him on horseback. Then with a deep sigh he set the sketches aside and jumped to his feet. "Enough of this. It's time for lunch."

When he reached for her hand, she didn't refuse. Whatever his father required of him, the older man was far away, restricted to reports by mail. She said so to him and he laughed.

"Maybe so, but I can't help feeling he's watching over my shoulder."

Chapter Twelve

Why had he revealed his insecurities to Linette?

She had been understanding and sympathetic, though.

But what did it matter what she thought? He would succeed. The house would soon be done. Margaret would come. Linette would accept defeat and leave. He shoved aside the questions as to where she would go and what would become of her.

Only one more thing he aimed to accomplish. Since he'd seen the Indians and their travois, he had been secretly working on a project that he hoped would convince Grady that men weren't to be feared. At least, not all men. He eyed the boy as he ate his meal beside Linette. "How long does he nap?"

"About an hour." Linette sounded puzzled by his question.

"Good. That's just about right." He spoke directly to Grady. "I'll have a surprise for you when you wake up."

"'Prise?" the boy spoke before he realized it was Eddie he addressed, and then he ducked his face into Linette's shoulder.

It was enough to give Eddie hope. It would only take some fun together for Grady to forget his fear of men.

"I ready for sleep." Grady scrambled down and disappeared into the bedroom.

The three adults exchanged looks and laughed. Linette followed the boy and a moment later came out chuckling. "His eyes are shut tight. Don't suppose you can tell me what you have in mind?" Linette's eyes filled with teasing lights.

"Nope. You'll have to wait just like Grady."

She laughed. "But I can't spend my afternoon napping like Grady, so it's harder for me to wait. Couldn't you give me a little hint?"

He leaned back on his heels and scratched his head, pretending to be in deep thought over her question. "I don't know if it would be fair. After all, I planned it especially for Grady. Of course, you'll have to come with him or he won't come." Would she latch onto the little nugget he'd dropped for her?

"Ah. So we have to leave the house? Will we be outside?"

"Best dress warmly." A grin tugged at his mouth as she narrowed her eyes and studied him.

"A ride? No, a walk? You've got something special to show us?"

Linette looked intrigued and tapped a fingertip to her chin.

That rhythmic movement drew his gaze to her chin. Its firmness signaled a determination that he already had firsthand knowledge of. She pressed her bottom lip into a thin line that made her look so serious he had to chuckle. "All I'll say is it isn't a cow." And if he hoped to have the surprise ready by the time Grady woke up, he would have to leave the house and head for the barn.

Yet his limbs refused to move and his gaze wouldn't veer from watching her fingertip.

She lowered her hand and shook her head. "I simply can't imagine what it might be."

He dredged up enough effort to turn and grab his coat. "I'll be back in about an hour. You'll have to wait until then."

"Maybe I'll go for a walk and see what you're doing."

She followed him across the cabin at his heels. Although he couldn't see her he felt her presence as clearly as sunshine on bare skin. He swallowed hard, promising himself he would not turn and meet her face-to-face. He knew if he did he would be close enough to see the way her eyes flickered from pale to dark brown as her emotions fluctuated. He hadn't yet learned to interpret those subtle shifts, but knew they signaled deep feelings—like anger, and maybe the opposite. Maybe if he turned, confronted her, they would darken with something else. He couldn't even explain what he hoped to see.

Best not to turn. Then he wouldn't have to witness anything or try to decipher what it meant. Or why it mattered so much. He should be thinking of Margaret anyway. She would have received their letters by now. Would she be eagerly packing and making plans? He grabbed the door. "Be a good girl and wait here."

Only after he'd pulled the door closed behind him did he realize he'd relegated her to the same status as Grady—a child. He hesitated. Should he go back and apologize?

A burst of laughter came from the other side of the door.

Linette wasn't offended by his remark.

A stampede of emotions raced through him. Pleasure at her amusement. Satisfaction that he had her interest.

And something unfamiliar that crept to the fore. A feeling unlike any he'd experienced before.

Connection?

He shook his head. That didn't make a lick of sense. He wasn't a bit interested in Linette. Didn't feel anything toward her but... He struggled to find a word.

Responsibility. That was it. He was stuck watching out for her—for Cassie and Grady too—until he could send them back.

Maybe he'd track down Grady's father and make him take responsibility for his son, though the idea of Grady being with someone who didn't value him didn't sit well.

And Cassie? Well, he'd seen the way Roper looked at her. She could do worse than marry a cowboy.

As for Linette, he would send her back to her father. A bitter taste filled his mouth as he thought of her married to an old man.

He went to the barn and set to work finishing his surprise. An hour later he returned to the cabin.

Linette must have been watching because she stepped out when he was still fifty feet away, Grady clutching one hand. Both were dressed warmly.

Eddie struggled to keep amusement out of his voice. "I see you're ready."

"Ready and waiting for your surprise," Linette called.

"'Prise?" Grady whispered.

Eddie stepped aside to reveal a toboggan. It was admittedly crude. Likely Linette was used to much better. "I did the best I could with what I had."

She clapped her hands and squealed. "You know what this is, Grady?"

The boy shook his head.

"A toboggan. It's for riding down the snow-covered hills. It's great fun. As much fun as racing horses."

"Another of your adventures with your brother?"

Her gaze brushed Eddie's and pink colored her cheeks. He didn't think it was from the cold. "My father was very displeased when he found out."

"And yet you sound totally unrepentant."

"I am. Like I said, I have no use for pretentious rules of conduct." Her chin went up. Her eyes flashed in challenge.

He heard distant warning bells. Echoes of his father's words. *A Gardiner always lives up to expectations. They are pillars of society.*

He ignored the distant call. He only meant to have a little fun and help Grady learn that men wouldn't hurt him. No one could object to that.

"Let's try it out." He headed for the hill. The snow on the north slope would make decent sledding. Linette fell in at his side. Grady carefully kept her between him and Eddie. But he came along eagerly enough.

They trudged to the top of the hill and stood on the crest looking down their intended path.

"I'll do a run first. Test it out. Then I'll take Grady down." And before Grady could protest, Eddie positioned himself on the toboggan, gave himself a little push and raced down the hill. He hit a bump, righted himself quickly and zipped to the bottom, coasting a hundred feet before he jumped off.

He waved at the pair watching from the top of the hill. Linette and Grady returned the wave and cheered. Now for the long trek back to the top. He leaned forward into the hillside and climbed. At the top, he paused to catch his breath. Again, Grady carefully kept Linette between himself and Eddie.

He plopped the toboggan down and waved a hand at Grady. "Your turn." Eddie sat on the back of the toboggan and patted the space in front of him. "You sit here and I'll keep you from falling off."

Grady whimpered and shrank back.

Linette squatted before him. "It's a lot of fun, Grady."

He shook his head, his eyes wide with what Eddie knew was fear.

"Eddie isn't going to hurt you. You know that."

Her complete confidence in him brought a grin to his mouth and a warm feeling to unfamiliar places in his heart.

But Grady wouldn't take another step closer. He looked down the hill where Eddie had ridden the toboggan, slid a glance toward Eddie and sighed deeply. Suddenly he brightened and grabbed Linette's hand. "You go, too."

Linette straightened and considered the spot in front of Eddie. "I don't think there's room."

How had she gone from touting how safe it was for Grady, to being as reluctant as the boy? Eddie wouldn't hurt either one of them.

He edged back and patted the wood before him. "Lots of room."

Grady tugged on Linette's hand.

She didn't move.

Eddie repeated her words. "'He isn't going to hurt you. You know that.'"

Her gaze darted past him, restlessly seeking a place to light, then she swallowed hard and met his eyes. Hers were wide with unnamed emotions. He knew his were challenging. He wondered if her mouth was as dry as his.

Grady waited for Linette to move.

Eddie wanted to take the pair for a ride. For Grady's sake. Only, it wasn't the thought of Grady sharing the toboggan with him that made him feel nervous with both anticipation and dread. He knew he would later regret this action, but at the same time figured it was worth whatever price he must pay.

She took a step toward him, her gaze never falter-ing from his.

He dared not blink for fear the pair would dart away like a couple of shy deer.

She reached his side, shifted her gaze. Pink stained her cheeks as she studied the small space they would have to share. "Come on, Grady." She eased down to the wooden seat and fussed about getting Grady settled.

"Ready?" She fit easily, as he expected she would, her head right at his chin, a familiar scent of flowers teasing his nose. He gave a shove. "We're off." Only, they didn't move.

"We seem to be stuck here." Linette giggled. With the added weight, it took both of them pushing off the snow to get them moving.

"Hang on. Here we go," Eddie said.

The toboggan picked up speed. Grady squealed once then was silent. Eddie wished he could see the boy's face to know if he was excited or scared.

They tilted to the right. The toboggan was harder to control with the others on it and he leaned hard to the left to keep them upright. They shot over a bump and flew off the ground. He couldn't see past Linette's head and had to balance them by feel. They landed on the edge of the toboggan. He threw his weight the other way, but it wasn't enough. They hit the ground, and snow blasted into their faces. They rolled in the snow, a tangle of arms and legs. When they stopped, Linette lay sprawled over his chest. He stared into her snow-dusted face just inches from his, her eyes wide...

"You okay?" he murmured, brushing snow from her face.

"I'm fine." She scooted away. "Grady?"

Eddie sat up and looked around for the boy. He lay spread eagle a few feet away. "Is he hurt?"

They scrambled to their feet and struggled through the snow to him. The boy's eyes were closed, and he shook all over.

"Grady?" Linette dropped to her knees at his side. "Are you hurt?"

Grady's eyes opened. He looked at Linette then darted a glance at Eddie.

Linette examined him with her hands.

But Grady pushed them away. "Fun," he wheezed.

"He's laughing." Eddie stared at the boy. "He's not hurt. He's enjoying this."

Linette sank to her heels. Eddie squatted beside her and they both studied Grady, who giggled.

Linette flopped to the ground and laughed as well.

Eddie shook his head. "You two are crazy."

"Crazy is fun." Linette managed to strangle the words out between giggles.

Amusement tickled his insides and gained momentum. A burst of laughter exploded, releasing something in his heart that had been tight most of his life.

He tried to stop. He almost succeeded, but then he looked at Linette and her giggle triggered an answering laugh from him. Finally he admitted defeat and flopped down in the snow next to her and let the laughter wash through him.

After a few minutes all three of them grew silent but no one moved.

Eddie couldn't say what the others were feeling, but he was relaxed and mellow. Then he grew aware of heat building in his arm, springing from where his elbow

brushed against Linette's shoulder. She'd been the cause
of him laughing so hard. She had a way of seeing the
fun, the possibilities, the positive in every situation.
He'd learned to appreciate that.

In his peripheral vision he caught a glimpse of the
big house. Margaret's house. He scrambled to his feet
and stared at it. He hadn't yet had a reply to his letter to
Margaret. But he had no doubt she would agree to come
once she heard of the fine place he'd built. He brought
his emotions under control. "Grady, do you want to go
down again?"

The boy hesitated, sought Linette's opinion.

"I think I'll stay at the bottom of the hill and watch,"
she said.

Her voice sounded strained. Was it from laughing so
hard? Or had she noticed his sudden withdrawal? He
wanted to explain, but what could he say? He'd enjoyed
the laugh. What's more, he enjoyed her company. But
nothing had changed. He still intended that she should
leave come spring and he still expected Margaret to
join him and become his wife. Surely she understood
that. Sometimes a man had to make difficult choices.

Now, if he could only persuade *himself* nothing had
changed. In hindsight, he realized things had begun to
shift days ago when she had fought off the wolves. Or
perhaps earlier when—

It didn't matter when or where or how.

It only mattered that he recognized it and must put
a stop to it.

He looked directly at the boy, avoided searching
Linette's face, afraid he'd see more than he cared to.

Or perhaps she would see more than he cared her to.

"Grady, if you want to ride down again, you'll have
to climb the hill."

Grady hesitated, darted a glance back and forth between the two adults and then plowed up the hill with Eddie at his heels. There was a moment when Eddie wondered if Grady would change his mind about sharing the toboggan for the ride down. But he climbed on in front of Eddie, all the while careful to avoid looking at him.

They rode down the hill without upset and zipped past Linette where she stood waiting for them.

Grady tumbled off the toboggan as they slowed to a stop and ran to Linette, squealing delight. "It's fun. You come again?"

"I think I'll stay here." She bent and hugged Grady. "I'm glad you're having fun." She smiled at Eddie. "The toboggan was a good idea."

He couldn't help noticing her smile didn't reach her eyes. Any more than he could miss the coolness in her voice. "Glad it's working out."

Only, he didn't feel as pleased about Grady's progress as he should.

Linette watched Grady return up the hill with Eddie. The boy was losing his fear of Eddie thanks to Eddie's efforts.

He'd be able to face life with a lot more confidence. Enjoy the fun parts of ranch life rather than clinging to the womenfolk indoors.

The smile curving her mouth at acknowledging these things did not reach her heart.

She'd known from the start she shouldn't get on the toboggan with Eddie. It was far too intimate. His arms about her, the feel of his breath on the side of her face, the tangle of arms as they rolled in the snow...

She swallowed hard against the tightness in her throat.

Freed by the moment, unexpected feelings had surfaced, only for a flash, but long enough for her to picture herself in the big house, filling it with dreams and life and—she gulped—love. Her unguarded eyes had surely revealed the overflow of her heart.

Eddie had read her growing regard for him. He'd jerked away as if stung. He did not return her feelings. Resisted the possibility.

Her insides twisted and she shifted her attention from the pair at the top of the hill. Feelings didn't enter into her plan. She only wanted him to see her as a partner. Capable. Suitable. She expected no less and wanted no more.

There was plenty enough time for the good Lord to change things, make Eddie see that she would make a better wife than Margaret any old day.

She didn't need any silly wishes for more. Such feelings left her vulnerable, uncertain of herself.

She shivered as Grady and Eddie sped past her on their downward journey. They tumbled from the toboggan, laughing together.

Eddie pulled the toboggan to her side.

She kept her gaze on the hilltop. But the sight of the track they'd recently sped down mocked her. Made it impossible to forget that moment in the snow when his eyes flew open and he looked deep into her gaze. His look had slipped past her reservations, past her control, past her pain, straight to a tender, aching spot in her heart that cried silently for his touch.

With the same stubborn determination she'd claimed as she crossed the rugged, unsettled continent, she pushed aside the foolish thought.

The pair climbed the hill. The toboggan raced past her again. Grady's giggles tickled her ears. Eddie had taken the boy from fearful to joyful. He would no longer need Linette to shield him from Eddie. The boy could accompany Eddie to the barn alone.

"I'm going indoors." She started for the cabin.

Grady scrambled after her. "I go with you."

She reached for his hand. Maybe he wasn't quite ready to move on without her. Shouldn't she regret the fact? But she didn't.

Eddie fell in step at her side. "It's a beginning."

A beginning for Grady, but was it the beginning of the end for her? Would she wind up trudging away from the ranch as dejectedly as she left the hill?

Right then and there she vowed she must protect her heart from wayward emotions and keep her eyes on the goal of getting Eddie to agree to a marriage based on rational decisions. She was surely the best woman for the job of being his wife in this appealing frontier.

Feelings did not enter into the situation.

When they reached the cabin, Eddie stayed outside. "I'll take the toboggan to the barn," he said.

Linette hadn't spoken as they crossed the yard, but she couldn't let him leave without acknowledging her gratitude for what he'd done for Grady. She faced him, her emotions hidden behind solid walls of determination. "Thank you for doing this."

"My pleasure."

She wouldn't read more into the words than a polite response.

"Grady, thank Eddie for the toboggan ride."

The boy hesitated.

Linette nudged Grady to reply.

"Thank you." His words were barely audible.

She realized the boy and man were much alike—hurt by fathers, uncertain about trusting. Perhaps she also shared the similarity. She silently prayed for God's healing for all of them.

Two days later, Eddie bit into a slice of fresh bread. "I could get used to this." She'd learned to make bread that gladdened a man's heart.

Linette grinned. "I could get used to success."

He concentrated on the meal before him. Success. What did that mean to her? Becoming his wife as she had said from their first meeting.

There had been no letters from home yet. Likely a number waited at Edendale. He and the men had been too busy to ride to town. Plus, the snow continued to build up. But when the letters did arrive, he was certain there'd be a reply from Margaret. She would come. He knew it. After all, he'd built the house to please her. Little did she know he'd taken note of the preferences she'd stated and incorporated many of them into the plans he and his father drew up. Margaret belonged here.

She would sit in the wingback chair near the window as she did needlework or cradled a child. She would serenely tell the cook what to prepare for dinner.

Would she struggle to learn how to cook bacon? Or to learn to bake bread?

Would she exclaim over the view? Want to capture it on canvas? Sketch it?

He shook his head. He would not picture Linette in the room. She simply did not fit. He would not tell her so, but his father never mentioned the Edwards name without getting a sour look on his face, as if he'd bitten into a fresh lemon.

He finished his meal and pushed from the table.

But before he could leave the cabin, a call came from outside.

"Hello, the house."

"Company," Cassie announced from the window. "A cowboy."

Eddie reached the door before the man could knock and threw it open. "Clyde, howdy." He shook hands with the cowhand from the OK Ranch. "Everything all right?"

"Dandy as can be. I'm not here looking for help but to invite you all to a Christmas party next week at the ranch." He glanced beyond Eddie to the womenfolk.

"Come in." Eddie introduced everyone as soon as Clyde shed his heavy winter wear.

"The boss figures this is a chance to get together."

Eddie nodded. "Good idea." He'd plan a similar event when the house was finished.

Clyde had coffee and they shared more conversation. As soon as he departed, Cassie and Linette peppered Eddie with a string of questions about the upcoming party. He couldn't blame them for being excited. They'd not been off the ranch for weeks.

They were ready to go. Linette tried not to wriggle and squeal with anticipation like Grady, but the idea of a party at the neighboring ranch thrilled her. The cowboys sat astride their horses, but Eddie had hitched horses to a wagon to carry the women and Grady. Cookie, Bertie and Cassie crowded together on the back bench. Grady and Linette sat beside Eddie on the front. The air shimmered with excited talk.

This was a chance for her to be with Eddie at a social, fun occasion. She intended to make the most of the opportunity.

Things between them had shifted though she couldn't say if was for the better. On one hand, he seemed to enjoy the evenings they spent together, sometimes with Cassie there, more often with her gone to bed with Grady. They often played chess. Just as often they simply sat and chatted. They liked to talk about the same places they'd visited in England.

"Seems odd we never bumped into each other," she'd once said and immediately wished she could suck the words back into her mouth when he grew serious.

"Not so odd, I suppose."

She heard what he didn't say—that his father would never knowingly, willingly cross paths with her father. Knowing she didn't fit into the well-planned life laid out for Eddie seemed an impossible barrier. It was up to her to prove otherwise. Make him see she could be accepted on her own merits. Tonight the social gathering and party atmosphere would hopefully provide a chance for him to see her in a different environment and to appreciate her.

She joined the conversation of the others in the wagon as they made the journey to the OK Ranch, but her mind hummed with possibilities. She'd primed Cassie to mention how well Linette had adjusted. Linette would tell the others how much she liked the country and not one word of it would be false. She fit here and Eddie needed to see it. To admit it.

They arrived at the ranch house—a long, low building alight with candles in every window and along the veranda.

Grady sucked in air and held it. He squirmed forward, reached out as if to touch the glow.

In the low light, Linette's and Eddie's gazes met and held. One thing they shared openly was a desire to make life good for Grady and they smiled at the boy's excitement. The look in Eddie's eyes, the glow in her heart shifted from Grady and Christmas to something beyond reason—a silent hunger she had no wish to acknowledge, much less name.

She tore her gaze away and turned to the open door where a man waited to welcome them.

Roper dismounted from his horse and hurried over to help Cassie down from the wagon. Linette watched the pair out of the corner of her eye. Roper had shown his interest at every opportunity, rushing to greet Cassie when they went to the cookhouse for coffee, escorting her across the yard, asking her to walk with him. He'd visited at the cabin several times both with and without Ward. Cassie was always polite but uninterested. She said she would never belong to another man.

"What happened to your plans to marry so you can have a man's protection?" Linette had asked her.

"I changed my mind. I see now I can make it on my own and I intend to."

Linette had understood and shared the sentiment. But if she didn't belong to Eddie and the ranch, her father would insist she belong to Lyle Williamson. It was a fate worse than imprisonment. At least on the ranch she could do something of value.

"Linette?"

Shaken from her thoughts, she realized Eddie waited to help her down. She sucked in raw air and rested her fingers in his palm. The cold air nipped at her cheeks. Her hands had cooled considerably on the trip, yet heat seared up her arm from his touch. Only nervousness, she informed her confused brain. If they married, touches would be common. She understood that. It did not need to set her heart to fluttering like a handkerchief held out in a brisk wind. Having so informed herself, she concentrated on the magic of the candlelight from the house and withdrew her hand as soon as she stood solidly on her feet.

Eddie waved to indicate they should all proceed to the house.

Linette followed the others, glad of the chance to shift her nervous reaction to excitement, though she was still acutely aware of Eddie beside her.

He led her forward. "This is Sam Stone, owner of the OK Ranch."

Mr. Stone welcomed them into the house. "Merry Christmas."

"Oh," Grady said, his one word full of wonder.

Linette's thoughts echoed his amazement. A huge tree stood in the far corner, adorned with red bows and white candles. Red bows swung from every doorway, every bookshelf. In the midst of the long room a U-shaped table stood draped in white, with a mixture of china dishes. The aroma of roast turkey and cinnamon filled the room. "It's beautiful."

"The credit goes to Miss Amanda Oake, my foreman's sister." He waved the pair forward to be introduced.

Linette immediately liked Amanda. Her eyes were clear and caring, her lips full and merry.

"Thank you. I love Christmas and have planned this for weeks."

Amanda and a shy-looking woman with very dark eyes and black hair were the only women, apart from those from Eden Valley Ranch. Amanda introduced the other woman as Mary, her kitchen helper. Linette guessed her to be Indian or Métis.

They circled the room, meeting and greeting the

others, then settled at the table. Eddie held a chair for Linette and she sat at his side. Roper made sure he did likewise for Cassie as she grabbed a place beside Linette. Grady was escorted to the kitchen to join Mary's little brother.

"You could do worse than Roper," Linette whispered to Cassie as she half turned away from Roper.

"You think marriage is an escape, but you don't realize it's only a form of control." Cassie's low whisper was harsh with disapproval.

Linette leaned closer. "Not if you don't give your heart."

Cassie studied Linette a moment, her expression disbelieving. Her gaze shifted past Linette to Eddie and back and her mouth twitched. "No doubt you believe you can achieve that."

"Certainly." She flicked her napkin to her lap. All she had to do was ignore the way her skin itched at his nearness, pretend she didn't jolt when he accidently brushed her elbow, convince herself all she wanted was an escape as Cassie said. "I will not be chained by emotions."

Cassie snorted.

Sam Stone rose to ask the blessing, making impossible any further conversation on the matter.

With Mary's help Amanda served mounds of creamy mashed potatoes, pitchers of succulent gravy, platters of tender turkey and a wide variety of vegetables.

Conversation buzzed around the table. For the most part, the men talked about the weather, the cows and the country until the food had all been placed on the table, then Amanda clapped her hands to get their attention. "Let's talk about Christmas. I want everyone to tell us a favorite memory of the season. I'll begin. I was a teacher at a girls' school and I enjoyed seeing the girls dress in their finest and be on their best behavior. I do believe if they'd acted more like that every day I would not have been so ready to give up my position." She laughed merrily and the others joined in.

She turned to the cowboy next to her.

He spoke in a soft voice, as if his memories were sweet. "I remember plum pudding and roast goose."

One by one, others shared memories. Then it was Roper's turn. "I grew up in an orphanage, so we didn't do anything very special, but every year some kind benefactor gave us each an orange for Christmas. Nothing has ever tasted better."

Linette nudged Cassie. "There. Don't you feel sorry for him?" she whispered. "He needs a family. You need a family."

Cassie gave her a dismissive glance before she turned to tell about the last Christmas before her husband died. "We lived in a little rental house. George had a job in a mill. I knit him a sweater that fit him perfectly. We didn't have much, but we were content."

The table was silent a moment at the knowledge of what she'd had and lost.

Then it was Linette's turn. She had to scramble to find a good memory. She'd allowed the later years to eat up those earlier pleasant times. "I remember the year my father took me out to see the stars on Christmas Eve. It was marvelous." Her voice caught and she nodded that she'd finished.

Eddie found her hand beneath the table and squeezed.

No doubt he thought she was homesick, but she was thinking how she'd felt special that night when her father took her in his arms and lifted her toward the sky

Eddie began to speak and she slipped her hand away.

"I believe my favorite memory would have to be the

year all four of my grandparents were with us. My eldest sister was a baby and the house rang with happiness." His voice ended suddenly.

Linette ducked her head lest anyone see the pain in her eyes as she wondered if Eddie thought the joy in the home was over a child belonging to both his parents—a joy that would never be extended to him. For a heartbeat she ached to reach out and squeeze his hand in sympathy and understanding, but she must guard her reactions to him. Seemed both her body and her heart had wills of their own.

She clasped her fingers into a tight knot and didn't move.

They devoured mounds of food then Mary brought in plum pudding and mince pie to cheers of appreciation.

"It's so nice to enjoy food I didn't prepare," Cookie said for the sixth time. "Besides, my food can't hold a flicker to this. You are an excellent cook, Amanda."

"Hear. Hear." Sam lifted his glass in a toast.

The whole crowd voiced their approval.

Amanda nodded serenely. "I had lots of help."

One by one the ladies finished and pushed their plates away. The men accepted seconds and some thirds of dessert.

Amanda shoved her chair back to signal the meal was over. "Let's move to one side while the table is removed." She signaled to the OK men who whisked the table away and arranged the chairs in a circle around the room.

Linette saw the expression of anticipation on Amanda's face and wondered what she had in store.

Amanda waited until everyone found a place to sit. "One of my favorite memories is when we played parlor games. So please help me in re-creating my fun time."

A murmur of protest came from many of the cowboys.

Linette kept her eyes lowered, not wanting to hurt Amanda's feelings, but she didn't want to play games. In her experience they often provided a chance to mock someone, usually her because she had dreams that, in her parents' opinion, exceeded possibilities.

Only a marriage based on mutual benefit would allow her to achieve even a fraction of the things she dreamed of. Yet, she feared she could easily forget she wanted nothing more than a business deal.

Amanda good naturedly ignored the protests and divided the group to play charades. The cowboys were good sports and let her forge ahead.

To Linette's relief the acting was humorous and any mocking was directed toward one's self. She could handle this. It was her turn. She unfolded the scrap of paper and silently read the words: "What Child Is This?" Too bad Grady was still in the kitchen. She could have used him as a prop. She stood and faced the others, cradled her arms and swayed as if rocking a baby.

"Baby?" Eddie guessed.

She nodded, smiling encouragement at him.

His gaze locked on hers. She couldn't pull away. If they married, would there be babies? Sweet little boys with dark eyes and dark hair. Precious girls with intelligence and spirit. If she had daughters she could encourage self-sufficiency and independence just as she was sure Eddie would encourage the same in sons.

Sons and daughters. Her tongue stuck to the roof of her mouth. She tried unsuccessfully to swallow.

"Baby?" Cassie prompted. "Baby Jesus?"

Linette jerked her attention to the other woman and shook her head. She made a motion as if playing the piano.

"Lullaby?" Eddie said.

Again their gazes collided. It took all her reserves of strength to jerk away. She made a questioning gesture and expression. Cassie guessed the name of the song and Linette gratefully returned to her seat, her ears burning with something more than embarrassment. She could not—would not—allow herself to think of being held, kissed, cherished by Eddie. His heart belonged elsewhere. She understood that. She didn't mind. She didn't want his heart. Only his name and a rightful place in his home.

Margaret would hate it here. She'd made as much clear to Linette. That freed Linette to pursue a marriage without love.

Exactly what she wanted.

The rest of the evening passed in a blur. She watched the proceedings without taking part any more than she must to keep anyone from commenting.

Then finally Eddie announced it was time to leave, signaling a sudden rush of goodbyes.

Linette had been quiet much of the evening. Eddie watched her out of the corner of his eye as they headed home. Had someone said something to hurt her? Had the holiday memories made her homesick?

Homesick was good. It could well provide the impetus for her to abandon this marriage idea and return home. But it felt so wrong. He wanted to hold her and comfort her.

They arrived back at the ranch and he asked Roper to take the wagon for him. "Cassie, would you take Grady? I'd like to show Linette something."

Cassie took the boy and ducked into the cabin.

"I should—"

He'd anticipated Linette's argument. "It's a lovely night. So clear."

She turned to study the sky. "It's beautiful."

"You should see it at the top of the hill." It was too dark for him to guess at her reaction. "Let me show you."

She nodded and he turned toward the path. She stumbled and he caught her elbow. He tucked her hand through his arm and felt her stiffen. There was a constraint between them he couldn't explain, any more than he could explain why he cared. Except he did. So much he wanted to stop right here in the dark and figure it out.

Instead, he led her across the bridge, past the pens and up the hill.

She dropped his arm as they reached the top and tilted her head upward. "It's beautiful. I feel like I could reach out and pluck handfuls of stars from the sky."

"Me, too." And if he could, he would fashion them into a necklace and hang them around her neck. It hit him like a blow to the head.

He had begun to care for her.

He took a step backward. When had this happened? When she'd made bread? Or when she had failed at her attempt? When she'd sketched a picture of the ranch for him? Or when he'd noticed the paintings she'd hung on the walls and realized she was the artist? It had happened slowly but surely from the first day when she'd stepped from the stagecoach with the expectation of becoming his wife.

She *would* make a great ranch wife. At the acknowledgment his heart plopped to the bottom of his boots. Except for one thing—he'd asked Margaret to reconsider. And until he heard from her, he wasn't free to speak of his feelings to Linette.

She sighed and faced him. "Thank you for bringing me here."

"I thought you might enjoy it. Thought it might remind you of happy times at home." He wanted to cheer her up. "You seemed a little unhappy at the party. Is something wrong?"

"Not at all. I suppose it was a little overwhelming. But didn't Amanda do a great job?"

"Indeed." He waited, knowing there was more to her quietness all evening, hoping she would tell him. "Linette." He touched her shoulder. "If there is anything wrong, I hope you would feel free to tell me. Would you?"

She kept her head downturned. "Of course."

Her answer came too quickly. He touched her chin and lifted her face to the starlight. Stepped closer so he could read her expression. Her mouth trembled. She seemed so sad his heart gave a vicious kick to his rib cage and he caught her with both arms and drew her closer. He studied her for a fleeting second then caught her trembling lips with his and steadied them with a kiss.

She gasped and pulled away.

He was as shocked by his actions as she. He backed up and scrubbed at his chin. "I'm sorry. I didn't mean that to happen. I just wanted to make you feel better."

She turned to stare down at the ranch where lights flickered in the cabin, the cookhouse and the bunkhouse. "It's me who should apologize. If we're to be married I expect we would kiss." She made it sound like bitter medicine.

"Seeing as that's not in my plans, my apology is even more heartfelt." He regretted that fact a thousand times more than the kiss, but as a man of honor he must stand by his word and his offer of marriage to Margaret. A Gardiner was, above all, honorable. "I'll see you to the cabin."

She managed her way down the hill without accepting his help. He left her at the door. "I have to make sure the horses are okay." The others would have seen to it, but he couldn't enter the cabin right now. Her presence was too close.

Chapter Thirteen

Linette prayed for sleep to block out her foolishness.

She'd seen his kiss coming. Had enough time to duck away. But she'd let him kiss her. It was true, if they married they would kiss. She'd wanted to know how it felt. Told herself she could keep her heart under lock and key.

But her good intentions had proven useless.

She pressed her fingertips to her lips. How could such a simple touch ignite such depth of longing? She pushed aside the feelings and questions. She only wanted to marry Eddie to escape her father's plans. At the same time she'd keep her heart intact so she could follow its dictates.

Lord, help me. Give me a secure heart. Keep me anchored in Your love. I need no more. I am safe in Your hands. Keep me strong.

A thought came to her mind. Why was she fretting so? Eddie made it clear he hadn't changed his mind. Oh, what a tangled mess she was in. Wanting to marry Eddie. Not wanting to love him. It seemed so simple at the start, but with each passing day she was discovering how complicated it was.

How could she ensure her emotional safety?

The next morning, Eddie was gone when she got up. He returned a little later for breakfast. Linette's gaze was drawn to him under cover of her lashes. He seemed unchanged by the kiss.

"The party last night made me realize I'm unprepared for Christmas," he said. "It looks like the weather will hold, so I'm going to Edendale to get some things. Anything you ladies need?"

Linette glanced at Cassie. Neither of them had any money. She'd given the last of her funds to the Indian lad on her way to the ranch. But she had supplies in her trunk. "We're fine."

When he left a few minutes later she watched him ride from the yard. Would he return with letters from home? One from Margaret saying the news of the big house convinced her to change her mind?

Even if such a letter came she still had until spring. God could work many a miracle in that time. Even in the heart of a man.

"I'm going over to see Cookie," Cassie said.

"Go ahead. I have a few things to do here."

"You want to come, Grady?" Cassie asked the boy.

"See Cookie?"

"Certainly."

The pair left. Linette hurried to her trunk and pulled out the shawl she had begun crocheting for Cassie. She lacked the skill Cassie had at knitting, so had tried this instead.

She glanced at the other gifts she planned to complete in time for Christmas. Time was drawing short, so she worked on them till suppertime.

That evening Eddie came home after dark.

His hands were full of mysterious parcels when

he entered the cabin. Linette waited to see if he offered mail.

"No mail has come through for several weeks. The roads are blocked by snow," he said in response to her silent question.

Relief flooded through her. A reprieve again. "Can we get a Christmas tree?"

He glanced about. "It would take up most of the room here."

"Maybe we could set up one at the cookhouse."

"I like that idea. Let's take Grady tomorrow and find a tree."

They set out right after breakfast, riding in the wagon. Linette could have refused to accompany him, but it would rob Grady of the experience. She had only one goal in mind—make Christmas enjoyable, thus proving in one more direction her capability and suitability as a pioneer wife. No, she mentally corrected, she had two goals. She also wanted to prove to herself that she could enjoy an outing with the man she hoped to marry without her emotions running awry. It should be easy with little Grady sitting on the wagon seat between them.

"First time," Eddie said.

She jerked about to face him, startled and confused by his words. "First time?"

Smiling, he tipped his head to indicate Grady perched between them and she understood his meaning. It was the first time Grady had sat beside Eddie without showing some nervousness. Instead, he leaned forward, anxious to find the perfect Christmas tree.

Linette grinned widely at Eddie, as pleased by Grady's progress as he and equally pleased to silently share the pleasure of the moment with Eddie. It made her feel as if they shared something special.

She sucked in air and turned to face forward as they headed past the barn and outbuildings up a trail toward the trees. She'd have to work much harder at keeping her emotions tucked away. But she was determined to do it. Linette Edwards could do anything she set her mind to.

"We get a tree here?" Grady pointed toward the first spruce they saw.

"We'll go a little farther," Eddie said. "If you think you can wait."

Grady edged back marginally. "Not too long?"

Linette laughed, her gaze drawn relentlessly toward Eddie. He laughed, too, and her pleasure deepened.

All because of the boy, she insisted, and turned her attention back to Grady. "Do you remember having a Christmas tree before?"

He nodded vigorously and turned his bright blue eyes toward her. "Mama take me to see Gramma and Gramps. They gots the biggest tree ever."

Eddie groaned. "The biggest tree ever?"

Grady nodded some more.

"How are we going to best that?"

Grady studied him a moment. Linette couldn't see the boy's expression but read tenderness and humor in Eddie's.

"It not have to be the biggest tree," Grady allowed.

"That's a relief." Eddie made a show of wiping worry from his brow.

His teasing brought a chuckle from Linette and their gazes collided with such force her lungs forgot to work.

She might have remained trapped if the wagon hadn't bounced. Perhaps it was best not to look directly at him until she figured out how to tame her wayward emotions. So she forced herself to keep her attention on the passing scenery. Not difficult except for the way his voice called to her as he talked about all the places up this trail he'd visited.

"A waterfall. Rushing rivers. And you should see the cows grazing in green valleys. It's a beautiful country."

"It certainly is." Almost beautiful enough to hold her attention.

"This looks like a good place." Eddie pulled the wagon to a halt and jumped down. Grady allowed Eddie to lift him to the ground. Linette would have gotten down by herself, but there was no graceful way to do it, so she took his hand and accepted his assistance.

Grady looked about. "Big trees." His words were spoken with awe.

"Bigger than the tree you had before?" Eddie asked.

Grady started to nod then stopped. "Maybe."

Eddie chuckled. "We won't cut down one that's too big to get into the cookhouse. Cookie might not like it if we push her out in the cold."

Grady giggled. "She whack you."

Linette laughed out loud. Eddie laughed, too, and their gazes caught and held. She couldn't help it. Nor did she regret it. The man had a nice laugh and when he smiled, his whole face appeared wreathed in sweetness. Oh, my. She was not doing well at teaching her emotions submission. Thankfully, Grady demanded Eddie's attention and the pair headed for the woods in search of the perfect tree.

"You coming?" Eddie called.

"The snow looks awfully deep. I think I'll wait here."

"Okay." He turned back to Grady. "You follow in my footsteps so you don't disappear in a snowbank."

"Okay." And with complete trust and confidence he

tromped after Eddie, who broke a trail the boy could follow.

Follow in my footsteps.

The words of a father to a son. *Oh, Lord, give this dear boy his father.* She'd left her address with Grady's father and instructions to contact her when he changed his mind. Perhaps the next mail delivery would include word from him.

In the meantime, Grady was learning to trust men and had a good example to follow in Eddie.

They went only a few feet and stopped. Slowly they circled a tree, looking it over with great concentration. Then they had a serious talk. Linette couldn't hear what they said, but there was a lot of head nodding. Then Eddie signaled for Grady to stand back, and with solid blows, he used his ax on the tree. It swayed and swished down. It took the combined efforts of a man and a little boy to drag it to the wagon. Linette allowed them to do it by themselves. She enjoyed watching them together too much to offer help.

The tree safely in the wagon, Eddie lifted Grady back to the seat then turned to Linette.

"Didn't expect you to let the men do all the work."

She could tell from his tone that he teased. "I was doing my share."

He drew back to stare at her. "How?"

She cocked her head to one side as if it should be obvious. "I was enjoying the entertainment."

He hooted and slapped his thigh. "So this was all for your amusement?"

"Absolutely. Didn't you know it?"

The way he looked at her felt like the sun warming her skin. "I do now. Happy to be of service." He touched the brim of his hat then held out his hand to help her onto the wagon seat. He whistled as he went to his place and took the reins. Every few minutes on the trip back he chuckled for no apparent reason and looked at her with laughter in his eyes.

Linette felt vastly pleased with herself that she'd made him laugh.

All too soon they arrived back at the ranch and he pulled up to the cookhouse.

Slim and Blue hustled toward them and helped carry the tree inside. It was soon standing in the corner of the dining room.

Cookie sighed. "It's just like home."

From the expression on the faces of the cowboys gathering in the room, Linette guessed they all agreed.

This was her chance to prove her abilities. "Who has decorations?"

Cookie nodded. "I have a few things."

Linette looked around at the others. "Everyone bring something and we'll decorate the tree right after lunch."

"What can I bring?" Grady whispered.

"We'll find something."

"Ma'am," Slim said. "What do you have in mind?"

She guessed they didn't have any fine ornaments, but she'd noticed how they often slipped a bright feather into their hatbands and she'd seen the colorful saddle blankets many of them used. She pointed it out to them. "Anything like that." It would take time to create things, so they agreed to meet and decorate the tree midafternoon.

Three hours later they again gathered in the cookhouse.

Grady wanted to be first. Linette had helped him color Christmas shapes on pages from her sketch pad then cut them out and put yarn hangers on them.

The cowboys had been very creative. Ward had a collection of feathers he tied to the tree. Slim had managed to tie bright threads from a blanket into bows. There were bits of ribbon and other assorted things. Cookie had six bright red Christmas balls. Linette added the ribbons she'd crocheted. Cassie had fashioned bits of colored paper into beads and hung them in clusters.

Only one person remained to contribute—Eddie—and everyone turned to him. He had something hidden beneath a wrap and now revealed it. "An angel for the top. I found it in the crate Mother sent."

Linette began to think that container held everything a person might want.

"Grady, you can help me put the angel on top." Eddie lifted the boy, and the two of them perched the angel on the uppermost branch.

They all stood back and admired the tree.

"We should celebrate with tea and cake," Cookie said.

No one argued.

Later that evening, after Grady and Cassie had retired to the bedroom, Linette and Eddie sat by the stove. She thought of suggesting they play chess, but neither of them seemed inclined to stir.

"You've made us all look forward to Christmas this year." He seemed to approve of her efforts. "Thank you."

"Being out in the West doesn't mean we shouldn't enjoy the season."

"I guess it takes a woman to plan it though." He shifted to consider her. "Not everyone would think to include the cowboys, too."

She nodded and caught a thrill of victory to her heart. "I'm not like everyone else."

"So I'm learning." He grinned. "Though you made

it pretty obvious from the start." His eyes twinkled. "Every time I see you in the big overcoat I am reminded. As if I need reminding. I don't think you'll ever give me a chance to forget."

She tried to think how to respond. How to make him see that women didn't have to live in the constricting molds from the old country.

Eddie lay on his bedroll. Today was Christmas—a day full of promise and possibility. He stared up at the still-dark ceiling and let his thoughts fill with pleasant prospects.

Grady rushed from the bedroom. "Get up. There's presents."

When Eddie didn't move, Grady yelled, "Get up. Get up."

Eddie grabbed the boy and tickled him. Grady was so excited about Christmas and gifts he didn't protest but squealed with laughter.

Linette stepped into the room, saw Eddie wrestling with the boy and laughed. She met Eddie's gaze and her smile crept into the bottom of his heart.

What was this strange feeling? Admiration? Certainly. Friendship? He hoped so and hoped it was mutual, though she seemed skittish around him as if she was afraid. Which made not one lick of sense. He'd never seen Linette afraid. Not even when they were attacked by wolves. His smile deepened as he thought how brave she'd been. If only he hadn't written Margaret and again offered her marriage. But he had and he would honor his word as he must.

Grady squirmed free and bolted to Linette's side. "Let's eat. Hurry."

Again Eddie's gaze caught Linette's. They smiled at

Grady's excitement. The air crackled with something more. She must have felt it, too, because she jerked toward the stove. Did it frighten her? Or entice?

Cassie joined the others at the breakfast table. Grady's excitement spread to all of them and they rushed through the meal, took only a few minutes to clean up then hurry across to the cookhouse.

All the cowboys gathered in the big room, dressed in their finest. Eddie wished he could take a picture of them staring at the decorated tree. A pile of gifts rested beneath the green boughs.

Cookie handed them each a cup of spicy tea mixture as they headed for the tree. All eyes turned to him. He was in charge.

He looked around the group. They were family now. And they accepted him. To them he was Eddie Gardiner, not the adopted, illegitimate son. He sucked in air to smooth the roughness in his throat. "I hope you don't see me as simply your boss, because we're family. Some of us have relatives in distant parts of the world. Most of them have no idea what our lives are like now. But we understand the demands of this new world. We know the necessity of working together, helping each other through the difficult spots. To each of you, Merry Christmas." He held his cup up in a toast and the others joined him. There was a clink of china against china and a chorus of "Merry Christmas."

"Now, who gets the first present?"

Grady's face almost disappeared in his big eyes.

"Grady?"

The boy nodded.

"Let's see what we can find." Eddie reached under the tree and pulled out the gift he'd made—a small wooden horse and a wagon for it to pull.

Grady tore the paper from the gift and yelled his approval.

Everyone laughed.

Eddie passed around gifts. Cassie and Linette had managed to make scarves for all the men. Cookie had made each a selection of candy. Grady got more carved animals from the men and a beautifully illustrated picture book made by Linette. The men had made each of the women a writing tray to hold their paper and correspondence.

Eddie pulled an unwrapped present from behind the tree and gave it to Linette.

"An easel," she said on an exhaled breath.

He couldn't tell if she was surprised or pleased. "I thought you might like to do some painting."

Her gaze burrowed deep into his. Was she remembering the afternoon she'd sketched a picture for him? Was she wondering if he considered her talent a silly pastime unsuitable for a pioneer woman? "This country is so pretty. I've often wished I could take a picture, but a painting is even better."

"Thank you." Her eyes darkened before she handed him a package.

He folded back the brown paper to reveal two pictures of the house on the hill drawn at different times of the day.

"Ward made the frames," she told him.

"Thank you. I'll hang them in the new house."

The air between them was heavy. With longing and dreams? No. He jerked away. She had only one purpose in mind—marry to avoid her father's despicable plans for her. And he had his offer to Margaret to honor. All they shared was the moment.

Winter set in for real after Christmas. Snow came

in blankets then disappeared in a warm Chinook. The temperature fluctuated. On warmer days Eddie continued work on the house, grateful for Linette's company and help. There was something isolating about being alone in the house. On colder days he made sure the cows were taken care of, fed the horses then stayed indoors, often playing with Grady as the women sewed and cooked. The place was warm and cozy and despite the crowded conditions no one complained.

But he liked evenings best. Cassie normally retired to the bedroom with Grady leaving Linette and Eddie to themselves.

Sometimes Linette painted, but after a few minutes would step back. "The light is too poor."

He didn't say much. He enjoyed watching her but knew it would make her uncomfortable if he said so. She viewed her painting as useless and would seldom paint in the daytime, saying there was work to do.

But whatever they did, they talked. He learned more about her home life. How her parents insisted on forcing her into a mold of their shaping.

"I wanted to join a mission and help the homeless and ill." Her half laugh, half snort held self-mockery. "You can imagine my parents' reaction to that. They threatened to put me under lock and key."

"It still surprises me they allowed you to come here." He couldn't imagine the place without her now. Her presence made winter enjoyable.

She lowered her gaze. The air seemed heavy and he wondered if another snow was about to descend, but the sky was clear. The heaviness came from her. "There's only one way I can escape my father's plans."

She expected him to be her means of escape. For her sake, he wished he could be. But he couldn't. Besides, what man wanted to be only a way to avoid an unpleasant fate? He changed the subject to ask about her brother. They both found talking about their siblings a pleasant topic.

They often discussed their faith and would spend time together searching out scriptures in his Bible. He came to look forward to those times, finding himself both challenged and encouraged by the depth of her faith in God's love and the extent of her knowledge of God's word. "My nurse taught me well. From her I learned to find answers to life's problems in God's word. No matter what, I know God's love is sufficient."

He realized he did not have the same rock-solid assurance she claimed. But over the winter months with Linette he found his faith growing like a spring garden warmed by the sun and watered by a gentle rain.

He told her much, too. About the things he'd faced as he'd started a ranch in the virgin land of northwest Canada. "I had to decide the best place for the buildings. I had to select the grazing land. Then there were Indians, wild animals and wolves to deal with. And no guidebook to show the way."

"God guided you."

"Seems He must have."

She tipped her head and studied him.

He wanted to escape her probing gaze but wouldn't allow himself to be a coward. Whatever she saw, whatever she measured, he was man enough to accept it.

"Your father would be proud. And rightly so. You have succeeded beyond what most have. Your ranch is solid. The animals are doing well. The men look up to you, trust you."

Her approval was honest, open. It watered his soul. "I hope my father sees it the same way."

One afternoon, he glanced up at the approach of a horse. One of the men from OK Ranch rode into the yard. "Got your mail." He handed him a bundle.

Eddie thanked him. He'd been pretending the roads were too muddy for a trip to town, but now the inevitable had come. Spring was here. He could no longer delay sending Linette back. It had been the plan from the beginning.

He flipped through the letters. He didn't see one from Margaret and sighed in relief. It only meant postponement.

He'd been playing a game of make-believe in order to see Linette in the cabin, to look forward to spending time with her, to picture her as the woman in the big house. But he wasn't a child controlled by pretend. It was time to stop playing and return to serious business.

He strode toward the cabin to deliver the three letters for Linette, all from the same return address but in different handwriting. No doubt each member of her family had written with news.

"Mail," he called as he stepped into the cabin.

She spun to face him, her mouth drooping as if reality had caught her by surprise as well.

If only they could stop time. Enjoy a few more days… weeks…months. But how long would be long enough? He was only avoiding fate.

He handed her the letters addressed to her and sat down to read the rest. There was a letter from an acquaintance wanting to come West and wondering if he might visit Eddie until he found a place of his own.

Jayne had written a letter full of wedding plans. She expected Eddie to return for the event though she still didn't give a date. He folded the pages and returned them to the envelope. Then he could find no more excuse for avoiding the letter from his father.

He slit it open and read words that made him feel as if he'd failed again. Instructions on caring for the cows. As if Eddie hadn't done so successfully for two years. Directions for every aspect of the house. Eddie had managed quite well without his father's supervision, though his father would no doubt wonder how it was possible. *I understand you are living like so many of the Northwest we hear about, ignoring legal and moral obligations and being consumed by the flesh. Furthermore, I hear you are still living in a cabin fit for a trapper but not a Gardiner.* He effectively made it clear the Gardiners held up a standard Eddie never quite achieved. *Mr. Edwards has expressed his shock that his daughter should be treated in such a fashion. He is threatening to take legal action against the Gardiners. He says he expects certain benefits in compensation even if you marry his daughter. I warn you, nothing good will come of this. Get rid of that woman immediately. Wash your hands of her.*

He turned the page over. Nothing had been said of Margaret. Did she intend to come? Was he expected to return to London to marry her?

He bolted to his feet. "I'll be back later." He strode up the hill so quickly his heart pounded by the time he reached the house.

Linette barely heard Eddie leave as she read her father's letter. It was full of threats. *I expect documentation about your marriage by return mail or I shall take severe action toward the Gardiners. I have it in my power to destroy them utterly and completely.*

Little did he know that Linette would be returning

without proof of marriage. Returning to her father's plans. She could only hope Lyle Williamson would find more suitable prey before she reached home.

She'd failed. Yes, she'd gained Eddie's respect for her as a suitable ranch wife. But not his offer of marriage. Now it seemed the best thing she could do was return home and deflect her father's intention of destroying Eddie's good name.

She'd prayed all winter for things to change.

They hadn't.

She must accept God had another plan for her. Perhaps like Esther of the Bible, she had something noble to achieve by accepting her father's will. *Oh, Lord, I submit to Your will but please, please may it be something other than marrying a man I despise.*

She glanced out the window as a horse rode by. It was Eddie headed toward the mountains. How long before he escorted her to town and saw her on the stagecoach back toward London?

The sun shone brightly and she headed outside. She ached to store up a well of memories of this place and this time. She wandered through the yards, paused to breathe in the sweet scent of the budding trees, then climbed the hill where she and Eddie had once tobogganed with Grady. She drank in the sight of the majestic mountains.

There was only one thing she would beg for and that was that Grady be allowed to stay with Cookie and Bertie. They would provide him with a loving home. She would take him with her except she knew her father would turn him out on the street as soon as she stepped into the house. Lyle Williamson would offer no more or she might view the marriage differently.

Cassie would likely be content to continue as

Linette's maid at least until they were back in the old country.

For some time she sat there praying and planning. Then she returned to the cabin and prepared a meal.

Cassie and Grady returned from the cookhouse. But Eddie did not come in. "We'll go ahead and have supper without him," she said after a considerable time. Had he decided not to join them? Or had he encountered difficulty in the hills? The men would surely know if they needed to go after him.

She tried to comfort herself with that knowledge, but as darkness fell and he still didn't return she pressed to the window, praying for a glimpse of him. She couldn't say how long she stayed there, only that her legs hurt from standing, her eyes ached from staring into the dark. Rain spattered the window and she shivered. *Lord, bring him home safely. Please.*

A noise outside the door drew her from the window. Eddie burst in, tossed his dripping Stetson to the hook and shed his wet coat. A puddle circled his feet.

She grabbed a towel and rushed to help him. "You're soaked."

"I'm fine." He took the towel and wiped his face.

"I'll make tea. I saved supper for you."

"I'm hungry."

She warmed the food, boiled water for tea and served him.

He thanked her and ate and drank in silence. Finished, he pushed his plate away. "Thank you. Now, if you don't mind, I'm tired."

Her cheeks stung at the way he dismissed her. She'd hoped he'd say where he'd been, but at least he hadn't told her to pack up for her return home. She gladly accepted the reprieve and ducked into the bedroom.

* * *

Eddie longed for her to stay. But he knew it was best if she left.

Unable to stop thinking about the letter from his father, he had left right after breakfast. He rode from the yard. The grass was greening in the lower pastures but the higher elevations would still be snow-covered. He didn't need to check them to know it.

He had to think. Sort out this confusion twisting his brain into a knot.

His direction took him away from the ranch. He'd ridden a few miles then reined in and studied the landscape. Wild. Open. Great for cattle if a man learned to work with the land instead of against it. He'd learned quickly he couldn't do things the same way they'd been done in the old country.

He turned his horse about and stared at the mountains.

Majestic. Bold. Unmovable. Unshaken by storms, by snow, by heat or cold.

I will lift up mine eyes unto the hills, from whence cometh my help. My help cometh from the Lord, which made heaven and earth.

Easily that passage came to mind. He and Linette had discussed it during the winter.

"God led me," she'd said, referring to her trip west. "I called to Him and He answered me and delivered me from all my fears."

Did she still believe God had delivered her now that spring was here and he had the onerous task of informing her she would have to leave?

He'd dropped from the horse, took the reins and walked. Over and over he'd informed himself it was time to tell her.

It had started to rain. But he'd stayed out rather than have to return and confront her.

He didn't want to tell her to leave. He didn't want to send her away.

But he'd asked Margaret to marry him.

The fact that she hadn't replied made him wonder how successful he'd been at convincing her. Perhaps he could write and retract his offer before she decided to come.

He stared at the mountains. Something about them made it impossible to avoid the truth.

It wasn't only because of his offer to Margaret that he hesitated. His father didn't like Mr. Edwards. His father had instructed Eddie to send Linette home. Actually he probably didn't care where Eddie sent her so long as it got her out of the Gardiner sphere.

Eddie had been trying all his life to live up to the expectations of that name. Would he ever succeed?

"Your father would be proud." "You've done a good job." "You're a good leader." Words he longed to hear, but they hadn't come from his father.

They'd come from Linette.

Linette who faced challenges fearlessly. Who played a sharp game of chess. Who painted and drew pictures that stirred his emotions.

Linette who showed kindness to all regardless of race and station in life.

He didn't need to prove anything to her. She accepted him as he was, not because he was the son of Randolph Gardiner. Her approval was honest, open, free.

Why would he send her away and lose all that?

Morning came and he still couldn't think clearly. He hurried from the cabin and saddled his horse. He meant to ride hard and far, but instead headed for the big house, approaching from the hillside so no one would note him. He strode into the house and went immediately to the windows overlooking the ranch.

He belonged here, was part of the developing country.

All his life he had worked for what he had here.

He knew who he was. Not a Gardiner by birth, but that no longer mattered. He was Eddie Gardiner, the man who built Eden Valley Ranch. The man who ran it successfully.

More than that, he was a man loved by God. Accepted by the One who created the mountains and plains. It was time he was honest to the depth of his soul. Here, in the wilds of northwest Canada, he had found acceptance such as he'd never before known.

One time he'd kissed Linette. One time only. But that one fleeting touch had been the most honest moment of his life.

He loved her. He wanted to share his life with her. He wanted to fill this house with a family they'd have together.

With every honest breath, his heart beat harder, more insistently.

He had one thing to do before he could ask her.

He must write Margaret and withdraw his offer then write his father and inform him he intended to follow his heart.

If that meant he had to give up running the ranch... well, so be it. With Linette at his side, he would start somewhere else.

His mind made up, he returned to his horse, rode to the barn, took care of his mount then hurried to the cabin and gathered up pen, ink and paper. The cabin was empty. He climbed the hill to the house and sat down to write two letters.

Before he began, he bowed his head and asked the Lord to guide him then he let honest words flow to the paper.

Finished, he sealed the letters and marched back down the hill. He found Slim and sent him to town with the missives.

Now to pick the right time to tell Linette of his decision.

It took determination to wait until after supper. "Linette, come for a walk."

She stopped, her hands clutching the pot she dried, sucked in air and tucked in her chin. "Of course." She put the pot on the shelf, removed her apron and hung it carefully on a nail by the washstand then reached for her heavy coat.

"It's warm out. Your shawl will be enough."

She rehung the coat and took her knitted shawl instead.

He held the door for her and fell in step beside her. He lifted an arm, wanting to pull her to his side, but she hurried ahead.

They passed the barn, crossed the bridge and went beyond the pens, up the hill to a spot they'd visited before. He knew she would welcome his offer. Hadn't she come for the very purpose of marriage to him?

He caught her hand and pulled her to a halt beneath the aspens heavy with the scent of spring buds. The sun was nearing the horizon. He turned her to watch the sunset—flares and ribbons of mauve and pink, purple and orange filling the western sky. And then the sun dipped out of sight, leaving the sky orange in its wake.

"It's so beautiful," she whispered.

He rested his hands on her shoulders and watched a moment longer. Then he slowly turned her to face him.

Her smile slid sideways and vanished.

He touched her cheek. "Don't look so afraid."

She lifted her chin and faced him. "I'm not afraid."

"I'm not about to tell you I'm going to send you home."

Her chin dropped hard. "You're not?"

"Linette, I want to marry you."

She blinked. "Really?"

He had so much to say but the words stopped halfway up his throat. "Not just because you've proved you would make a good ranch wife. I want you to stay. I want you to be part of my life."

The uncertain, surprised look in her face made him realize he was doing a poor job of saying what his heart felt.

"Linette." He took her upper arms in his hands and bent closer. "I love you. I want to share my life, my dreams, my heart with you."

She splayed trembling fingers over her chest. She looked so vulnerable. So uncertain.

Had he surprised her so much with his confession of love? "I know you look at marriage only as an escape. You weren't expecting an offer of love. Maybe you don't even welcome it. But it doesn't matter. I love you. And if you can't love me back, it's okay. I'll still love you." He hoped somewhere inside her lay a tender feeling toward him. He prayed there was a tiny seed of sweet regard that, with nourishment, would someday grow into love. He intended to provide the nourishment.

Giving her time to refuse, rejoicing when she didn't, he caught her mouth with his own, letting his kiss say all the things he felt, hoping, trusting she heard his silent promises. He lifted his head, smiled at the confusion in her eyes. "You will marry me?"

She nodded. "I told you you'd change your mind."

Chapter Fourteen

Linette's breath stuck halfway up her throat.

He'd offered marriage. Exactly what she wanted. But he'd offered more than she bargained for. His heart.

She couldn't decide what to think except it frightened her. She hadn't expected love. Didn't know if she was prepared for it. Love meant so much more than a marriage of convenience. It meant relinquishing her dreams in deference to his plans.

But in return, she'd get his devotion. The thought reached into her heart and squeezed it, flooding her veins with a combination of anticipation and caution.

"What about Margaret?"

"Let's sit."

They sat on the crest of the hill as the light faded from the sky.

"I wrote Margaret and my father, informing them of my choice." Eddie's laugh carried a note of regret and he took her hand between his. "Father suggested you might not be suitable to become a Gardiner."

"I guessed as much."

"Sorry. Remember my father isn't sure *I* am suitable to be a Gardiner."

Her defense on her own behalf died. "I can't imagine always feeling the need to prove yourself. Besides, he is so wrong. He needs to visit and see for himself how well you've done."

"He'd only see what he wanted to see." His expression brightened. "But I came to a conclusion this afternoon. I know who I am. God made me and He's in charge."

"Amen. He holds you in His hand and directs your steps."

"Like a good shepherd."

She laughed. How often had they discussed the Twenty-third Psalm over the winter months, considering the differences between raising sheep and cattle?

But what would Eddie do if his father forbade their marriage?

"How soon can we be married?" he asked.

She hesitated but a second. "As soon as possible, I suppose."

They talked about how their marriage would change things.

"What about Grady?"

"He'll live with us in the big house."

His ready answer gave her the strength to dismiss her fears.

They didn't return to the house until late. At the door, she stopped. Did they kiss again? What were his expectations?

As if he'd read her mind, he gently turned her into his arms, allowing mere inches to separate them. "I'm willing to do things your way. Whatever you're comfortable with is fine with me. I pray at some time you'll grow to love me, but if you don't, we can still have a great marriage. I promise."

She sighed her relief and rested her head against his shoulder. He wanted her to say she loved him but she could not squeeze the words from her fearful heart.

"I'm sorry." Love frightened her, but how could she explain it to him when she didn't understand it herself?

"I'm not complaining." He cupped his hand to the back of her head and held her gently. He pressed his cheek to her hair and she was almost certain he kissed the top of her head.

"I will be a good wife," she murmured against his jacket front, breathing in his warm scent. "I'll work hard."

"Linette, you don't need to prove anything to me. I love you just the way you are."

He held her a moment longer then led her down the hill and shooed her away to bed.

In the dark, she whispered to Cassie, "He said he'll marry me."

Cassie bolted upright, making Grady murmur a complaint. She settled back down. "I don't believe it."

"It's true."

"Will we all get to stay, then?"

She found Cassie's hand on top of the covers and squeezed it. "What would I do without you and Grady? Of course you get to stay."

"I'm happy for you. It's what you wanted."

"Thank you." She shifted to her side and stared into the darkness. It was why she'd come West—to marry a man who would allow her to escape her father's plans. She hadn't counted on him falling in love with her.

You don't need to prove anything to me. I love you just the way you are.

Love? What was that? Didn't it turn her into a pawn, the way she'd been as her father's daughter?

Eddie was not like her father.

But she couldn't push away the fear of giving herself wholly and completely to another. Unless she retained control of her heart, she feared she would lose who she was to him.

The next morning, she accompanied Eddie to the cookhouse where he called for attention. "Linette has agreed to become my wife."

Nice of him to put it that way when they all knew she'd come with the specific intention of marrying him. But it pleased her that he made it sound as if it had been his idea.

"Didn't I tell you so?" Cookie exclaimed as she engulfed Linette in one of her massive hugs.

Eddie managed to keep his arm about her shoulders and protect her from some of Cookie's enthusiasm, then she turned to pat Eddie's back in congratulations.

Linette felt the thuds clear to her fingertips and feared Eddie would suffer internal injuries.

One by one the cowhands who were present filed by shaking Eddie's hand and taking hers in a polite gesture. All of them said they were glad she was going to stay and help Eddie run the ranch. Even Ward offered his congratulations.

"Guessed you weren't interested in my little ranch."

At first she giggled at their comments then she began to squirm. "Eddie has done quite well without my help so far. I expect he could continue to manage without me."

Eddie squeezed her to his side. "They know a woman's touch makes all the difference. Especially a woman as wise and generous as you."

She waited until they were alone to question him.

"What did you mean about me being wise and generous?"

He laughed hard. When he noticed she didn't join in his merriment, he sobered. "You really don't know?"

She shook her head, not caring her fears and uncertainties likely showed in her face.

He took her hands and pulled her close. She tipped her head to search his eyes as he spoke.

"Linette, you show kindness to all, you try to help people no matter what their race or color or social standing. You speak your mind but in a way that causes people to respect you. You stopped my men from hanging an Indian who didn't deserve such a fate. And brave? I never expected to see a woman stand up to the wolves the way you did." He pressed a kiss to her nose. "I understand you think you have to prove you are something more than a beautiful woman who can be used as part of a business deal." His voice deepened as if the words pained him and her heart did a slow tilt toward him.

"But my dear sweet Linette. You don't need to prove anything to anyone. You are beautiful." He kissed her on each cheek. "But you are so much more. And I cherish each and every bit of you—your personality, your faith and your…" He paused, eased back a few inches and touched her chest over her heart. "Who you are inside."

She swallowed hard several times, struggled with a sense of breathlessness as his words washed over her, cleansing away self-doubt and fear, leaving her whole.

She loved this man for the gift he'd given her.

But when she tried to say the words, they stuck in her throat.

If he noticed her struggle he didn't say anything, just pulled her close again and held her gently. "I need to go." He caught her chin with his fingertip and lifted her face to kiss her sweetly and quickly. "I'll be back later and we can talk more."

But it was easy in the following days to talk about other things. She sensed his patient waiting but the knot in her throat would not let go. In fact, it seemed to extend to her heart and bind her feelings behind prison bars.

One day she glanced up to see a line of Indians riding by and realized winter had begun to relinquish its hold on the land.

Eddie came from the pens and stood at her side.

"They're moving out to hunt for food. Unfortunately there is little left for them. Buffalo hunters have killed most of the huge herds. And now the people are confined to specific areas. It's a tough life."

"I hope they'll be safe. I wonder how Bright Moon, Red Fox and their boys are."

They watched the long line snake by. A man turned aside and headed down the hill toward them, a woman at his side. "It's them," Linette squealed, running to meet the family.

Bright Moon showed them the baby, wearing the sweater Linette had given him.

"His name Little Shirt." A chuckle accompanied Red Fox's announcement. "White woman give little shirt."

Linette grinned, happy at their choice of name. The baby had put on weight. In fact, they all looked considerably better than last time she'd seen them.

"Mother has gift," Little Bear said.

Bright Moon handed her a pair of baby moccasins, ornately decorated with beads.

Linette choked up. "Thank you," she managed to say past the tears clogging her throat.

"You are great white woman," Red Fox said, holding his hand out as if in benediction.

From the hill came a cheer. The whole tribe faced them.

Linette waved then thanked Red Fox and hugged Bright Moon and the boys. The family returned to the others and the Indians continued their journey. Linette watched until they were out of sight.

"The great white woman. I like that." Eddie had his arm about her shoulders and pulled her close to rest his forehead against hers. "You are appreciated by men of both races. How does it feel?"

She considered his question. "It feels fine."

He gave her a little shake. "And yet you still doubt. Linette, my love. When will you believe you are accepted and more…honored and loved?"

She shrugged. "I don't know."

He kissed her forehead. "I pray for the day but until then know this, I love you just as you are."

"Sounds like a wedding vow."

"It is. I am yours for as long as I live. You have my heart, my love, my everything."

"Eddie…" Her voice broke. "I don't deserve so much."

He gave her another little shake. "But you do."

She nodded as tears gathered in the back of her throat.

How she wanted to believe him. Say to him the words he wanted to hear. Was it stubborn pride that prevented it?

Lord, help me. I came for a marriage of convenience. That's all I wanted. Now it seems I must choose if I want more. But something in my heart is stuck. Broken, even. Show me how to fix it. Please.

She was tired of the constant warfare between what she wanted to give Eddie and what she wanted to keep for herself.

Her heart.

Later that day Eddie went to Linette. "Let's inspect the house." He wanted her to see it as hers. He wanted to feel her joy in making plans. "It's yours now. You can choose how to use the rooms, how to decorate them."

They climbed the hill to the house and she went immediately to the window overlooking the ranch as he knew she would. "I want this to be our main room so we can enjoy this view every day."

He chuckled. "Why doesn't that surprise me?"

She would have stayed there, content to ignore the rest of the house, but he took her hand and drew her away. She inspected the kitchen as if seeing it for the first time. "I can see myself working here."

"I expect it will be a pleasant change after the cramped quarters of the cabin and the tiny stove, which you've managed to cook very nice meals on."

"I enjoyed it." She faced him. "Are you sure about this?"

He looked at the wooden worktable. "Is something wrong with it?"

"What if I never say the words you want?"

She'd read his longing so clearly. He ached for her to say she loved him. Wondered what held her back. Not that he had any reason for complaint. She was gentle, loving and kind to him. Just as she was to everyone.

He pulled her to his chest, pressed her head to the hollow of his shoulder where he'd discovered it fit very nicely. He rested his cheek against her hair. "Linette, I love you enough for the both of us. Yes, I pray you will someday learn to love me, but so long as you can accept my love I'm okay with this arrangement."

She wrapped her arms about his waist and held him tight. "You are a good man."

It had to be enough for now. But someday, God willing, there would be more.

A few days later, Linette turned as Eddie strode into the cabin. Her lungs tightened with—

She couldn't say what. Or perhaps she didn't want to admit it.

"I'm going to help the men move the herd up to new pasture." Eddie pulled Linette into his arms and searched her face with hope. But she couldn't give him the words he wanted. Yes, he'd said he would wait. No demands. Yet she felt his longing as clearly as she felt the air fill her lungs. "Take good care," she said, and boldly lifted her face and kissed him.

He hugged her tight then hurried away.

She watched him go then climbed the hill to the house.

The house was almost finished, but Eddie said he would complete the work before they were married. They hadn't yet set a date. She knew he wanted to hear back from Margaret, officially freeing him from his offer. But she wondered if he also waited for a reply from his father. What if his father forbade the marriage? He would never choose her over his father's approval.

She went immediately to the row of rooms upstairs. They were in a separate wing from the family rooms. Meant for the Gardiner family. But she saw them as suitable for an entirely different purpose. A place of healing and rest for the hurting and weary. She had already moved cots into two of the rooms and now she mentally furnished them and imagined them occupied.

Racing horses' hooves caught her attention. She hurried to a window in time to see Slim race to the barn and throw himself from the saddle even before the horse stopped. The horse was lathered in a way Eddie would frown on. Slim raced to the barn and pushed the big doors open.

Something was wrong.

She dashed from the house and jogged down the hill in time to see Slim rattle from the barn in the wagon.

"Wait," she called.

He saw her and shouted, "…hurt." But he didn't slow down.

Had he said Eddie was hurt? She was certain he had and she sank to her knees to watch the wagon bounce along the trail. She didn't move until it disappeared from sight.

And then she returned to the big house to the windows that allowed her a view of the ranch. From where she stood, she could see the wagon before it reached the barn. Before it could be seen from the cabin or any of the buildings below her.

Lord, keep him safe.

Her knees failed and she sank to the chair, never taking her eyes from the window.

How badly was he injured? Her heart beat double time.

What if he was worse than injured? The blood congealed in her veins.

She couldn't imagine life without him. She'd give up every dream, every desire, if it meant she could share the rest of her life with him.

The truth hit her with such force she groaned.

She loved him. But she'd never told him.

Why had she waited so long? Perhaps she would never get the chance now.

She'd held back her words because of her father. Fearing Eddie would somehow turn into a man like him. See her as currency to be used in a business deal. But Eddie was not her father. Never would be. Eddie loved her. And she knew her heart was safe in his care.

Oh, why had she been so stubborn? So prideful?

Why had she feared so much to love a man? A verse her nurse had taught her came to mind. *There is no fear in love; but perfect love casteth out fear...he that feareth is not made perfect in love.*

God's love was perfect and complete. It enabled her to love a man, to say the words to him.

Tears washed her soul.

She'd wasted so much time. Maybe lost her chance.

Lord, forgive me. Please give me a chance to tell him how much I love him.

She remained at the window until she saw a twist of dust far to the north then dashed from the house and down the hill to await the wagon.

She prayed it wasn't Eddie, but if it wasn't him it would be one of the other men or some unfortunate stranger. She couldn't guess how badly the poor injured party was, only that the injury was severe enough to send a man back for the wagon.

The wagon drew closer, surrounded by a guard of men. It took her only one quick glance to see Eddie wasn't among those on horseback and with a cry straight from her fractured heart, she raced forward.

Ward dropped from his horse and caught her in his arms. "He looks worse than he is."

"Let me go." She struggled in his arms, straining toward the wagon.

"Best let us clean him up first."

"I must see him." She broke from his grasp and made it to the back of the wagon before anyone could stop her.

"Eddie." His name wailed past her teeth.

He lay motionless on the wooden wagon bed. Blood covered his face. She scrambled up beside him, kneeling at his head but not touching him. Afraid to, lest she hurt him further. "What happened?"

"His horse stumbled in a hole and threw him into a rock. Knocked him out cold."

Ward touched her back. "We need to get him inside."

She thought of the bedroll where he always slept and quickly made a decision. "Take him to the big house. He'll be more comfortable there." The bed she'd pictured as respite for a wounded stranger was about to hold the one she loved.

The wagon jerked forward and Linette pressed her palms to the floor to keep her balance. "Eddie, wake up," she whispered.

But he showed no response.

Blood wept from his hairline and she lifted her fingers but drew back without touching his skin. Would she make things worse? She didn't know and wished she'd defied her father and entered a hospital to train as a nurse.

"Let us carry him in."

She hadn't noticed they'd pulled up to the house and she shifted aside so four men could tenderly lift Eddie from the wagon and carry him up the stairs. She rushed ahead, grabbed a handful of blankets from one of the storage crates and tossed them to the bed.

Through it all Eddie made not one sound. Didn't even flinch.

Linette pressed her lips together to keep from crying out. She sucked in air and pushed resolve into her trembling body. "I need water. A basin. Towels."

Someone put a chair next to the bed and she sank into it, never taking her attention from Eddie's face. *Please, Lord, let him open his eyes.*

Ward set a small table beside her, along with a basin of water. Eddie still did not stir.

She wet a cloth and tenderly, gingerly, patted at the blood. "I can't tell where it's coming from." Her voice shook like a wind-battered leaf. She rinsed the rag out and finished cleaning his face. He was so pale. So still. Only the rise and fall of his chest assured her he was alive.

Fresh blood flowed down his cheek and pooled in his ear. She sponged it off and pushed his matted hair aside to search for the wound. It gaped a few inches above his ear, blood flowing steadily. She tried to push the edges together but there was too much swelling. She rinsed the cloth again then pressed it to the wound. The blood flow stopped.

She ran her gaze over the rest of his body. "Is anything broken?"

"Don't seem to be," one of the men replied.

"He's been out a long time," Ward said, his voice tight with worry.

Worry Linette shared. Eddie was too quiet. Deathly still. "I don't know what we can do but wait. I'll watch him until he wakens."

Roper stepped back. "Come on, boys. The boss will expect the work done when he wakes up."

One by one they slipped away until only Ward remained. "You'll be okay on your own?"

She nodded. "I'll give a holler if I need anything."

He nodded. "We'll check on you in a bit."

Then she was alone with Eddie and she let the tears flow unchecked. "Don't you die on me, Eddie Gardiner. I never got a chance to tell you I love you."

She checked the wound. It still oozed and she applied pressure again. *Please, God. Please, God.* She couldn't form any more of a prayer but knew God heard the cry of her heart.

Cassie stepped into the room, a covered plate in her hands. "Any change?"

"He hasn't moved. Not once."

"You need to eat." She handed Linette the plate.

Linette stared at it. "What's this?"

"Supper."

"It can't be." She glanced toward the window. The sun almost touched the mountaintops. "How long have I been here?" She'd been vaguely aware of one or another of the cowboys slipping in and leaving again. Cookie had come once, tsked and left again.

"At least six hours."

She turned toward Cassie. "Six hours and he's still unconscious." Her voice caught. "That's not a good sign."

Cassie shook her head. "Everyone is praying."

Linette nodded, but strength seeped from her body. She set the plate on the table lest she drop it.

"I'll be back after Grady is asleep." Her friend patted Linette's shoulder then slipped away.

Linette fell on her knees at the side of the bed, clutching Eddie's limp hand in hers, willing him to waken. "Eddie, I love you. Don't leave me. I'm so sorry I didn't tell you sooner. Don't leave me. Please, God, don't take him from me."

She wasn't aware darkness had fallen until Ward entered and set a lamp on the table. She didn't recall returning to the chair, but she sat close to the bed still holding his hand.

"I'll sit with him while you rest," Ward offered. "Cassie made up the bed across the hall."

"I can't leave."

"You'll be close. I'll call if anything changes."

Still, she didn't move.

"You need to keep up your strength."

A cry filled her mouth and she clamped her fist to her lips to stop it from escaping. Did he mean Eddie could remain like this for a long time? Or did he mean Linette might be faced with a funeral and the sorrow accompanying it?

She bolted from the room, threw herself on the bed and sobbed into the pillow.

She must have dozed off, because she was startled by a sound from the other room and dashed across the hall. "Eddie?"

It was Slim. "Sorry, Linette, there's been no change."

"I'll be back in a moment to sit with him." She did a quick toilet and rushed back to the house. Dawn spread fingers of pink across the sky as she threw back the door.

Upstairs, the men had gathered.

"He's not going to die." She stared hard at each in turn, not shifting until each had lowered his eyes. "Is there a doctor in the area?"

Slim shook his head. "Don't know. Never heard of one. Closest is Fort Benton."

She turned to Ward. Eddie had often said he was

the best rider. "Ward, ride to town and ask around. I don't care how far you have to go. Bring back a doctor if there's one anywhere at all."

"It's several days to Fort Benton. Do you want me to go that far?"

"Go a reasonable distance. But hurry."

He was already out of the room.

She turned back to the others. "Now, go about your business and stop hanging around as if it's a death watch. I'll stay with him."

They hesitated until she shooed them away.

Finally, alone again, she sat at Eddie's side. Someone had brought fresh water and she gently washed his face and hands, as much to have something to do as anything. As she worked, she talked softly. "Eddie, I know God's in control, but it's hard to trust Him when you're lying here so still. Please wake up. I know you can't hear me, but I will say it anyway. I love you. Wake up and hear me. I love you."

The men came, one by one, and left again. She knew they were concerned about their boss.

Cassie brought tea and toast. Cookie lumbered up the stairs and wheezed a few minutes before she sighed sadly and left again.

Linette wanted to order all of them to stop acting as if Eddie was dying. He couldn't die. *Please, God.*

From outside she heard a horse gallop into the yard. She sprang to the window. Ward had returned, but he was alone. She searched the back trail for a slower horse, a buggy or wagon, but saw nothing. She turned as Ward clattered into the room.

"Ain't no doctor within a hundred miles."

She sucked in dry air that made her cough. "Then we'll wait and pray."

"Brought the mail." He set a bundle of letters on the table.

She glanced at them. Saw the return addresses. Randolph Gardiner in bold letters. Eddie's father had written. Would he threaten dire consequences to Eddie if he proceeded with his plan to marry Linette?

She recognized the handwriting on another letter as Margaret's.

She jerked away. Nothing mattered but seeing Eddie wake.

The day slipped away without him moving. Again, Slim insisted she lie down in the other room. And again, she fell asleep crying and praying.

She bolted awake. The room was dark. Silent. Her heart raced. Eddie had called. She'd heard his voice as if he stood at her bedside. She raced across the hall to Eddie's room where a lamp on the table gave the place a golden glow. Roper sat on a chair at the bedside. She dropped to the floor at Eddie's side. "Eddie?" But he didn't move. Didn't show any sign of response.

Her heart still beat a hard tattoo against her ribs. What had wakened her? "Eddie." She spoke his name louder. "Eddie, wake up."

Nothing. She sank back on her heels. No sign of a response.

Roper guided her to the chair. "It will soon be morning."

She shook her head. "It's dark as coal out there."

"It's always darkest before dawn."

His words slid through her like life-giving rain to a drought-stricken desert. He hadn't likely meant them as anything more than an observation, but they gave her hope. She would not give up even though there'd been no change.

Vaguely she realized the light in the room increased, that Roper turned the lamp off and slipped away.

But her every breath, every thought, every energy focused on Eddie, willing him to live. Over and over, she murmured his name. Sometimes gently, other times demanding as if she could order him to wake up.

"Eddie, I love you." She would say the words again and again in the hope he would waken and hear them.

Her head fell forward. She jerked upright. She must stay awake. If he only regained consciousness for a second, she would not miss it. She would not miss her chance to tell him she loved him.

Chapter Fifteen

Cassie brought Linette food. She ate it because Cassie wouldn't leave until she did. As soon as Cassie left she knelt by the bed, clutching Eddie's hand and praying.

She squeezed his hand tight.

His fingers curled against hers.

Had he moved or had she imagined it?

She jerked back to look at him. His eyes were open. They were clouded with confusion and perhaps pain. He struggled to keep his eyelids open, but he was awake. She cupped his face in her hands. "Eddie. I love you."

"I love you, too." He closed his eyes.

"Eddie?"

But he didn't respond.

She dashed away tears she hadn't known she shed. Was it a sign he was returning or—she groaned from deep in her soul—was it goodbye? She clung to the belief he would recover. But at least he'd heard her words of love.

He opened his eyes again before dinnertime and smiled at her before he drifted off again. Her heart overflowed with gratitude, which grew and multiplied as he wakened several more times throughout the evening.

She didn't want to leave him when darkness fell, but Slim insisted. She lay on the bed unable to sleep despite fatigue that numbed her bones. *Thank You, God. Thank You.* She couldn't stop saying the words.

The next day he wakened for longer periods and was able to take a bit of nourishing broth provided by Cookie.

The following day he tried to sit up, groaned and grabbed his head.

She eased him back to his pillow. "Lie still. Give your head a chance to heal."

"Right." He breathed hard then grabbed her hand. "I dreamed I was in a dark tunnel and you called me. I followed your voice back." He fell asleep without releasing her hand.

She gladly sat at his side, their hands together on his chest. A bit later he stirred again.

"I dreamed you said..." He didn't finish.

She realized how desperately he needed to hear her words, how he feared to believe he'd heard them. "It wasn't a dream. I should have told you before, but I was stuck in my fear and pride." She cupped her palms over his cheeks and leaned closer, drinking in the hunger in his eyes, the strength of his features. "Eddie Gardiner, I love you." She pressed a gentle kiss to his lips, fearing she would hurt him. He smiled beneath her kiss and pulled her to his chest.

Slowly in the following days, he gained strength and stayed awake for longer periods. But the letters on the table haunted her."You have letters. Margaret and your father wrote."

He groaned. "Read them to me."

"I don't know if I should."

"I don't intend to have secrets from you. Read Margaret's first."

She nodded. Her fingers trembled as she opened the letter and unfolded the one page.

Did Linette not make it clear that I am not interested in leaving the comforts of London? I thought you would have married her by now. She is by far more suited to that life than I. I wish you both the best.

Linette smiled at Eddie. "I tried to tell you as much."

"So you did, but I had to make sure Margaret hadn't changed her mind." He sounded weary.

She considered delaying the news in the next letter until he was stronger.

"Read Father's letter. I won't rest easy until I know what he's said."

She couldn't refuse after that and she quickly opened the envelope and read the words aloud.

Eddie.

No "Dear Eddie." Not a good beginning.

I forbid you to marry that woman.

Your duty is to obey me.

And a bold signature. *Randolph Gardiner.*

The trembling had spread to her stomach and she wished she hadn't eaten.

"Linette, would you get pen and paper?"

With leaden feet she did as he asked and held the items to him.

"Would you mind writing as I dictate? I fear I am not up to doing it myself."

"Of course." She could think of nothing she wanted less to do.

"Dear Father, I received your letter today. All my life I have done my best to honor you, not only because I wanted to be a good son but because God has instructed us to honor our parents. However, I fear I must disobey you in this matter."

Linette ducked her head over the paper. Could he mean he would choose her over his father?

Eddie continued and she wrote again.

"It is my honor and privilege to have met Linette Edwards and I can assure you she is more than worthy of marrying any man…even a Gardiner. I intend to make her my wife as soon as preparations can be made. New paragraph, if you please. I realize you might want to make other arrangements for the ranch, but I invite you to examine the records, ask others in the area about the operation and you will discover that I have done an excellent job. If you find my work satisfactory I am willing to stay on but not as a foreman or supervisor. I will stay on in one condition—you make me a full partner. Awaiting your pleasure in this matter."

"Eddie, you can't mean it. Where will you go? What will you do?"

"Don't you mean where will *we* go?"

"Of course."

"We'll manage fine. We could start a small place like Ward has. Now hold the paper for me to sign."

She did so then sealed the letter in an envelope.

"Get one of the boys to take it to town today."

She found Slim and gave him the letter then returned to Eddie's side.

She perched on the edge of the bed. "Are you sure about this?"

"All this—" he waved his arm to indicate the house, the ranch "—means nothing without you to share it with."

A smile threatened to split her face. "Is it any wonder I love you?"

He caught her hand and pulled her close to kiss her. "I will never grow tired of hearing those words. Now, when can we get married?"

She laughed. "Don't you want to wait until you can stand?"

A month later

Everyone from OK Ranch had come. At Eddie's request a minister had come from Fort Calgary for the occasion.

Linette wondered aloud if Eddie was ready. It had taken him ten days from the accident before he could stand without dizziness and another ten days before he could ride a horse. But he insisted he was back to normal. They'd had so many sweet times as he recovered.

She told him how she'd wakened, as if shaken by an unseen hand, in the middle of the night, and knelt at his bedside calling to him. He insisted it was her voice calling his name that enabled him to fight his way from the darkness of unconsciousness.

They talked about what they would do if Eddie's father asked them to leave the ranch. She'd tried to share Eddie's optimism but couldn't deny a bit of sadness. She had come to love the place, the residents and the house. But the fact that he would give it all up for her filled her heart with sweetness.

Eddie had invited others from around the area to the wedding.

Linette laughed in surprise as the stagecoach she'd arrived on rattled into the yard and men jumped off the top and climbed from the coach. "You seem to have the regard of everyone in the area." She hugged Eddie's arm.

She and Eddie stood on the bridge, facing the visiting minister and the gathered crowd. The trees were dressed in spring finery and the water rushing under the bridge filled the air with gurgling music. Cassie and Roper stood at their sides. Roper barraged Cassie with longing glances. Linette smiled. Roper had a tough journey ahead of him, but if she could change Eddie's mind, if Eddie could teach her to love, then Roper could win Cassie's heart.

The minister spoke and drew her attention to the dear man at her side. They exchanged vows and sealed them with a kiss full of promise and trust.

Cookie insisted she would provide a meal to rival the Christmas feast at the other ranch and she did them proud.

During the meal, the stagecoach driver sidled up to Eddie and Linette. "All winter I wondered if Eddie here would come to his senses and see what a prize you are. Glad to see he came round."

Eddie pulled her close and pressed his cheek to her hair. "Not half as glad as I am."

She wrapped her arms about Eddie's waist. "Nor half as glad as I."

The driver sauntered away, his eyes on the cinnamon buns Cookie put out.

Grady considered Linette with a worried look. She pulled him to her side. "What is it, little man?"

"I stay with you?" He addressed Linette, but darted a quick glance toward Eddie.

She'd assured him over and over that he had a home with them, but he needed to hear it again.

Eddie drew the boy closer. "You will stay with us."

Grady nodded. "You be my new papa?"

Eddie hugged the boy. His eyes glistened as he met

Linette's gaze over Grady's head. "I would be honored to."

"I love you," Grady said.

"I love you back," Eddie replied and opened his arms to pull Linette into a three-cornered hug. "I love you both."

"Me, too," she whispered. "Me, too."

Grady edged free to grin at the assembled people.

Linette turned her face up to Eddie. "I suppose this is a good time to admit I was more than a little in love with you even before I came."

His eyes flickered amusement and heart-stopping love. "You don't say? How is that possible?"

"From the letters you wrote to Margaret I kept thinking, there's a man worth loving."

He cupped her chin. "It took your faith in me for me to see I deserved more than my father's name."

They still hadn't heard from Eddie's father, but she refused to let the concern about what he'd said mar her day.

"Our future is in God's loving hands," Eddie said.

It didn't surprise Linette that he'd read her thoughts. "I am so happy."

"Me, too." He kissed her, a sweet, promising kiss.

Whatever the future held, she could gladly, eagerly face with Eddie's love and God's care to guide her.

Epilogue

Linette wandered through the house checking each room. She straightened the covers on each bed, adjusted the curtains at a window and paused to admire the china in the dining-room cupboard—a gift from the owners at OK Ranch. She had grown to love the house, but nowhere as much as this room with the windows overlooking the ranch, and her footsteps returned there as if drawn by a cord to her heart.

Below, Roper rode into the yard and waved a bundle at Eddie. Eddie took it, glanced at it then turned his gaze toward the house, unerringly finding Linette in the window. He waved a long white envelope.

Linette clutched her arms about her. It was the long-awaited, dreaded letter. She looked over her shoulder and mentally began saying goodbye to the room and mentally began packing their belongings.

Eddie found her sitting in the wingback chair before the window. He knelt in front of her and wrapped his arms around her. "Whatever this says, nothing changes so far as I'm concerned. I have all I want right here in my arms."

"Open the letter," she begged.

"Not before you tell me it doesn't matter what it says."

She stared into his eyes, deep into his heart and saw the promise of his faithful love—a love she had grown to cherish more with each passing day. "I only care because I know the ranch is important to you."

"Nothing matters but you and me together."

"If you're happy, I'm happy." Her heart overflowing with joy, she leaned forward and kissed him. "Now open the letter."

He sat at her knees and carefully broke the seal on the envelope to withdraw a sheaf of official-looking papers.

Her heart kicked against her ribs. "He's removing you from the ranch."

Eddie read the documents. "I don't think so." Suddenly he laughed. "He's made me half owner. I will be in complete control of what he calls 'Northwest Canada operations.' He will retain control of major monetary investments over five thousand dollars." Eddie whooped. "He's basically given me the ranch." He bolted to his feet and pulled Linette up to face him. "The Lord has done great things for us."

"Above and beyond what we thought possible."

They hugged each other and kissed then Eddie turned to the rest of the mail. "There's a letter to you."

She took it. "From Father." Inside she found a note and explanation that the funds of her dowry had been placed in Eddie's name at Fort Macleod.

Eddie barely glanced at the letter. "It's your money to do with as you want. I have no need of it and don't want you to ever think I had an eye to gaining this by marrying you." He kissed her to prove he was teasing.

"I know exactly what I want to do with it."

Eddie chuckled. "Let me guess. First, you want to

finish furnishing the rooms in the guest wing then make them available for people in need and you want to use the money to help them."

She giggled. "What are you, sir? A mind reader?"

His eyes flashed humor. "Wouldn't take much of a mind reader when you talk about it every chance you get. Well, Mrs. Gardiner, you have my complete approval to do whatever you want."

She wrapped her arms about his neck. "Is it any wonder I love you so much?"

He sobered. "Your love will always be a wonder to me."

She nodded, equally sober. "And yours to me." They searched each other's gaze for a moment, found the assurance they knew they would and kissed—a kiss full of promise and hope and joy and so many more things.

* * * * *

Dear Reader,

There is a highway not far from us called Cowboy Trail. It's one of the prettiest drives I've ever gone on and I do it at least once a year for the sheer beauty of the view. Along that trail are mountain vistas that take my breath away and historic ranches such as the Bar U. I can't see all this without feeling drawn to the setting and history, so Bar U has become the basis for the fictional setting of these ranch stories. I hope I can in some small way make you glimpse the beauty of the scenery and the magnitude of what early ranchers and settlers faced as they settled the land. I love to hear from readers. Contact me through email at linda@lindaford.org. Feel free to check on updates and bits about my research at my website www.lindaford.org.

God bless,

Linda Ford

Questions for Discussion

1. What challenges did Linette face in leaving England and heading for the new West? How was she equipped to deal with them?

2. Why does she help Grady and Cassie? Do you think her motives are pure?

3. When did you suspect she loved Eddie even though she continued to deny it?

4. Linette has some very strong opinions about what she wants out of life. Why does she feel this way? Are her motives pure?

5. Does she find Eddie portrays what she feels a man will expect of her or does he surprise her and if so, how?

6. Eddie also has very clear objectives in mind. What are they? Are they based on truth or misunderstanding? How?

7. Why does he want to marry Margaret and not Linette? Are his reason valid? Why or why not?

8. What does Eddie feel about Grady? What does he do about the boy? Does that have any bearing on the romance?

9. What does Eddie learn about Linette that makes him see her as more than an outspoken nuisance? How does that shape his feelings toward her?

10. What lesson did they each learn that enabled them to trust love? Do you need to learn lessons to learn to trust love—both God's and man's—more fully?

COMING NEXT MONTH
from Love Inspired® Historical
AVAILABLE FEBRUARY 5, 2013

BLESSING
Deborah Bedford

Disguised as a boy, Uley Kirkland must testify as a witness to attempted murder, but when she falls for Aaron Brown, the defendant, she realizes she'll do whatever it takes to save Aaron's life—even risk her own.

COURTING MISS CALLIE
Pinewood Weddings
Dorothy Clark

Ezra Ryder, disillusioned by women seeking him for his wealth, disguises himself as a stable hand. But when he falls for the beautiful Callie Conner, his deception may ruin their hopes of happiness.

THE RELUCTANT EARL
C. J. Chase

Leah Vance risks social ruin by selling political information to pay for her sister's care. When Julian DeChambrelle, the dashing former sea captain, catches her in the act, they're both pulled into a world of danger.

GROOM BY ARRANGEMENT
Rhonda Gibson

Eliza Kelly is mortified when she mistakes blacksmith Jackson Hart for the mail-order groom her friend arranged for her. Both are afraid to fall in love, but could a marriage of convenience make them reconsider?

LIHCNM0113

REQUEST YOUR FREE BOOKS!

2 FREE INSPIRATIONAL NOVELS
PLUS 2
FREE
MYSTERY GIFTS

Love Inspired

HISTORICAL
INSPIRATIONAL HISTORICAL ROMANCE

YES! Please send me 2 FREE Love Inspired® Historical novels and my 2 FREE mystery gifts (gifts are worth about $10). After receiving them, if I don't wish to receive any more books, I can return the shipping statement marked "cancel." If I don't cancel, I will receive 4 brand-new novels every month and be billed just $4.49 per book in the U.S. or $4.99 per book in Canada. That's a saving of at least 22% off the cover price. It's quite a bargain! Shipping and handling is just 50¢ per book in the U.S. and 75¢ per book in Canada.* I understand that accepting the 2 free books and gifts places me under no obligation to buy anything. I can always return a shipment and cancel at any time. Even if I never buy another book, the two free books and gifts are mine to keep forever.

102/302 IDN FVXK

Name   (PLEASE PRINT)

Address   Apt. #

City   State/Prov.   Zip/Postal Code

Signature (if under 18, a parent or guardian must sign)

Mail to the Harlequin® Reader Service:
IN U.S.A.: P.O. Box 1867, Buffalo, NY 14240-1867
IN CANADA: P.O. Box 609, Fort Erie, Ontario L2A 5X3

Want to try two free books from another series?
Call 1-800-873-8635 or visit www.ReaderService.com.

* Terms and prices subject to change without notice. Prices do not include applicable taxes. Sales tax applicable in N.Y. Canadian residents will be charged applicable taxes. Offer not valid in Quebec. This offer is limited to one order per household. Not valid for current subscribers to Love Inspired Historical books. All orders subject to credit approval. Credit or debit balances in a customer's account(s) may be offset by any other outstanding balance owed by or to the customer. Please allow 4 to 6 weeks for delivery. Offer available while quantities last.

Your Privacy—The Harlequin® Reader Service is committed to protecting your privacy. Our Privacy Policy is available online at www.ReaderService.com or upon request from the Harlequin Reader Service.

We make a portion of our mailing list available to reputable third parties that offer products we believe may interest you. If you prefer that we not exchange your name with third parties, or if you wish to clarify or modify your communication preferences, please visit us at www.ReaderService.com/consumerschoice or write to us at Harlequin Reader Service Preference Service, P.O. Box 9062, Buffalo, NY 14269. Include your complete name and address.

LIHI3

The wrong groom could be the
perfect match in

GROOM BY ARRANGEMENT

by **Rhonda Gibson**

Eliza Kelly thought her humiliation was complete when she
identified the wrong train passenger as her mail-order groom.
She was only trying to tell Jackson Hart that the madcap scheme
was *not* her idea. When the blacksmith decides to stay, he offers
the lovely widow a marriage of convenience. Between caring for
an orphaned youngster and protecting Eliza, Jackson feels whole
again. If only he can persuade Eliza to marry him, and fulfill
their long-buried dreams of forging a real family.

Available in February wherever books are sold.